"I KNOW who's after us."

"You do?" That didn't exactly make Rodney feel better. "By reputation, or personally?"

Again the hesitation before Ronon answered. "Personally. And we have to watch our every step from here on out."

"Who is it?" Rodney wanted to know. Well, no, deep down he didn't want to know at all. But he needed to know.

The answer was one he hadn't expected. "Runners."

"Other runners?" Rodney stared at him. "Like you?"

He felt the air move as Ronon shook his head. "No. Not like me. Not any more."

"Then like what? Who are they? How do you know them? What do they want?" Rodney was both horrified and fascinated. Before they'd met Ronon they'd never even heard of a Runner, but apparently the concept was legendary among all the worlds touched by the Wraith—a lone individual, caught by the Wraith but released and then hunted down. For sport. Most Runners didn't last very long, a week or two at most—they were said to be chosen for their cunning and their skills but the Wraith had been hunting and killing for centuries.

Ronon had been a Runner for seven years.

If these others were even half as good at hunting and fighting as he was, they had a serious problem on their hands.

STARGATE
ATLÄNTIS™

HUNT AND RUN

AARON ROSENBERG

FANDEMONIUM BOOKS

An original publication of Fandemonium Ltd, produced under license from MGM Consumer Products.

Fandemonium Books
PO Box 795A
Surbiton
Surrey KT5 8YB
United Kingdom
Visit our website: www.stargatenovels.com

STARGATE
ATLANTIS

METRO-GOLDWYN-MAYER Presents
STARGATE ATLANTIS.
JOE FLANIGAN   TORRI HIGGINSON   RACHEL LUTTRELL   JASON MOMOA
with PAUL McGILLION as Dr. Carson Beckett and DAVID HEWLETT as Dr. McKay
Executive Producers BRAD WRIGHT & ROBERT C. COOPER
Created by BRAD WRIGHT & ROBERT C. COOPER

WWW.MGM.COM

ISBN: 978-1-905586-44-8
Printed in the United States of America

For Dave, Peter, and Jenness, who let me bounce ideas off them — and for Jen, Arthur, and Adara, as always.

PROLOGUE

"IS EVERYTHING set?"

A shadowy figure moved through the dark, feet placed precisely to create no sound and leave no trace. She stopped beside two other shadows; these crouched down, fingers flickering as they worked.

"Almost, Lanara," one replied softly.

"Good here," the other, Misa, added, straightening.

"And here," the first one, Adarr, agreed, standing as well.

"Fine. Move out." Lanara turned and retraced her steps just as silently as before, now with two additional shadows at her back. "Ready, Nekai," she called as she neared.

"On your mark," a new voice answered, its words emerging without a point of origin.

Lanara shifted, sliding beyond the edge of the dark. She paused only long enough for Misa and Adarr to join her. "Mark."

Behind them, a light began to blink on a panel. And somewhere, a klaxon began to wail. But here there were none but shadows to hear it.

"Now," Lanara whispered as they departed, "we wait."

CHAPTER ONE

"OKAY, this is ridiculous," Rodney commented as he strapped himself in. "Does anyone else think this is ridiculous?"

"No, Rodney, no one does," Sheppard replied, most of his attention on the console as he powered up the Jumper and signaled the monitor crew to activate the gate. "It's just you."

"What's ridiculous?" Teyla asked, and Sheppard rolled his eyes at her. Why did she have to encourage Rodney's rants? Ronon, at least, knew better than to answer.

"This." Rodney indicated the Jumper and them. "This mission. Some ship we've never heard of before sends out a distress call and we go running to the rescue? Why? What are we, the interstellar version of AAA? 'Oh, don't worry, ma'am, it's just your drive coil — we'll have you flying again in no time'?"

"We help people," Sheppard reminded the scientist through gritted teeth, even as he maneuvered the Jumper through lift-off and through the gate in front of them. The familiar distortion kept him from adding anything else for a second. "It's what we do," he finished after he'd recovered from the disorientation. As always, he wondered if that would ever disappear — would he ever be able to pass through a gate without his brain and his senses taking a few seconds to adjust?

Probably not.

Now that he was able to focus again, however, he started checking their surroundings. The gate they'd come through was the free-floating kind, he saw, and it hung in outer space, its rippling surface and the glowing sigils around it edges providing weak illumination against the stark backdrop of space and distant stars. There wasn't any sign of a ship nearby, so he began scanning for the distress signal. There!

"I've got a lock on it," he told the others. "Maybe ten, fifteen minutes away. Hang on." And he set the Jumper to close in on the other ship's coordinates.

"Yes, but why do we do it?" Rodney was insisting. "It's a valid question, you have to admit. Why do we help these people? Our mission is to explore this region, to catalog everything we find, and to improve our own knowledge, technology, and resources. How does fixing the flat on someone's space jalopy add to any of that?"

"They might be a new race we have not encountered before," Teyla pointed out. "And by helping them we earn their good will."

"Great, that and two bucks'll get you a cup of coffee," Rodney muttered.

"It's karma," Sheppard told him. "You help them and sooner or later it comes back to you. That's how the universe works." At least he fervently hoped so — admittedly he was still waiting for returns on many of those investments.

"It's not about getting something back," Ronon announced. Sheppard turned around, surprised the big guy was even participating — usually he stayed silent during these constant arguments, watching the rest of them and frowning as if they were behaving like idiots. Which, admittedly, they often were. Teyla and Rodney were staring at the Satedan as well. "You help because it's the right thing to do," he continued. "That's what separates us from animals."

Not surprisingly, Rodney recovered from the shock first. "Wow, thank you for that staggering insight," he sneered. "Ironic, hearing a lecture on morals from an unfeeling caveman." Ronon glanced at him, not even a glare really, and Rodney shrank back but didn't apologize. Then again, when did he ever?

"Ronon is not unfeeling," Teyla defended her friend. She ignored the 'caveman' comment — they were all used to Rodney's snide remarks, especially toward Ronon. "He has feelings just as anyone else does. But he has learned to do what is necessary, and to do so without that hesitation which could be fatal."

"A fact," Sheppard hastened to point out, "that's saved your butt more than a few times."

"Yes yes, I'm grateful for his reflexes and his martial skills," Rodney acknowledged. "But that has nothing to do with this. We help others because it's right? Because it shows we're not animals? That's just an excuse not to think about it. Really, I want to know — what do we get out of this?"

"Maybe," Sheppard growled, reaching the all-too-familiar limit of his tolerance for Rodney, "they'll have some magic way to shut you up. That would be worth any price."

Teyla laughed and even Ronon grinned.

"Oh, ha ha," Rodney grumped. But at least he didn't continue the argument. Sheppard estimated it would take at least a minute before the scientist burst out with something inane again.

By then they'd be at the other ship. Hopefully that would keep him too occupied to speak further.

"There she is," Sheppard pointed out a few minutes later, cutting Rodney off mid-breath and mid-argument. The silence had only lasted a minute before Rodney had felt compelled to pick up the same whine as before. But seeing the ship materialize on-screen brought his scientist self to the fore, and cut off any other complaints he might have been about to make.

"Standard configuration for a local ship," Rodney confirmed after a second of scanning the readouts. "Short-range, too. What's it doing way out here? Have we got any planets within range?"

"A few," Teyla responded, tapping her own console for confirmation. "But none inhabited. That is strange."

"Are you picking up anyone onboard?" Sheppard asked. He

was already looking the other ship over, trying to decide the best angle from which to approach. They'd use the Jumper's ceiling hatch rather than the rear cargo door—it was smaller and wouldn't leak out as much of the cargo bay's atmosphere. There were ports on both sides, so he'd pivot the Jumper, bringing it in on its side so the ceiling hatch lined up with one of those. It would be easiest to come at it from the far side, looping under and around. That'd also give him a chance to make sure there wasn't anyone lurking beneath it, too. He'd had a few too many ambushes sprung on him not to be cautious.

Behind him, Ronon obviously shared his concerns. "No outward weaponry," the Satedan pointed out. "No shields, either. Definitely not a military vessel or even a proper scout ship. Most likely civilian, possibly merchant."

"Which again begs the question, what is it doing out here?" Rodney interrupted himself as his console chimed. "I've got life-signs!" he announced. "Seven of them, all strong."

"Hailing now." Teyla was already typing in commands. "No reply," she said after a moment.

"We're still getting the distress beacon," Ronon commented, "but they may be unable to respond further."

"I'd say so," Rodney told him, "seeing as how responding would require power and they haven't got any!"

"If it's powered down—" Teyla began, but Sheppard had jumped to the same worry himself.

"—then they've got no life-support," he finished for her. He kicked their speed up a notch, and began the arc of the turn. "I'm bringing us in fast as I can—every second could count here!"

The others began suiting up while he piloted. Their MOPP gear wasn't actually a spacesuit and wouldn't last long in a total vacuum, but they would serve to get from the Jumper to the injured ship. Once inside, they'd keep out any airborne contaminants and could regulate body temperature. Each suit also had a small air canister and could recycle that for ten to twenty minutes if there wasn't any other air present. Hopefully that would be enough. They did have one actual spacesuit on the Jumper, but Sheppard didn't want to use that unless it was absolutely necessary. "I see no signs of damage," Ronon pointed out once he had his protective suit in place. He was leaning on the back of Sheppard's chair, peering over him out the front, but Sheppard had neither the time nor the energy to care. Besides Ronon knew better than to get in his way while he was flying. And he was right, anyway — the distressed ship looked structurally intact. No blast holes, no missing pieces, not even any major dents. Hell, it was in better shape than their Jumper!

"So if it's not hurt," Rodney asked, "why is it just floating here?"

"There could be any number of reasons," Teyla reminded him. "The most likely is some form of internal power failure."

"Or poison gas," Ronon added darkly.

That earned him a glare from Rodney. "Oh, great! You just had to say that, didn't you? What if our gas masks aren't enough to deal with something like that? What if it's acidic and eats right through our suits? Huh? What then?"

Ronon shrugged. "Then we die."

"That's your answer? Just like that?"

Sheppard could feel Ronon shrug again through the chair. "Hopefully," he agreed. "It could be long and drawn-out and painful instead."

"If you're so eager to check," Rodney managed after a moment of stunned silence, "maybe you should just go in by yourself!"

"We're all going in," Sheppard told him sharply. He spun the Jumper lightly on its axis, and eased the engines off just as their roof nudged up against the side of their target. The impact wasn't even rough enough to count as a scrape. Damn, he was good! "The MOPP suits can handle it," he assured Rodney as he stood and accepted his gear from Teyla. "And if the suit scanners do pick up anything beyond their rating we'll back off at once and quarantine the entire ship, okay?"

"Fat lot of good that'll do us after we've already been exposed," Rodney muttered, but he fell into line a minute later as Sheppard led them through the bulkhead door into the cargo hold, and then to the Jumper's ceiling access hatch.

"All set?" Sheppard asked everyone. He got two nods and a grumble he took to mean yes. "Then here we go." He reached up and punched the release switch, and the hatch hissed open. The shuttle's door was right beside them, inches away, and he simply grabbed the handhold beside their hatch and pulled himself up so he could hit the door's access panel. It slid open — good thing it didn't open outward! — with a faint hiss. Beyond it he could make out only darkness.

"Hello? Anybody home?" Sheppard hauled himself through both doors, taking a second to let his body reorient so the shuttle floor was 'down.' "Avon calling!"

"If we die," Rodney warned as they clambered one after the other into the distressed ship, "I'm blaming you!"

"Fair enough." Sheppard stepped to the side once he was through, allowing the others in, then closed the door behind them. No sense letting any possible contagions onto the Jumper if they could avoid it. Rodney was a coward and a complainer, but he wasn't stupid and he did occasionally have some valid concerns. "Okay, let's have a look around."

They split up, though in a ship this size that didn't mean much — even when he had reached the far hull Sheppard could turn around and see the others' faces within their helmets. The Jumper had room for a crew of four and perhaps another six to eight passengers. This ship would be lucky to fit eight total. Especially since it didn't have any seats in the back section.

"Light cargo," Ronon guessed, completing a sweep of the interior. "Only the two seats up front, pilot and copilot, and the rest is cargo space."

"And no sign of anyone," Teyla added. "No bodies, no remains, nothing."

"I'm not seeing any interior damage, either," Rodney pointed out, sweeping a handlight along the walls and particularly over the panels. "I'd have to crack everything open to be sure, but at least on the surface there's nothing to indicate why this thing isn't zipping along somewhere."

"Distress beacon was activated," Sheppard reminded them, gesturing toward the front console, where a small light blinked on and off. "Somebody hit it. And this thing is dead in space, so something happened. We just need to figure out what." Something about all this was bugging him, though. He just couldn't put his finger on it right away.

Rodney didn't have any such problem. "There's nobody here," he declared suddenly.

"I think we got that," Teyla told him.

"No, listen," the scientist insisted. "There's nobody here. So where did those life-signs come from?"

It was Ronon who answered — sort of. "We need to leave," he announced. "Now!"

"What? Why?" Sheppard turned but the Satedan was already striding back toward the shuttle door. "Hey, hold up, big guy! What's going on?"

"We need to get off this ship at once," Ronon insisted. "And touch nothing!" That last comment was directed sharply at Rodney, who had been in the act of reaching for an instrument panel near the front console.

"But if I can get in here —" Rodney started to protest.

"Leave it!" Ronon repeated. "Or viruses will be the least of your worries!"

That shut Rodney up and got him moving in a hurry. By the

time he reached the rest of them Ronon had the door open. He ushered them all through before leaping back into the Jumper himself. Then he pulled the shuttle door shut again, but he didn't shut the Jumper's ceiling hatch.

"We need to push off," he said instead. He gestured toward one of the collection nets that hung from a rack above one of the rear seats. "Sheppard, give me a hand."

Sheppard knew better than to argue — Ronon never did anything without a darn good reason, and most of the time that reason was their immediate survival. The Satedan had survived seven years as a Runner, after all — and if being chased nonstop by the entire Wraith empire didn't teach you to recognize danger signs, Sheppard wasn't sure what could!

He handed Ronon the net and watched as the Satedan reversed it and used the butt of its handle to shove off against the shuttle's hull. He could see Ronon's muscles straining, and after a second the constant pressure nudged the two ships apart. Once they were separated the Jumper's own slight momentum carried it further, and the impact against the empty ship forced it to drift in the opposite direction, widening the gap.

"Be ready to engage the ship's drive," Ronon warned as he finally pulled the ceiling hatch closed and air began to filter into the cargo hold again. Their MOPP gear had held — barely. "But don't activate it until we've gained more distance."

"Got it." Sheppard hurried back into the cockpit and slid into his seat, not bothering to remove his suit, and began but didn't finish his preflight checklist. "So, want to tell us what's going on?"

"Later," was the only answer he got. "Once it's safe."

Couldn't argue with that, Sheppard decided. The rest of the team had joined him back in the cockpit and had closed the bulkhead door behind them, slipping into their usual seats. He sat impatiently, one hand poised over the engine controls, until he caught Ronon's nod. Then he fired everything up and immediately spun the ship around, putting its back to the other vessel —

— which was why the blast propelled them forward when the distressed ship exploded.

Even though he'd been half-expecting it, Sheppard had to fight the controls as the Jumper bucked and fought, the shockwave tossing it about like a leaf battered by a hurricane. The fact that they'd already turned had definitely saved them, though — if they'd still been alongside their viewports would have been shattered by the blast, and most of the Jumper's systems fried as well. As it was, warning lights were flaring up all across the console, and klaxons were screaming through his helmet.

"We've got damage to the thrusters!" Rodney was shouting at him, "and to life support! Communications are out! Engine coolant levels are plummeting — we must have a crack in one of the lines somewhere! We need to set down!"

"Can we make it back to the gate?" Sheppard asked him, still battling the helm.

He got the answer he'd been half-expecting and completely dreading. "Not a chance! We'll be out of power in minutes. Six at most." And the Stargate was at least ten minutes away. Damn!

"There is a planet within range," Teyla informed them quickly, her fingers dancing across the computer panel on her suit's arm — at the moment it was a more stable option than the ship's own systems. "I will enter the coordinates." She tapped them into the ship's navigation, and Sheppard nodded as it came up on-screen. Definitely closer than the gate. The only question was, would it be close enough?

"Not like we have much of a choice," he muttered. "Okay, hang on — I'm going to floor it!" He stopped fighting the controls and settled for maximum speed, letting the ship's own momentum carry it part of the way. Better to put that velocity to work, even if it wasn't a smooth ride. They all still had their suits on, which was also a good thing — no telling how long the life-support would hold, and every little bit helped.

Hopefully, it would be long enough. Then, of course, they'd just have to figure out what to do next — stuck on an uninhabited planet in the middle of nowhere, with a dead ship, unable to reach the nearest gate, because someone had set an empty vessel as an ambush.

He sighed. Much as he hated to admit it, and never would out loud, Rodney was right for once. This really was ridiculous.

CHAPTER TWO

THE INSTANT Sheppard set the Jumper down — a little unsteadily but more or less in one piece — Ronon was on his feet and charging back through the cargo hold to the rear door. "We need to find cover!" he shouted over his shoulder. One hand was tapping the open command. The other had his laser pistol drawn. "Right now!"

"Now, hold on there, chief," Rodney argued, clambering out of his own chair and following Ronon but at a distance — he knew the Satedan well enough by now to give him a wide berth, especially when he was this agitated. "What's the rush? We're on the ground, and that exploding ship is half a light year away — what's left of it."

"That isn't the danger," Ronon told him brusquely. "Not anymore."

"What is the danger, then?" Teyla asked. She stepped up beside Ronon and rested one hand on his forearm, gently pushing his gun down until it pointed at the floor. "Ronon, if there is a threat here you must let us know. How else can we ready ourselves for it?"

"I —" It was rare to see the Satedan at a loss for words — he didn't speak much, but when he did he was very concise. To see him pausing now made Sheppard uneasy. But after a second Ronon shook his head and holstered his pistol. "It's just a feeling," he claimed. "I don't think we're out of danger yet."

"I tend to agree with that," Sheppard offered, rising as well and joining the rest of them, "if only because, as long as the Jumper's this banged up, we're sitting ducks. But our first priority has to be getting the ship up and running again, and getting back through the gate. We can send a military unit back to investigate the wreckage from that vessel, see what they can tell us about who set it and why — they'll be better equipped to deal with any additional threats."

Teyla nodded. "I agree — we should return to Atlantis as soon as possible."

"No argument there," Ronon admitted. His hand still rested on the butt of his pistol, though.

Rodney couldn't keep quiet, of course. Especially since he had gotten his way. That put him in a good mood, which made him talkative. Of course, when he didn't get his way he became grumpy, which also made him talkative, just more whiny. Really, Sheppard thought, there weren't a lot of things that didn't make Rodney talkative. Other than sleep and maybe strong tranquilizers.

"Well, now that we've all agreed," he suggested, rubbing his hands together, "is it all right if I actually get to work? Or did we want to sit and bicker a bit more?"

"Shut up and get to work, Rodney," Sheppard told him. "The rest of us will look around, see what sort of dirtball we've crash-landed on."

"You and Teyla go," Ronon corrected with a grimace. "I'll stand guard."

That earned him a stare from Rodney. "Over me? You're going to guard me?" If anything, Ronon's grimace became more pronounced, and that woke an answering grin from Rodney. "Well, now I've seen everything."

"There's air," Teyla reported, and Sheppard saw that she'd tied her suit's computer into the cargo bay door. Smart — that way she'd used the Jumper's external sensors to run an analysis on their surroundings but her suit had done the processing. "Thin, but breathable. Temperatures are within comfortable ranges. No sign of any toxins. We won't need the suits."

"Great — let's get them off." Sheppard immediately started stripping his off, and the others followed his lead. The MOPP suits were great but they had a limited air supply, so if the air outside was breathable they were better off conserving their resources. And the suits hindered movement and obstructed vision, something he didn't want to risk when they were scouting an unfamiliar location like this.

"Better—definitely better," Rodney exclaimed once he'd hung his own suit back on the rack. "I hate wearing that thing—I feel like the inside of a glove. Yuck!"

"Just get the Jumper up and running again," Sheppard instructed as the door lowered and they all filed out. "And get our comm link back up so we can call Atlantis—we haven't hit our window yet but once we do Woolsey's going to start worrying."

"That's a good thing, right?" Rodney asked, automatically raising and closing the Jumper's door again behind him. "He'll send troops through to find us?"

"And what if whoever set that ship to explode is still here?" Ronon demanded. He'd dropped into a crouch the minute he was outside, pistol back in hand, eyes scanning the area. "What if they ambush the troops as they come through?"

Rodney turned pale and stared all around. "Right, comm link," he whispered. "Got it."

Sheppard slapped him on the back. "Stay out of trouble." He exchanged a nod with Ronon. "Keep him out of trouble."

"Be careful," Ronon returned. He'd straightened slightly but hadn't lowered his weapon. "I still don't like this."

"We'll watch our backs," Sheppard assured him. "Ready?" he asked Teyla. She nodded, and together they turned away from the Jumper and their friends. "Then let's see what this lovely little mudball has to offer!"

"Not really a mudball at all," Sheppard muttered to himself an hour later. "More like a big dirty rock."

It was true—they had been scouting the area around their impromptu landing site, and everything he and Teyla had seen so far confirmed that basic impression. This wasn't a planet, not in the sense of proper landmasses and full ecosystems and weather patterns. Oh, it had dirt and water and plants and a breathable atmosphere — but only barely. There was some dirt but mostly it was rock, and they'd been hiking through craggy hills and shallow valleys for the past twenty minutes or more. A short distance away those same hills rose to become a low mountain range, and Sheppard was sure he saw dark openings here and there along the sides. Caves. He hated caves.

There was some moisture here and there — narrow little streams trickling along, small muddy puddles collected in small depressions — but he suspected that was from ice-covered meteorites small enough to get sucked in by this place's low gravity. A few plants poked up as well, mostly scrub brush and tough vines. He figured the dirt was the result of countless meteorites, asteroids, and other bits of space debris, and some of it must have held a few seeds — there was sunlight aplenty, though the "sun" was a small star with watery white light, and without competition the few plants here had managed to eke out a basic subsistence. They didn't have enough water or soil to flourish, however, and most of this place was still just bare rock.

"It's a hiker's paradise," he added, hauling himself up onto a small boulder and straightening up to survey their surroundings. "Too bad I left my good hiking boots back on Atlantis."

"At least you have your canteen," Teyla pointed out. She raised hers in salute before taking a quick swig. Sheppard did the same, careful to only drink a mouthful of the warm water. No telling how long it would take Rodney to fix the Jumper, and the last thing he wanted was to risk dehydration.

"The good news is, I'm not seeing any signs of other life," Sheppard commented, still scanning the horizon. "I'd say we're alone out here."

Teyla nodded. "I have not see anything either." Then she

frowned. "Except perhaps for that." She pointed off in the distance. Sheppard followed her gesture and after a second his eyes picked up a glare. Something over there was reflecting the sunlight — something metallic.

"Could just be a piece from the Jumper," he argued, hopping down from the boulder. "I'm sure we lost a few bits of the hull in that explosion, and passing through this place's joke of an atmosphere might have been enough to tear it loose."

"Perhaps," Teyla admitted. "In which case Rodney might need it in order to complete his repairs. But what if it is not from our ship? It could be random debris, pulled here by this planet's gravity well — or it could be something left behind by whomever set that ship to explode."

"Why would they be here, though?" Sheppard wondered out loud as she headed in the reflection's direction. "They could have flown that ship over there, rigged it, and flown off in a second ship they had following it. They wouldn't have needed to set down on a planet at all. And they'd probably be safer not landing here — jostling explosives is never a good idea, and you risk having the thing blow up in your face before you can clear the atmosphere."

Teyla only shrugged. "We do not know who set the ship or for what purpose," she pointed out without slowing her pace, "and so we have no way of knowing their motivations for anything. But perhaps whatever is up ahead will provide us with some clue."

"Yeah, or it could just be a discarded candy wrapper," Sheppard said softly. But he followed her anyway. There wasn't anything else to see out here, and Ronon's earlier paranoia still had him a little on edge.

They spent the next few minutes without speaking, picking their way over rocks or around them. "You may be correct after all," Teyla said finally. She had increased her lead and was now a good twenty paces ahead of him. The shiny object was perhaps another twenty paces past her, Sheppard judged, and he still couldn't tell anything more about it than the fact that it was metal or at least metallic, and probably no bigger than his fist. It had been sheer luck that Teyla had spotted it in the first place — a slightly different angle, or a different time of day, and they'd never have seen the glare it gave off.

"What, it is a candy wrapper?" Sheppard called out. His stomach rumbled. "I don't suppose it's unopened?" He had emergency ration bars on him, of course, but didn't want to eat those if he didn't have to. They had better rations back on the Jumper, anyway. As soon as they'd inspected this thing, whatever it was, he planned on heading them back there. Hopefully Rodney at least had a diagnosis by now. Assuming Ronon hadn't shot him yet.

"It may be," Teyla agreed. She had slowed a few feet from it. "All I can be certain of is — " her words cut off abruptly as the ground suddenly vanished beneath her and she disappeared completely from view.

"Teyla!" Sheppard burst into a sprint, making for her last location, and covered the rough ground in a flash. There was a crevice of some sort there, long but narrow. How had they missed that?

"I am unharmed," her voice floated up from that gash in the earth. "This appears to be a natural formation, and it ends in a ledge some eight feet down. Be careful, however — there is a tarp here with me."

"A tarp?" Sheppard had reached the edge and dropped to his knees, peering down. Sure enough, there was Teyla less than ten feet below him. She was holding one edge of a wide, stiff cloth that also piled below her boots. It was the same color as the rocks around them both, and even from here Sheppard could tell it had some texture to it as well. Someone had deliberately covered the crevice, and had placed that shiny object there as bait!

"It's a trap!" he muttered, spinning around, his P90 sub-machine gun in hand as he scanned their surroundings. But he didn't see anyone, or any movement. As far as he could tell, they were alone.

"A well-set one," Teyla agreed. "I did not notice the difference in the ground until I felt it give way beneath me."

"But why?" Sheppard wondered. He swept the area again, then slung the P90 back on his shoulder and lay flat on his belly, arms extended into the hole. "Why put this here? Who were they expecting? Us?"

"Perhaps whomever answered the distress beacon," Teyla offered. She took a few steps away, then turned, ran back, and leaped. Her powerful legs propelled her upward and she caught Sheppard's outstretched hands easily, her own locking onto them with a powerful grip. Before he could move she had slammed her feet against the crevice wall, pushed off, and flipped up and over him to safety.

"Okay, well let's talk about this back—" Sheppard suggested, rolling over—and stopped short, all sound and motion cut off by the rifle barrel pressed against his chest. A dark figure, silhouetted against the sun, offered him a hand up. Past the stranger's shoulder Sheppard saw another one securing Teyla's hands behind her back. "Hi. You must be the welcoming committee."

"Up," the stranger commanded. The barrel didn't waver in the least.

"Doesn't look like I have much of a choice," Sheppard acknowledged. He took the hand and let the stranger pull him to his feet. Male, Sheppard guessed, and in good shape, but beyond that he couldn't tell—both of the strangers wore what looked like armored hooded jumpsuits, patterned in desert camouflage to blend in with the dirt and rock around them, and face-masks and goggles completely concealed their features. "Nice setup," he admitted. "So where were you hiding?" he glanced down into the crevice, and — as he'd hoped — his captor's gaze flicked to the hole as well. And so did his gun barrel.

"Now!" Sheppard yelled. He pivoted to the side, one hand grabbing the rifle and keeping it aimed past him while the other landed at the back of the stranger's neck. The blow knocked the man forward a step, and Sheppard's tug on the weapon continued the motion, causing the stranger to stumble — right into the crevice.

Turning, he saw Teyla flip her own captor over her shoulder. She landed on his abdomen as he hit the ground, her knee knocking the wind out of him, and his head bounced off a rock a second later, leaving him stunned. In an instant Sheppard was at her side, his knife out to sever her bonds.

"Let's get out of here!" She nodded and fell into step beside him as they took up a quick march back toward the Jumper. She'd retrieved her P90 from where it had fallen and his had never left his shoulder, so they both covered the area as they moved quickly but carefully. The last thing they needed now was to stumble and shoot themselves in the foot because of some loose rocks.

They had made it away from the crevice and back to the boulder where they'd first seen it when a shot from somewhere zinged past Sheppard's head, just missing his left ear. "Down!" he ordered. Teyla dropped to a crouch and he did the same, taking up cover behind the boulder. He returned fire, but he wasn't entirely sure which direction the shot had come from. Their assailants could be anywhere.

"We need to get back to the ship!" Teyla offered, shooting past the boulder as well. But Sheppard had had time to think, and shook his head.

"No," he decided. "We don't want to lead them to the Jumper. If Rodney can get it up and running again, he and Ronon can call Atlantis for help. But if we get pinned down there, we're sunk." Teyla nodded, as he'd known she would. She understood tactics well enough to see his point. "Right now," he continued, "our job is to give them as much time as possible to effect repairs. And maybe take down whoever these guys are in the process." He squeezed off another round.

"We can stay here for now," Teyla pointed out, "but they know this land and we do not. They have the advantage."

"I know." Sheppard rubbed at his temple. "And we can't contact Ronon and Rodney, in case they're monitoring—it's possible these guys haven't noticed them yet, and I'd like to keep it that way." He frowned. "We'll think of something."

He ran out of time, however, as the boulder shuddered in front of them. And then shifted—toward them.

"Run!" he shouted, leaping to his feet and backpedaling rapidly as the boulder began to roll—directly toward him and Teyla. They abandoned all hope of cover fire and dove to the sides as it rumbled across their path and down the mild incline, narrowly missing them both.

"Nice trick," Sheppard admitted, pushing himself back up to his hands and knees. He wasn't surprised to find another gun barrel in his face, and let hands strip away his radio and submachine gun without a fight. "You probably had that boulder rigged for just that purpose, right? Best cover around, so you knew we'd hide behind it, and then you send it after us and catch us with our pants down." The strangers didn't reply, but he could sense their smiles even through their mottled facemasks. "Smart." One bound his wrists while another kept him under guard. Two more did the same with Teyla.

"So which one of you did I push into the crevice?" Sheppard couldn't resist asking. The one with the gun stepped forward slightly, the barrel poking him in the chest. "Yeah, sorry about that." He shrugged. "Can't really blame me, right?"

They still didn't answer. Instead the one who had bound his wrists nodded to the others, and they turned toward the hills. The gunbearer shifted behind Sheppard and prodded him in the back, forcing him into motion. Teyla was ahead of him, the two of them kept ten paces apart. These guys were well-trained, Sheppard had to admit. Well-trained and well-equipped, and clearly after something.

The question was, what?

He only hoped Rodney was making headway on the Jumper. And that Ronon had heard the shots. Right now, that was all he could ask.

Time would tell if it was enough.

CHAPTER THREE

"DID YOU hear that?"

Rodney glanced up. "Did I hear what?"

"That." Ronon wasn't even looking at him — the big mus-
cle-bound Satedan was staring off into the surrounding hills,
his whole body tensed, head up, nostrils flared. He looked
like a hunting dog and any second he expected the big man
to go bounding off and return with a duck hanging from his
mouth.

"I didn't hear anything."

"There!" Now Ronon did glance at him, more of a glare really
from beneath those heavy brows. "That! That was gunfire!"

Rodney frowned. Had he heard something just then? It was
hard to be sure. He thought he might have, but maybe it was
just because Ronon had told him there was something to hear.
Sounds — or the absence thereof — could work that way. You
could hear things just because you were listening for them.
Especially if they were already supposed to be faint.

"I don't know," he admitted finally, much as he hated that
particular phrase. "Maybe." He glanced around. "You think
Sheppard and Teyla are in trouble?" Ronon wasn't listening to
him. He had gone back to gaze toward the horizon. "Ronon?"
Rodney didn't care for it when the big oaf stared at him, but he
liked being ignored even less. "Are they in trouble?"

"Yes, they're in trouble," Ronon replied after a minute. He
shook himself and turned his attention fully upon Rodney,
making him squirm. "And so are we. We need to leave here.
Now."

"I've only just started isolating the damaged areas," Rodney
protested. "It'll take me another few hours to get the Jumper
operational again — at the least!"

But Ronon wasn't listening. He simply grabbed Rodney's arm and began hauling him away from the ship. "We can't stay here," he explained softly as he moved toward the hills.

"What? Wait!" Rodney tried to free his arm, but it was like a fly struggling against a vise grip. "We can't just leave the ship here!"

"That's exactly what we can do," Ronon retorted. "We're too vulnerable here."

"Then we should get it up and running as soon as possible," Rodney argued. "The sooner we're off this world the better."

Ronon was already shaking his head, and he hadn't stopped moving. "Too late for that," he said. "There's no time."

"Are we going after Sheppard and Teyla, then?" That did make some strategic sense, Rodney admitted to himself — three guards instead of one would afford him more protection while he worked. He could get the comm link up and running first, and let Sheppard or Teyla call in to Atlantis while he moved on to the navigation and propulsion systems. But his self-appointed shepherd was shaking his head again.

"We can't go after them."

"What? Why not?" Rodney struggled against the Satedan's grip again. "Come on, you said they were in trouble!"

"They are."

"So we need to help them!"

"It's too late for that," Ronon replied. He still hadn't slowed down. The Jumper was almost completely lost in the shadows behind them now, because this world's sun was already drifting down toward the horizon.

"Too late?" Rodney felt a chill wash over him. "You mean they're —?"

"I don't know," Ronon admitted. "Either they've won free, in which case they'll find us later, or they've been captured, in which case we will need to plan their rescue."

"You don't think they're dead?" That was a relief! Rodney

might enjoy busting Sheppard's chops from time to time — okay, so most of the time — but he actually respected the commander. And Teyla was one of the few people in Atlantis he actually liked.

"Not dead, no. They're bait."

"Bait? For what?" The chill grew worse. "For us?" He yanked on his arm again. "I can walk on my own, you know — I'm not an infant!"

Ronon released him suddenly, making him stumble and barely catch himself. "Then keep up." The Satedan drew his sword with his newly freed hand — the other already held his pistol — and lengthened his stride. Rodney had to jog to keep pace.

"So you think they've been captured?" Rodney asked again a few minutes later. They were in the hills proper now, and it was getting dark enough that he barely caught Ronon's answering nod. "And whoever did it is using them as bait to lure us in?" Another faint nod. "Why?"

"They know we're still out here," Ronon answered absently. "They need to take care of that. This is how they do it."

Rodney studied the bigger man's back. "You seem awfully sure of that," he noted. "What's going on here?"

"I'm trying to keep us alive," was the answering growl.

That kept Rodney quiet for a minute — but only a minute. "No, really," he started again as they clambered over some rocks and up a small cliff face. "You know something. Don't you?" He felt as much as saw Ronon tense. "I'm right, aren't I? Of course I am. You do know something! I thought so! You've been acting strange ever since that ship." He grabbed Ronon by the shoulder, but quickly let go as the bigger man swung back to face him. "Tell me!"

"I recognized the trap," Ronon admitted softly. "The 'ship in distress' gambit. I've seen it before." He shook his head, his long braids whipping about. "It took me too long, though. I should have noticed it at once."

"You saved our lives," Rodney pointed out.

"But not our ship," Ronon snapped. "And we're still stuck here. Still being hunted. I was sloppy."

"Okay, so you were sloppy. You still saved us. Again." Rodney glanced around, not sure what he expected to see — the sun had set completely now, and it was dark enough that he could barely make out his companion's glare in the deepening night. "But that's not all of it, is it?"

Even without being able to see it fully he knew Ronon was glaring at him — he'd come to recognize the feel of that particular response. "No," the Satedan ground out after a long pause. "I know who's after us."

"You do?" That didn't exactly make Rodney feel better. "By reputation, or personally?"

Again the hesitation before Ronon answered. "Personally. And we have to watch our every step from here on out."

"Who is it?" Rodney wanted to know. Well, no, deep down he didn't want to know at all. But he needed to know.

The answer was one he hadn't expected. "Runners."

"Other runners?" Rodney stared at him. "Like you?"

He felt the air move as Ronon shook his head. "No. Not like me. Not any more."

"Then like what? Who are they? How do you know them? What do they want?" Rodney was both horrified and fascinated. Before they'd met Ronon they'd never even heard of a Runner, but apparently the concept was legendary among all the worlds touched by the Wraith — a lone individual, caught by the Wraith but released and then hunted down. For sport. Most Runners didn't last very long, a week or two at most — they were said to be chosen for their cunning and their skills but the Wraith had been hunting and killing for centuries.

Ronon had been a Runner for seven years.

If these others were even half as good at hunting and fighting as he was, they had a serious problem on their hands.

"Not now," Ronon answered shortly. "Not here. We're not safe."

Rodney took that in. "Okay, yes. Safe. Safe would be good," he agreed. He was babbling, he realized, and forced himself not to say another word. Instead he followed as Ronon continued into the mountains, taking a winding path Rodney knew was meant to throw off anyone trying to track them. At last they paused, and Ronon knelt, brushing dirt and small rocks and dead brush back from the stone wall beside them. Behind the debris was a small dark opening.

"Get in," he told Rodney. His tone made it clear this wasn't a request.

Rodney's first impulse was to argue. He didn't like small dark spaces, and he didn't like being ordered around, and he didn't like not being told everything at once. But he also didn't like being shot at or taken captive, and he was fairly sure he would like being killed even less, so he held his tongue, dropped to his knees, and crawled through the opening.

It widened slightly about twenty paces in, and the ceiling rose enough that he could sit up without bashing his head on the rocks above. Beyond that it narrowed again. Far enough, Rodney decided, and leaned back against the cool stone. He heard rustling from the opening.

A moment later Ronon joined him. "I covered the opening again," he explained quietly, his voice little more than a gruff whisper. "They won't find us here."

"Good." Rodney closed his eyes and took a deep breath. Then he opened them again and fixed Ronon with the sternest glare he could muster, especially considering he could barely see the big lug. "Now talk. Who are these Runners, how do you know them, and why are they doing this to us?"

For a second he thought Ronon was going to refuse. But then the big Satedan seemed to reach a decision. He nodded slightly, and grimaced as if in pain. Then he began to speak.

"It was seven years ago," he started, his voice soft and his eyes somewhere far away. "I had just been captured by the Wraith . . . ."

CHAPTER FOUR

"I'LL KILL you! I'll kill you all!"

Ronon lashed out blindly, tears still stinging his cheeks and blurring his vision. But his fists did not connect and he spun around from the force of his empty blows, toppling himself to the ground. He lay there for several seconds, groaning, just letting the pain and rage and grief overwhelm him.

"Melena," he sobbed. He could still picture her face, still see her when he closed his eyes — and still gape in horror as she died inches from him, torn apart by one of the many explosions that had wracked their planet. Melena was gone. So was Sateda. He was all that remained.

Why hadn't the Wraith killed him as well? That was the question that tore at him. It was one of the few things that had kept him going, burning inside him throughout the torture and the taunts and the waiting. Why was he still alive?

The Wraith were hardly known for their mercy. Nor could it even be called mercy, taking a man and sparing his life after slaughtering his entire world and killing the woman he loved. That was the worst kind of torture. But that didn't explain why they had let him go.

Because they had let him go. Ronon was under no illusions about that — they hadn't allowed it. He hadn't escaped, hadn't outsmarted or outmaneuvered or outfought them. He had been caught, he had been toyed with, and he had been released.

But not unscathed.

He rolled over, gritting his teeth at the pain as the rocks and dirt rubbed against the raw skin of his lower back. The Wraith who had tormented him had done something there, something that had pierced Ronon with a sharp agony beyond any he'd previously experienced. It was a purely physical pain, however, and so he had tightened his jaw and endured. That was what Satedans did. That was what Ronon Dex did.

Not that the Wraith had been fooled. "It hurts, does it not?" it had inquired, leaning in close and leering, showing all its sharp teeth. Ronon had struggled against the bonds that clamped him to the table, but of course they had been fastened tight. No one could say the Wraith were stupid.

"The pain must be extreme," it had continued. "Good." Its grin widened even as its eyes narrowed. "Shall I tell you what I have done?" And then it did.

The incision point was still raw now, a day or so later, but most of the pain had fallen to a dull throb. It was a pain Ronon could live with. Not that he expected to live much longer.

After all, he was now the object of a Wraith hunt. The tracking device imbedded in his spine would reveal his precise location to any Wraith equipped with the appropriate frequency. They would be coming for him even now.

So be it. Ronon bit back a scream as he pushed himself onto his stomach, got his hands under his chest, and heaved himself back to his feet. He swayed there a second, almost falling again, before straightening into a half-crouch. He would die on his feet, like a man. Like a warrior. Like a Satedan. And then he would be with Melena again.

But that didn't mean he was planning to go without a fight. No, the Wraith that came for him would know they had fought Ronon Dex. And the ones who survived would remember his name.

He glanced around. They had stripped away his Specialist armor when he had been captured, and his weapons, his sword and his pistol, were likewise gone. All he had were his fists, and they would not be enough. Not against the Wraith.

They had dropped him on some planet, he had no idea which one, but there was dirt beneath his feet and trees and bushes nearby. No rocks big enough to function as weapons, nor any flint or slate he could chip into a spearhead — not that he would necessarily have time for such a venture anyway. No doubt the Wraith were already on their way. He would need to find a weapon quickly.

Ronon's eyes wandered to the trees again. They were deciduous, with wide trunks and curving branches and thick clusters of broad leaves. The branches began perhaps ten feet above his head, and he studied the possibilities before selecting one that looked sturdy. Then he leaped for it.

He missed, and fell to the ground again, cursing under his breath as the impact jarred his bones and sent fresh lancets of pain radiating from his back. But after a few seconds he picked himself up, took a deep breath, and tried again.

This time his fingers brushed the branch before he dropped back to earth.

A third time. Ronon was gasping for breath, his chest heaving, sweat dripping into his eyes, pain coursing up and down his spine. He doubted he would be able to make a fourth attempt. He shook his head, flinging the sweat from him, and snarled. He would not fail! He was Satedan! Using all his remaining strength he crouched and then uncoiled, hurling himself upward. His hands, fully extended, wrapped around the branch and clamped on, digging into the rough bark. Yes!

Now he was hanging from a tree, his feet dangling several feet above the ground. If a Wraith came upon him now, he would be helpless.

But Ronon did not intend to stay this way for long. Instead he tightened his grip and then swiveled his body sideways, legs scissoring in the air. He had judged the distance well, and his feet slammed into the tree's trunk, almost jolting him from his precarious perch. But the branch shook as well.

Again. His feet hit the trunk hard, his fingers clung to the branch, and everything shook. But through the pain and the fatigue Ronon thought he heard a faint creak above him and to the side.

He hung for a second, catching his breath, and then kicked the tree a third time. Yes, this time he heard a definite sound. It came from the juncture of the trunk and the branch. And it was growing louder.

A fourth kick, and the creak became a groan and then something akin to a scream. The branch, unable to withstand the constant abuse of both Ronon's weight and his attacks on the trunk, shrieked and tore loose, the wood at its base splintering away from the tree and showering the area with a flurry of small splinters. Ronon dropped to the ground, the branch plummeting with him. Only his tight grip on it, and his flinging his arms over his head as he fell, kept it from smashing in his skull.

Ronon lay on the ground for a good minute after that. He could barely breathe, choked by sweat and tears and possibly blood and flecks of tree bark. He could barely see, his thick braids matted and covering his face like a shroud. His entire body ached, the aches turning to twinges of pain as he moved.

But he had a weapon.

Groaning, he forced himself to his feet and hefted the branch. It was good solid length of wood, heavy enough to do real damage, rough enough for a secure grip. An excellent club. He swung it a few times, getting its weight and balance. Not perfect, but it would cave in a head or shatter a limb nicely. He couldn't bite back the grin that tugged at his lips. Now let them come for him. He would take at least one of them with him before he fell.

"Nice club." The voice startled Ronon and he dropped into a crouch, raising his new weapon and gripping it tightly with both hands. "Won't do you much good, though."

A figure stepped from the trees. Ronon stared — he had not heard anyone, had not seen anyone, yet the man moved casually, comfortably, as if he were in no hurry and at no risk. He did keep well enough back that Ronon would not be able to reach him, however. Not a fool, then.

And not a Wraith, either. The man was human, shorter and more solidly built than Ronon, with skin of a redder hue and short hair the color of a deepening sunset. He wore clothes rather than armor, though the way he moved suggested they were reinforced in strategic locations. At his side were a long knife and a pistol, but his hands were empty.

"It'll crush the first Wraith foolish enough to charge me!" Ronon snapped in reply, his words fading to a growl as he thought about the joy he would take in breaking at least one Wraith before they got him. But the stranger shook his head.

"They're not stupid enough to get that close," he answered. "Not right away. They'll shoot you first, most likely in the leg — bring you to your knees, both so you can't run and because it amuses them to break their victims first. Then the shoulder — no way you can wield that branch with only one arm, so you'll drop it. That'll leave you defenseless." He shrugged. "Then they can pick you off at their leisure."

"You have a gun — give it to me!" Ronon demanded. "With that I can kill several before they can close! Or I'll wait, lure them in, and then shoot them!"

The man shook his head again. "They'd still kill you, in the end," he pointed out. "You might get a few of them, but not enough. Not enough to make a difference."

"It would make a difference to me!" Ronon roared back. "They killed my world! They killed my wife! I have nothing left to live for!"

"I can give you something to live for."

Ronon turned his back on him. He was almost out of time, he knew. The Wraith would be here soon. He refused to let himself be distracted.

"Will you listen?" the stranger called from behind him.

"Please?"

"Go away," Ronon growled over his shoulder. He hefted his club again. "I have matters to attend to."

He heard the stranger sigh. "Fine. We'll do it the hard way."

Before Ronon could wonder what the man had meant, he heard an unmistakable sound. The sound of an energy pistol being fired. Even as the noise registered, his body convulsed, the club flying from his grip as his entire frame shook with pain.

Then the darkness swarmed in, enveloping Ronon. He tried to fight against it, but it was everywhere, and his world went black. He didn't even feel the impact when he hit the ground.

CHAPTER FIVE

"DRINK this."

The words shattered the silence, and Ronon blinked reflexively, turning toward the voice. His motion became a wince, however, as flickers of light stabbed beneath his eyelids , and the act of shifting his head sent jolts of pain arcing up from his neck to his temples and back.

"Easy, easy," the voice continued. "Just relax. Cup's right by your mouth. I'll hold it, you drink." He recognized the voice now — the man in the forest, the one who had mocked his plans for vengeance.

The man who had shot him.

"I'll kill you," Ronon managed to whisper. His lips curled in a snarl, and brushed against something smooth, wide, and curved. The cup. The parched agony of his throat betrayed him then, and he felt his lips part slightly, jaw trembling. The man said nothing as he pressed the cup closer and angled it, letting cool water trickle into Ronon's mouth and down his throat. Ronon gulped it gratefully, and felt his senses waken again as some of the pain eased.

"I'll kill you," he repeated, squinting against the brightness and trying to force his eyes to focus on the man in front of him. "They were coming and you took me away from them."

"I took you away so you wouldn't die," the man countered. "What good would that have done anyone?"

Now Ronon was able to open his eyes fully. "It would have ended my suffering," he growled back. "And it might have ended one or more of them as well!"

The stranger shook his head, but his eyes narrowed in a look Ronon knew well. The man was appraising him. "Maybe it would, at that," he admitted after a few seconds. "You've shaken off the stun blast faster than I expected, and snapping that tree limb took a lot of strength. So yeah, you might have taken one of them with you." He leaned forward, gray eyes intent. "But what good would that have done, in the long run?"

Ronon glared back at him. "There is no long run," he insisted. "Not for me. Not anymore."

"There could be again," the man replied.

"How?" Ronon reached for the cup, annoyed at the sight and feel of his arm shaking, but managed to take it from the stranger and raise it to his lips without splattering himself. "Even if the first one falls, they will send others. And they will always know where to find me."

Now the man smiled. It was a cold expression, with very little humor behind it. "Maybe, maybe not." He leaned back. "I can help you. And you can help me, too. Together, we can help each other — and make the Wraith pay."

Draining the cup, Ronon tossed it aside and wiped his mouth on his forearm. "You want to help me? Fine. Give me your gun."

That at least got a laugh from the stranger. "What good would it do you?"

"You already know the answer to that." Ronon stood, warily at first but his balance was still solid and the world stopped spinning after a few seconds. He took a deep breath, then another, and closed his eyes. When he opened them again, he swiveled to stare down at the stranger. "Will you give me the gun or not?"

The stranger laughed. "I like you, I really do — you've got a lot of willpower. But that's not going to be enough to deal with the Wraith."

"It will if I have a gun."

"I don't think so. They'll still — urk!" That last sound leaped from the stranger's throat when Ronon turned and slammed his hand palm first into the other man's stomach. It knocked the wind out of the stranger, propelled him several feet, and left him slumped on the ground against the back wall of what Ronon now realized must be some sort of small cabin, possibly a hunting lodge. The cramped space had three rickety chairs, a small circular table, several old sleeping pallets, and nothing else.

Right now, though, Ronon didn't care about the cabin or its decoration scheme. He was too busy grabbing the stranger's pistol and bolting for the door. He'd hit the man hard enough to stun him for a few minutes, but that meant he had to be well away from here — wherever "here" was — before he lost this window of opportunity. Ronon didn't waste any time — by the time the door slammed shut he was already twenty paces away, and broadening that gap with every second.

Once he was back among the trees — it looked like the cabin had been nestled into a small clearing, and Ronon felt more comfortable with proper cover — he took stock. His head still ached but not enough to do more than slow him down. Same with the rest of him — sore but serviceable. He didn't have any food or water, and he had no weapons beyond the stranger's pistol.

It was a handsome-looking pistol though, Ronon thought as he studied the piece more closely. Longer and sleeker than most laser pistols he'd seen, a bit more solid and significantly better balanced. It had an indicator switch along the left side, just below a pair of tiny lights. So the gun had multiple settings! That was good to know. One of them must be the stun setting the stranger had hit him with, and one must be a standard "kill" setting. Ronon clicked the switch and the small red light lit up for an instant. Perfect.

Then he selected a clump of trees, took up a stance behind them, and waited.

As he'd suspected, it didn't take long. Ten, perhaps twenty minutes passed and then he heard heavy footsteps approaching from the front. They weren't the stranger's either — he had moved through the trees without a sound.

And there had been only one of him.

Ronon took a quick glance around the tree, pulling back smoothly so no sudden movement would tip them off, and frowned. Three Wraith were rapidly approaching his hiding place. He could feel his blood heat up at the sight of them, with their pale green skin and long white hair.

Two of them wore heavy, segmented armor chestplates and strange ridged helmet-masks that completely covered their faces. They carried bulky rifles, the wide stock taking up most of the weapon's length, a glowing energy beam visible through its center. They were soldiers, warriors, and Ronon had faced their kind back on Sateda. They were powerful but slow and not clever. Armed as he was, taking out both of them would not pose a problem, not even in his current state.

The one in front of them, however, was slighter in build and moved more easily, almost catlike in his grace. He wore a long, flowing black jacket and pants rather than armor, and his head was bare, exposing his pallid features and yellow eyes and strange facial slits. His long pale hair hung over his shoulders and midway down his back, and he carried a small pistol of some sort in one hand. That one would be the dangerous one, Ronon knew. His eyes were everywhere, darting from tree to tree, searching. He was a commander, and he would be far more intelligent and resourceful than his two companions.

Ronon targeted him first.

He leaned out from behind the tree and snapped off a quick shot. His pistol flashed red, firing a matching red beam that struck the lead Wraith square in the chest. The creature staggered but did not fall, and its mouth opened into a wide grin, revealing all its sharp teeth.

"Ah, the prey bites back!" It called out, looking directly at Ronon despite the tree between them. "Good, I enjoy a more

spirited contest. Come out and face me, Ronon Dex of Sateda!"
Its grin spread. "Or did all the true men of your world die
when we attacked?"

Ronon knew it was a deliberate goad but that couldn't stop
him from rising to the bait. "The last real man of Sateda is
here," he snarled, stepping away from his cover and present-
ing himself to the three Wraith. "Come and see what kind of
spirit I possess!"

The Wraith eyed him up and down. "Indeed I shall." It did
not gesture or speak to its companions, but they raised their
rifles as one and sighted on Ronon. "Run now and I will give
you a moment's head start, to make this more sporting."

Ronon shook his head. "I'm done running." He fired on the
warrior to the left, but the blow glanced off its heavy chestplate. "And this isn't a sport to me." He aimed for the commander again, but this time the Wraith sidestepped the crimson bolt.

"Your choice," it said with a hint of disappointment, raising its own weapon. "But I had hoped for a bit more enter-
tainment first."

Then it shot him.

Ronon's body convulsed and he almost fell to his knees.
Pain! The feeling was almost exactly like when the stranger had
shot him, only not quite as intense, and he wondered about the
pistol he now held. Where had the man gotten it, and why was
its stun setting more powerful than the Wraiths'? Regardless,
he managed to maintain his grip on the weapon and hefted it
again. This time the Wraith commander was not expecting
return fire, and took the hit square in the chest. It staggered
back, smoke rising from the hole in its armored jacket.

"You dare?" It growled, eyes narrowing. "For that I will flay
you alive before draining your life from your bloody flesh!"

And it sprang at him.

Ronon managed to fire once more before the Wraith was

upon him, knocking his pistol aside. It had holstered its own weapon and now one fist slammed into Ronon's jaw, jolting him and blurring his vision, while the other clamped onto his throat. The Wraith's momentum knocked Ronon off his feet, and he landed on his back, the creature leaning over him and holding his head and torso up by that neck grip.

"Now you will die slowly," it hissed at him. Its second hand raised again, but this time it opened the hand wide, revealing the narrow opening upon its palm. That was how the Wraith fed, Ronon knew — they sucked out a victim's life force through that opening. And it was reaching toward him with deliberate slowness, taunting him with his inability to break away from the death that crept toward him inch by inch.

Then a burst of crimson light flashed across the Wraith commander's head, lighting it with a halo of red. Its eyes widened in surprise before they glazed over, and the creature slumped, its grip on Ronon going limp. He shrugged off the body in time to see a second crimson bolt strike one of the Wraith warriors in the neck, between helmet and chestplate. The warrior gurgled and collapsed.

That was all Ronon needed to see. His own pistol had fallen by his hand and he quickly scooped it back up and hit the remaining Wraith warrior in the throat, dropping it instantly. Only then did he sit up and rub his own neck, coughing against the rawness the attack had produced.

"Feel better now?" It was the stranger, of course, sliding from behind two trees a few feet to the left.

"A bit," Ronon admitted. He glared over at the man, then shook his head. "Thanks." He was honest enough to admit he would have been dead without the man's help.

"Now do you see that your way will only get you killed?" the man asked, brushing aside Ronon's thanks. "Even with a pistol you weren't able to take them on."

"I didn't know their weaknesses," Ronon pointed out.

"Now I do."

"Now you know some of the weaknesses," the stranger corrected, approaching and crouching down so he could speak to Ronon face-to-face. "Wouldn't you like to learn more? To know them all?"

Despite himself, Ronon was interested. How many more Wraith could he kill if he knew all their weaknesses?

Apparently his thoughts were easy to read on his face. "I can teach you how to kill them," the man explained. "I can help you kill them. Together we can wipe out dozens of them, maybe more. Possibly even eliminate whole Hives!"

Ronon nodded and clambered to his feet. "I'm listening."

"Good." The man glanced around. "But not here. There are probably more Wraith on the way. I know a place we can go to buy ourselves some time. Come on." He turned to go, then paused and shifted back, extending his hand. "My name is Nekai."

"Ronon Dex." Ronon accepted the grip. It was firm, no-nonsense, and quick—the handclasp of a warrior.

"A pleasure." Nekai favored him with a brief smile before turning away. "Come on then, Ronon Dex. Let's go talk about how to kill more Wraith."

He led the way into the trees, and Ronon eagerly followed. He spared only a single glance at the three dead Wraith behind them. You are but the first of many, he swore silently. And each of your deaths will feed the soul of my people, that all Sateda may one day know peace.

With those bloody thoughts in his head, Ronon took off after Nekai, already impatient for the knowledge the other man claimed he could provide.

CHAPTER SIX

"WE SHOULD be safe here — for now." Nekai had led Ronon away from the forest and into a row of short hills. They had continued on through those, never stopping for more than a minute to catch their breaths and drink from nearby streams, until they had found a rockier plain beyond. The hills were lower and more angular here, and Ronon's new guide had paid particular attention to their bases — Ronon wasn't sure what he was looking for until the man had nodded, crouched, and brushed some dirt aside to reveal a small opening. A cave.

They had crawled inside, Ronon going first at Nekai's insistence, and now they were huddled in a dark, dank little hole within the rock itself. Ronon didn't like it — he was used to open spaces, and being trapped like this made his skin crawl. It also struck him as strategically lethal — there was only the one entrance. All it would take was the Wraith finding that hole and they would be completely trapped.

"Relax," Nekai assured him, shifting about and folding his legs in front of him. "You're thinking like a warrior. Don't."

"That's who I am," Ronon snapped, though quietly — he was afraid too much noise might cause the ceiling to collapse upon them. "It's how I think."

"No," his new companion corrected him. "It's who you were. That's not who you are anymore. Not if you want to survive."

"I already told you, I don't care about survival," Ronon growled back. "I just want to kill as many of them as I can before they take me."

"And the longer you survive, the more you can kill," Nekai pointed out. "But in order to do that, you have to change the way you think. A warrior charges into battle, even against

overwhelming odds. That'll just get you killed, and quickly."
He leaned forward, his eyes locked on Ronon's. "You need to
become a hunter."

"A hunter?" Ronon considered that. "I know nothing of
hunting," he admitted softly. "My people do not hunt. We
raise domesticated animals for meat." He paused. "Or at least
we did."

"I can train you to be a hunter," Nekai assured him. "You
have the reflexes for it, certainly, and the stamina. It's just a
matter of learning a new way to think, a new way to look at
situations — seeing things as predator and prey rather than
warrior versus warrior." He shrugged. "Once you learn that,
the rest is easy."

"And to what end?" Ronon demanded.

Nekai grinned, a quick flash of white teeth in the near-
darkness. "So you can hunt the Wraith, of course. Isn't that
what you want?"

"They're the ones hunting me!"

"I know." The smile vanished as quickly as it had appeared.
"But that's exactly what makes them vulnerable. They know
you're a warrior — that's why they made you a Runner. They
expect you to stand and fight, just like you did back there.
Twice."

"You knocked me out the first time," Ronon pointed out,
rubbing the back of his head at the memory. It still ached.

"I had to — otherwise they'd have killed you immediately
and that would have been the end of it." Nekai studied him.
"I saved your life."

Ronon could hardly deny it. "I am in your debt."

His companion waved that off. "I don't want your debt, Ronon
Dex. I want your friendship. I want your skills. I want you hunting at my side, as an equal." He returned to his original line of
thought. "They think you are a warrior. When you become a
hunter, you can use that against them. They won't be expecting

it, and so you'll have the advantage. Prey turned predator." His grin this time was far nastier. "You'll be able to take them down before they have time to adapt to the change."

Ronon studied the man in front of him. Nekai seemed at ease most of the time, his posture relaxed, but he was always alert as well — his eyes were constantly on the move, sizing up the small space around them. His hand never strayed too far from his pistol. And there had been real anger there when he spoke of the Wraith.

"Why do you care so much what happens to me?" Ronon asked softly. "Why should any of this matter to you?"

"Why?" For a second Nekai seemed startled by the question. Then he leaned forward again. "Because, Ronon Dex — I was just like you." He nodded at Ronon's expression. "Yes. I am a Runner as well." Nekai shifted around and raised his jacket and shirt slightly — even in the dim lighting Ronon could see the massive scar across the other man's back. It looked to be right about where he bore his own recent wound.

"My people, the Retem, resisted the Wraith's dominance," Nekai continued, restoring his clothes and leaning against the wall again. "The Wraith slaughtered them and destroyed our planet completely. It is little more than cinders now." The bitterness in his voice was unmistakable. "Those they did not kill they captured, to serve as slaves — and as food." He glanced away. "I was one of those they took alive — they felled me before I could throw myself upon my blade. I had been one of our people's finest warriors, and had killed several Wraith before they were able to subdue me, so they decided to make me an example." His lips twisted in what Ronon took to be grief and pity and possibly disgust. He was starting to see that there was far more to this man than he had realized.

"They made you a Runner?" Ronon prompted, when Nekai fell silent, no doubt as haunted by his memories as Ronon was by his own.

The question roused Nekai again. "Yes," he agreed. "Implanted the tracker in my back, just as you have in yours, and released me on the nearest planet. Then they hunted me." He met Ronon's gaze again. "I stood and waited for them, just as you did. I wanted nothing more than to throw myself upon them and die in battle, so that I might join the rest of my people in the afterlife of our forefathers."

Ronon was almost afraid to ask. Almost. "What happened?"

To his surprise, Nekai laughed, a grim sound but one with some genuine humor. "The first Wraith to catch me was too disappointed to kill me. 'There is no sport in this,' he complained when I hurled myself at him. 'Run away, little human, and keep running. Give us a reason to chase you. Show us you are the warrior we took you for, not a sniveling coward who throws his life away for no reason.' And then he walked away."

Ronon blinked. "I would have torn his heart out for speaking to me in such a way!"

"I felt the same way," Nekai agreed. "His contempt made me furious. But then I thought about it, and realized he had been right." He nodded. "Yes, he was right. Trying to get myself killed like that was the coward's way out. A true warrior would do as much damage to his enemy as possible, for as long as possible. And that's what I was determined to do."

"So you went after him and killed him?"

Nekai shook his head. "No. I ran." This time his laugh was entirely at Ronon's expression. "Are you horrified? But if I'd attacked him again right then, he just would have killed me or recaptured me and that would have been that. In order to do serious damage to them, I needed to regain my strength and find a way to fight back. That meant time to plan, time to heal. And in order to gain time, I had to keep out of their reach. So I ran."

"For how long?"

His companion sighed. "Two years."

Ronon stared at him. "Two years?"

"Yes. I had little choice — no weapons, no armor, no allies. My only hope was to keep moving and to hope something changed."

"So what happened?"

"I got lucky," Nekai admitted. "I found one of the ancestral rings — you know of them?" Ronon nodded — they had the strange circular portals on Sateda as well, and the elders knew the secret of activating them. "I'd seen them back on my home-world," Nekai continued, "and when no one else was around I snuck over to this one and managed somehow to get it open. That took me to another world. The Wraith came after me fast, before I had a chance to really get my bearings, but I managed to active the ring again, this time to a different world, and fled through that to one as well. That continued for a while — I'd reach a world and stay only long enough to find whatever food and water I could, then flee to the next before the Wraith could arrive. Usually I just foraged for fruit and nuts and, when I was lucky, meat. But finally one time I passed through and spotted a curl of smoke not far away." He smiled, remembering. "It was a village. Not big, but big enough for my needs. They were hunters and fishermen, judging by the trappings, and everyone except a few women and children were out when I reached the outer-most hut. They were a bit primitive, technologically speaking, but I found a dagger, a spear, and a bow and arrows." His smile turned sharp. "And now I had weapons."

"You fought back." It wasn't a question.

Nekai nodded. "Oh, yes. The same Wraith came for me, the one who had let me live that first time. He found me hud-dled over and growled 'Still you throw your life away? Then this time I will not refuse such a gift!' And then he grabbed my shoulder, no doubt to drain my life from me and toss my shattered body aside."

"But you were feinting," Ronon guessed. "Drawing him in."

"Exactly. As soon as he touched me I spun around and impaled him on my new spear. Then, while he was staggering back clutching at it, I grabbed his own gun and shot him with it. In the head. Three times." Nekai's smile wasn't pleasant. "Then I cut off his head, just to be sure."

Ronon nodded. He could hardly blame the other man. If he ever faced the Wraith who had released him, he would no doubt be just as brutal. Some things could not be forgiven.

"Now I had real weapons," Nekai concluded. "A Wraith pistol to go along with my spear and bow and knife. And I also had this." He tossed something at Ronon, who caught it reflexively. It was a small tablet, the entire front a small blue screen. There was a grid patterned across it, with a glowing green dot in the center, and around it a pulsing red circle.

"What is it?" Ronon studied the image. "What is this dot and why is it throbbing?"

"It's not." Nekai glanced around again, listening carefully. Then he gestured. "Come on." And he began crawling back out of the cave.

"I thought we needed to stay out of sight," Ronon asked even as he followed the other man. He was happy to get out of that tight space, to breath fresh air again and to stand up straight, but at the same time he didn't want to present the Wraith with an easy target. Not now, when he was just beginning to believe that it might be worth surviving a little longer.

"We do, but a minute or two won't give them enough time to pinpoint us, and I can't show you how this thing works if we're that close together." Once they were out, Nekai moved away, stopping perhaps forty paces from Ronon, who still stood right by the mouth of the cave. "Okay, look at it again."

Ronon glanced at the screen and saw that now there were two red circles. One was still around the green dot but the other was a short distance away. And neither of them were pulsing—they both glowed steadily.

"It's a tracking monitor," Nekai explained. "It shows the tracking devices they implanted in us. This is how they find us."

"Not much of a range," Ronon commented, studying the screen again. Given the distance between them, and the spacing on the monitor, he guessed it had an effective range of a mile, perhaps less.

"It's set to close-range right now," Nekai replied. "It took me a while when I first acquired it, but I eventually figured out how to scale in or out. Trust me, it's got enough range to cover the entire galaxy." He gestured at the device. "That's how they find me no matter what planet I go to. Once they reach the planet themselves they can zoom in to pinpoint my exact location."

Ronon frowned. "But before, in the cave, it was pulsing."

"Exactly!" Nekai started walking slowly back toward him. "Keep your eyes on the screen," he instructed. Ronon did so, and saw that as the two circles—his and Nekai's—overlapped, their edges began to waver. They flickered more and more, their shapes wobbling, until Nekai was standing beside him again and the circle was only a faint shape brightening and dimming randomly around the green center dot.

"I met another Runner once," Nekai said, taking the monitor back from Ronon. "I'd just happened to look at the monitor—not much point in it usually, since it just shows my own location—and there was a second circle! I used the thing to find him, and that's when I discovered what happens when two Runners are less than ten meters apart. The circles overlap! Apparently the Wraith never expected Runners to meet, so they didn't take any precautions against it—the tracking devices cancel each other out when they're this close together."

Ronon understood the implications at once. "So as long as we stay close, they can't track us."

"Exactly!" Nekai grinned, a predatory look, and Ronon

knew his own expression matched it. "We can get the drop on them."

"Excellent." Something didn't make sense, though. "What about that other Runner?" he asked. "The first one you found? Where is he? Two are strong but three would be stronger."

Nekai nodded. "They would, yes." He looked away. "I found out something else that day, too. Because the first thing we did when we met and realized we were both Runners was agree to remove each other's tracking devices. Then they wouldn't be able to track us at all."

Ronon nodded. It made perfect sense — render the trackers useless, or better yet remove the tracking devices but keep them operational. Then you could use them to bait an ambush. "What went wrong?" Obviously something had, since Nekai still had his tracking device.

"They're rigged, the devices," Nekai answered quietly. "If you tamper with them — they explode." He didn't have to explain beyond that. "But if we can't remove them, at least we can negate them," he added, shaking off the memory. "Which means we can turn the tables on the Wraith." He studied Ronon. "So, what do you say now? Still want to throw yourself at the nearest Wraith and go out in a blaze of glory?"

Ronon smiled and stroked the pistol at his side. "No. Not any more." He faced the smaller man. "Teach me how to hunt. Then I will show these Wraith what happens when they allow a Satedan to live."

"Good." Nekai clapped him on the back. "We'll start at once. But for now —" he gestured to the cave entrance. "We should get back inside. They might have noticed us while we were separated."

Ronon nodded, but hesitated a second before crouching and ducking back into the cave. "Is this part of being a hunter?"

"What, sitting in narrow spaces for extended periods?" Behind him, Nekai laughed. "Oh yes, my friend. A very big part."

Ronon sighed. Still, if it meant being able to kill many Wraith, it would be worth it.

CHAPTER SEVEN

"YOU'RE dead."

"What? No!" Ronon rose from his crouch, but slowly. It wouldn't do to move too quickly — not with a pistol pressed against his temple like that.

Nekai lifted the pistol, then holstered it. His reply was a single word: "Again."

Ronon was still processing recent events. "How did you find me?" he demanded. "I was careful!"

"Not careful enough," his mentor told him.

"I watched where I stepped." Ronon insisted. "Nothing but solid rock. No tracks."

That got a smug smile from the other man. "Too bad you didn't look up."

Ronon glared at him. "Explain."

"You did a good job with the tracks," Nekai agreed. "But you forgot that the ground isn't the only way to keep track of someone's progress. You brushed against branches, vines, tree trunks — you bent leaves and disturbed moss." He shook his head. "It was even easier than following footprints — at least this way I didn't have to stoop."

Ronon sighed. "This isn't working," he complained, leaning against the nearest tree. "It's been weeks, and I'm not getting any better. Actually, I think I'm getting worse."

"Learning to hunt takes time," Nekai told him, but he perched on a nearby tree root himself. "There's a lot to cover. And I've got to unlearn you a lot as well."

Wasn't that the truth, Ronon thought, idly drawing, spinning, and holstering his pistol in a single move. Before Nekai, he had thought he was an expert fighter, a trained warrior and strategist capable of handling any combat situation. But it turned out that was only true for open warfare. This was hunting, the art of tracking prey and then moving in silently, striking without warning and killing quickly and quietly, and for that he had no background. In fact, much of his prior military training directly contradicted what he needed here — he'd been taught speed over stealth, maximum damage instead of subtlety. This was all different. He really did have to forget half of what he knew so that he could learn a new way of doing things.

Fortunately, Nekai was proving to be a patient teacher. No, that wasn't really true — he wasn't patient, not in the sense of waiting for Ronon to figure things out on his own or leaving him time to get things right. But he was persistent, and dogged. And he yet to explode at Ronon, to insult him or belittle him or call him stupid — all standard tactics in Satedan military training, getting the recruit angry enough to focus past the pain and fatigue. Nekai kept telling Ronon he was doing well, that this took time, that he had fine skills and excellent potential, but he also never let up. This, too, was a whole new way of doing things.

Case in point — Nekai leaned back on his perch and shut his eyes. "Two hundred," he announced softly. "One ninety-nine. One ninety-eight. One ninety-seven . . ."

Ronon rose with a groan. He had already learned that Nekai didn't kid about training, not at all. If he was counting down, he meant it — and when he reached "one" he would open his eyes and shoot Ronon where he stood if he was still in sight. And the Wraith stun-pistol Nekai used — apparently his backup weapon, but since Ronon now had his usual pistol and no intention of ever giving it back Nekai was using the stun-pistol entirely these days — hurt like hell when it hit you. It didn't stun Ronon completely, not on the first shot, but it did stop him in his tracks, and Nekai had no compunctions against following that first hit up with two or three more to make sure he'd put Ronon down.

One of these days, Ronon swore to himself, he was going to
turn the tables on the stocky Retemite. He was going to sneak
up on Nekai and stun him instead. That thought was now just
as powerful a motivation as the idea of killing more Wraiths
in keeping him moving and training.

Which meant that perhaps Nekai's way wasn't all that different from Satedan methods after all.

Ronon woke up at dawn two months later to discover that he
was alone. That wasn't entirely unusual — Nekai often woke
before him and scouted the area, or found some sort of food.

Food — that had been another new experience. Ronon had
never hunted before. Now he was learning how to hunt Wraith,
but he was also learning to hunt animals. They kept moving,
switching to a new planet every two to three days so the Wraith
couldn't pinpoint their location during the times when they
were far enough apart that both their tracking signals would
be clear, and Nekai could tell at a glance whether a planet held
edible flora and fauna. Ronon was learning how as well. It had
to do with recognizing various plants, noticing telltale hints
of poison in their fruit or nuts or roots, but also in searching
for and reading animal tracks, teeth marks, dung, and other
signs. Now he knew the difference between marks made by a
small burrowing mammal and a large, poisonous reptile, and
could tell whether fluttering overhead was from harmless birds
or dangerous bats or deadly winged snakes.

Even so, the first time he'd had to shoot an animal he had
found it incredibly hard. He had lowered his pistol several
times before finally taking the shot. And it had been set on
stun, because a killshot from the weapon would have charred
the creature and left it inedible.

"Why is it," he had wondered out loud after the beast had fallen
and he and Nekai had crouched beside its still form, "that I can
shoot a man or stab him or cut him without a second's hesita-

tion, but I could barely bring myself to shoot this thing?"

"Because the man was trying just as hard to kill you," his mentor had pointed out. "This beast wasn't doing anything to us. It couldn't hurt us if it tried." Judging from the sharpened horn gracing the animal's brow, Ronon wasn't entirely convinced of that, but certainly it had made no move toward them. It had raised its head in alarm when Ronon had lowered his weapon the second time, its delicate ears swiveling toward the faint noise, but had looked poised to run away rather than to charge.

"Don't feel bad for not wanting to kill it," Nekai had assured him. "That's natural. It means you're not mean-spirited — you kill it because you have to, not because you want to. But you do have to. We need to eat to survive, and this creature wasn't smart enough or fast enough to escape you. That makes it prey." He'd pulled a knife from somewhere — Ronon was never entirely sure where his mentor stashed all the knives he seemed to carry — flipped it over so the blade was resting atop his palm, and had offered it hilt-first to Ronon. "Now you have to finish the job."

Ronon had forced himself to slit the creature's throat, making sure the cut was fast and smooth so it felt no pain. He had lost whatever food had already been in his stomach the first few times Nekai had shown him how to skin, gut, and dress an animal, but by then he was able to handle the chore without difficulty or pause. Nekai was right — they needed to eat. And any beast foolish enough to be taken down by them probably deserved it. Especially since they never killed more than they needed, which meant it was only the slowest, stupidest animals around that became their prey. That had made it a little easier, but not a lot.

This morning, however, was different. Ronon knew that at once, because not only was Nekai gone, so were all traces that he had ever been there. All except for one.

Sitting atop a small rock not far from his head was a device

Ronon had never seen away from Nekai before. The tracking monitor. And under it was a single scrap of paper.

"You have two hours," he read as he picked up both the monitor and the scrap. "Find me before I find you."

Great. Another test. Of course. As their training had progressed and Nekai had pronounced himself pleased with this or that aspect of Ronon's new education, these little tests had become more frequent — and more difficult. But this was a new one. Usually Nekai told Ronon how much time had and where he had to go or what he had to do, then they split up. For Nekai to have left before Ronon was awake, and to have removed his tracks as he went, and to leave the monitor behind — this had the feel of a final exam. All or nothing.

Ronon studied the monitor in his hand. He could cheat, of course. Turn it on and use it to pinpoint the other man within minutes. Not that Nekai wouldn't lay some sort of trap for him, but he was confident he could find his way around or through that. And using the tracker was how the Wraith would come for them.

The Wraith! Ronon glanced up and around quickly, his free hand going to his pistol. How long had Nekai been gone? If there was a Wraith already in the area, and the creature had one of their tracking monitors, he would have noticed both Ronon's signal and Nekai's. They might not have much time.

But Nekai knew that better than anyone. That's why he was only allowing Ronon two hours. Two hours from dawn, presumably — he knew that was when Ronon woke if not awakened by something else beforehand. So Nekai must have felt that they would be safe for those two hours. Or safe enough.

Ronon nodded to himself and slid the tracking monitor into his pocket without switching it on. He wouldn't cheat. Nekai had probably known that. But he needed to know he could find the Retemite on his own, using just the skills Nekai had taught him and his own instincts and senses. He needed to know he could do this without any help.

Crouching down, Ronon studied the ground around him carefully. No footprints, no drag marks — Nekai was careful. Maybe too careful. He grinned as his eye registered a swathe of dirt that was a little smoother than its neighbors. Gotcha.

Straightening and dusting his hands off on his pants legs, Ronon drew his pistol, made sure it was still on stun, and headed into the scrub brush surrounding the little clearing. He was on the hunt.

Some time later, he glanced up at the sky, gauging the time from the position of this world's sun. At least that was a skill he'd already been taught in the military, even the calculations necessary to adjust for a sun's size and a planet's proximity to it. Right now, he'd say it had been at least an hour and a half since he'd left the spot where they'd camped the night before, and possibly closer to two. Which meant Nekai would be hunting him soon instead of just the other way around.

He'd followed the brushed-out trail at first but had quickly lost it as the undergrowth had thickened, making it unnecessary to hide footprints. The ground here was covered in dry leaves, wet leaves, creeper vines, moss, and occasionally flower petals. The trees were close enough together to provide excellent cover but far enough apart to allow a man to slip between them without difficulty. Low branches offered concealment from above, as did hanging vines, and the foliage filtered the sun so only speckles of light shone through, dancing across dust motes and creating constant shadows. It was a perfect place to hide — or to hunt someone unsuspecting.

Fortunately, Ronon was well aware of that. Unfortunately, so was Nekai.

He had picked up the Retemite's trail twice more, once when the shorter man had nudged aside a hanging vine and disturbed its place on the branch above and once when he had brushed leaves back into place behind his feet but had flipped one over, leaving it the only dry leaf among a patch of damp ones. Both times the trail had vanished again a few paces later, but Ronon had kept to the same general direction, sure Nekai meant to put as much distance between them before doubling back. The trick would be noticing when he did begin that wide turn, otherwise Ronon would keep right on going and Nekai would be able to come at him from behind.

Nor had his mentor left the area unprepared. Twice Ronon had noticed snares, once just barely in time — his foot had literally been an inch off the ground when he'd spotted a vine with a little too much tension in it and had realized it was a rope concealed among the true foliage. He'd been forced to roll forward to avoid stepping into the trap, which had taken him safely out of harm's way but had meant he'd spent several minutes concealing all the marks he'd left from that tumble. He knew Nekai would probably circle back and hunt for him along his own previous path, so there was no sense making it easy for the other man.

Given the time, Ronon was sure Nekai had already begun his turn. He hadn't seen any evidence of that, but he could feel it in his gut. Which just left the question of which way to go. If you were simply running from someone, you'd want to turn away from the sun so you could better see what you were doing and where you were going. But if you were hunting someone — or evading someone hunting you — you'd do the opposite. You'd turn toward the sun, using its glare to dazzle your pursuit so you could duck away and sneak up on them more easily.

Ronon turned toward the sun. Even through the thick canopy above the sudden light made him blink, and he ducked behind a tree as he waited for his eyes to adjust. Then he glanced around —

— and noticed a faint sheen to the bark on the tree beside

him, a handspan or so below his eye level.

He broke into a slow grin. Nekai had done the same thing he'd just done, stepped behind a tree while his eyes got used to the increased light. That tree. The sheen was where Nekai's shoulders had rubbed against it, staining the sensitive outer bark ever so slightly. Ronon stepped away from his own protective trunk and glanced at it. Sure enough, he'd left a similar sheen. There was no way to conceal that — rubbing at the bark would only make it worse — but at least now he knew he had chosen correctly. Nekai had gone this way, and had turned at exactly this point, two hours in.

Which meant the other man was somewhere ahead of him, and just beginning the process of sneaking back around to strike at Ronon.

But Ronon was ready for him. He stroked the pistol at his side. This time, he was going to teach his mentor a thing or two about hunting. Mainly that sometimes a good thing was simply too good to be true.

Ronon cursed. And for good reason. He was currently hanging upside down. His left foot was trapped within a vine loop he'd triggered by stepping into it, and the pressure of his weight had knocked loose the counterweight and jerked the vine and the branch holding it — which had been bent downward and pinned in place — up rapidly, yanking him from his feet and upending him to hang here trussed like a fatted calf.

Just waiting for a hunter — or a Wraith — to stop by and finish him off.

A faint rustling caught his attention, but it was behind him and Ronon couldn't exactly turn around. Still, he wasn't surprised when a voice cut through the silence of the forest a second later.

"I thought I'd trained you better than that," Nekai commented as he emerged from the bushes. Even listening hard,

Ronon could barely hear his footsteps as the stocky Retemite came closer, pistol raised and leveled at Ronon's chest. "You were doing so well, too — picking up on my tracks, avoiding my snares, covering your own traces well." Ronon was sure the other man was shaking his head now. "Then you got careless."

"Must have," Ronon admitted. "I'll do better next time."

"What makes you so sure there will be a next time?" There was no humor in Nekai's tone, and Ronon felt a chill run down — or up — him.

"What're you saying? That I failed?"

"I don't know," the other man admitted quietly. "I really am surprised by you. I thought you'd do better than thi —"

The rest of Nekai's words were cut short as his foot came down among a clump of wet leaves — and they shifted beneath him. Ronon had managed to twist and sway enough that he could see his mentor off to the side of his vision, so he had at least a quick glimpse of the shock on the other man's face as Nekai realized what was happening. Then Ronon's snare had closed around his ankle, the counterweight had fallen, and the Retemite was being hoisted into the air. The sudden force of the ascent knocked the stun gun from his hand, and it fell to the leaves below as Nekai hung there, swinging from the built-up momentum of his rapid rise.

"How?" he sputtered as Ronon bent his left leg, pulling himself higher. Then he bent and reached up with both hands, grasping the vine just above the loop. The added pressure above the knot forced it to loosen and he pulled his foot free, then swung both legs down and dropped easily to the ground. His own pistol was securely in its holster, and he drew it now, covering Nekai even as he crouched and collected the fallen Wraith stun gun.

"I spotted the snare without a problem," Ronon admitted, straightening and taking a few steps away from his strung-up mentor. No sense getting within range of the man's knives. "So I rigged one of my own just a few steps away from it." He shrugged, trying not to grin. "Then I stepped into yours and waited for you to hear the commotion and come running." The grin slipped free anyway. "Which you did."

"You couldn't know which direction I'd come from," Nekai insisted.

"No, but I knew you'd circle around until you were behind me," Ronon pointed out. "So I positioned the snare where I wanted it, then adjusted my own orientation until it was directly at my back." His grin widened. "The rest was easy."

Nekai studied him for a second — then laughed. "Nicely done," he admitted. "You used my own planning against me, and I fell for it. I am impressed."

"Then I passed?" Ronon asked, lowering his pistol slightly but still not moving too close. "Can I cut you down, or are you going to try for me anyway?"

"You definitely pass," his mentor assured him. "The test is over." Ronon holstered his pistol and drew a knife, slicing through the vine with a single quick overhand slash. Nekai fell to the ground, twisting and curling into a ball to lessen the impact. He was on his feet a moment later, and Ronon handed him back the stun gun without a word.

"You've learned well, Ronon," Nekai told him once he was armed again, and had removed the snare's loop from his ankle. "There's only one thing left now, one final step."

"You said I passed," Ronon reminded him, his grin fading a little bit. How many more tests would he have to endure?

"This isn't a test," Nekai answered. "More like a proving ground. It's time."

"Time for what?" But deep down, Ronon already knew the answer, and his mentor echoed it a second later, a predatory grin crossing his face.

"Time to hunt a Wraith."

CHAPTER EIGHT

SNAP! Ronon tensed, then forced himself to relax. He uncurled his fingers from around the butt of his pistol, unclenched his stomach muscles and his jaw, lay flat again, and forced himself to breathe slowly. Patience. He had to have patience.

Where were the damned Wraith? Why weren't they here yet?

It had been over three hours since he and Nekai had separated. Nekai had suggested they wait another day, until they had both eaten and slept and Ronon had recovered from the stress and tension and effort of their recent mutual hunt. But Ronon had refused.

"Now," he'd insisted. "I want to do this now."

Nekai had decided not to argue. Probably he had seen the determination — what Melena had often called the "stonewall stubborn" on his face. Or maybe he had just accepted that it would be better to get this out of the way once and for all.

Besides, resting hadn't really been an option. During the hunt there'd been the risk that the Wraith might detect their signals and come looking for either or both of them. Disguising the tracking devices now would only intrigue any Wraith already in the area. They'd either have to flee to another planet immediately — or let the Wraith come, and deal with them once they arrived.

Ronon was all for the latter. He'd been itching to kill Wraith since they'd first attacked his homeworld, and that itch had grown into an all-consuming rage once they'd killed Melena and the rest of Sateda and taken him captive. He'd suppressed the desire while training only by constantly reminding himself that what Nekai was teaching him would make him better able to kill Wraith and in much greater quantities.

Well, now it was time to put that to the test.

So Nekai had headed back toward a cave he'd selected for just such a purpose — the minerals in the walls would make him more difficult to pinpoint, he claimed. And Ronon had selected a likely spot, set a few snares and other traps, and settled in to wait.

And here he was. Waiting.

He hated waiting.

What if there hadn't been any Wraith in the area already, he wondered for the hundredth time. What if none of them were within range to detect his tracking device? What if he was laying in wait for an enemy that would never show? How long could he wait? A day? Two? Eventually he'd need to move, if only to find food and water. Otherwise when a Wraith did show he'd be too weak to deal with it.

Snap!

Ronon went completely still. His ears strained, trying to pinpoint the location and source of that sound. It had been nearby, certainly, but not right beside — definitely within visual range if he dared to turn his head and look, which he did not. There were dry leaves and small twigs littering the ground here, which was one of the reasons he had chosen this spot. It was all but impossible for anyone to sneak up on him here.

Snap! Crunch! Crack!

Too many sounds, too close together, Ronon decided. More than one pair of feet tromping through the forest on this fine cool day. If they were Wraith there would probably be three of them, two soldiers and one commander, just as there had been before. The last time, Ronon had needed Nekai's help to finish them off. Not this time.

At least, he hoped not. He had hunted animals without a problem, and had even gotten the drop on Nekai himself this morning. But that had been one man. This was three Wraith. He had never hunted multiple targets before, and suddenly

Ronon found himself cursing Nekai's oversight. Why hadn't they gone after small packs and prides and other groupings, to get experience for exactly this sort of situation?

True, he had a plan. He thought it would work. But there was no way to be sure. Not until it happened. And if the plan failed? Well, that would be very, very bad.

Ronon waited, unmoving, and listened for more noises. They came soon enough, and confirmed what he had already guessed: three of them, all moving in this direction, all walking together. One of them was a little better at stealth than the other two, who didn't care what they stomped on or how much noise they made.

Wraith.

Ronon grinned. Let them come, he thought. His hand tightened on the pistol but he still didn't draw it. Not yet.

He had learned to be patient. At least patient enough to make sure his prey was exactly where he wanted them before he struck.

The noises were drawing still closer, and now Ronon thought he could make out actual footsteps mingled with the other sounds. Two sets, at least — the third was almost more an absence than a presence, a noise that did not accompany one-third of the dry-stick sounds that reached his ears. The commander was not bothering to avoid dry leaves or twigs, he could clearly care less about being undetected, but his step was naturally light enough not to register.

Still, the other noises and the sounds of the two soldiers made tracking their progress incredibly easy.

Ronon finally allowed himself to tense a bit as the three strangers passed into his line of sight. Wraith, just as he'd thought. And they were moving in the same configuration as the first trio he'd met, the commander in the lead and the two warriors flanking and slightly behind him.

Perfect.

Ronon had to force his hand away from his pistol. He had always been an excellent shot, and his time in the Satedan military had honed that skill to a razor edge. Then Nekai had honed it further. Military training taught you to aim for vital organs, to cause the most damage in a single shot. But that often left an opponent bleeding out and staggering around — they were no longer a threat so you didn't much care how far they got before they finally dropped. Hunting was different. You wanted your prey to stay close — the further it got the harder it was to chase it down again, and the more likely some other predator would try to claim it. So you aimed for incapacitation, joints and killing blows — if you couldn't kill right away you sought to immobilize your target so you could finish it off quickly.

Plus there was the whole issue of shooting from cover. That had been a completely new experience for Ronon — he had never been the "hide in the bushes, then attack by surprise" type. His attack formations had usually involved head-on charges, shooting and slashing all the way. But his last encounter with the Wraith had proven better than any lecture that such a technique would not be effective here. He couldn't overpower three Wraith, not by himself. And he could never count on outside help or reinforcements, not even from Nekai. Especially not while hunting — if the Wraith ever figured out how their signals overlapped, they might devise a way to counter that, and then Ronon and Nekai would lose their one advantage, not to mention their one measure of cover.

So Ronon had to take out all three Wraith as quickly as possible, as quietly as possible, and by himself.

Which meant not shooting any of them. Not yet. He couldn't guarantee he could take them all down before one of them tagged him, or called in help. And he couldn't take that risk.

Instead, he slowly, quietly shifted his hands forward and lifted the vine he had coiled just in front of his head. It was the strongest one he could find, strong enough to withstand his yanking on it with no ill effect, and he had looped a section of it and made a crude but very effective slipknot. Now he shifted his weight slightly on the thick branch he had chosen for his perch, and raised the loop, gauging the distance to the figures approaching his tree.

They had a tracking monitor, of course. Which meant they could find his position, no matter how carefully he hid.

Fortunately, it had apparently never occurred to the Wraith to look up.

They were about to learn the folly of that particular oversight. Too bad they wouldn't survive the discovery long enough to pass it along to the rest of their kind.

He would snare the one to the right — a quick toss would put the loop around the warrior's neck, a sharp tug would tighten it, cutting off the warrior's air, and then a solid pull would lift him off his feet and into the air, hiding him within the thick canopy. To his companions it would seem as if the warrior had simply vanished. At the same time, a branch snare would strike the warrior to the left, knocking him off his feet and distracting him long enough for Ronon to kill the snared warrior and then shoot the downed one as well. That would leave only the commander, confused and alone. He'd be searching the trees for Ronon by then, but Ronon would have switched perches as soon as the first warrior was dead, and for all their skills the Wraith were hardly woodlands masters. He would be able to escape the Wraith commander's detection, sneak around, and take him out from behind before the Wraith could figure out what to do next.

Assuming everything went according to plan.

Time to find out, Ronon told himself. He hefted the loop. The Wraith were almost directly beneath him now, and he tossed the vine down and out, making sure to give it a small snap of the wrist so the loop floated wide rather than closing up.

It settled perfectly around the warrior's neck.

Ronon gave the rest of the vine a sharp tug, and it tightened obediently —

— and caught on a protrusion of the warrior's heavy breastplate.

Nine hells!

The vine went taut as the warrior pulled it to its full extension, and the impact stopped him short. It didn't lift him off his feet, however, and with the loop snagged it didn't interfere with his breathing at all. All it did, in fact, was alert him and his companions to the fact that there was someone or something in the trees just overhead.

Not surprisingly, the warrior raised his stun-rifle and opened fire on the canopy.

The second warrior stepped forward, shifting to get past his commander and get a cleaner line of fire — and the branch snare struck him full in the chest. Exactly as planned.

Only he didn't fall down.

He did stagger back from the force of the blow, but his rifle rose at the same time and he began shooting into the foliage around him. The Wraith weapons were designed to stun rather than kill, so that the Wraith could then feed upon the helpless victim, but they did still produce some kinetic impact, and so the shots tore at the branches and leaves all around.

The commander, meanwhile, had taken a step back. He surveyed the plant carnage calmly, studying the scene — and then he looked up. Right at Ronon. Their eyes met, and the Wraith smiled, showing all his pointed teeth.

Nine hells.

Ronon was up off his branch in an instant. He hurled himself forward, landing full-force on top of the commander before the Wraith could raise his stun-pistol. Rolling forward, Ronon came to his feet just behind the two warriors, who were still firing wildly and had just started to realize there was a foe standing among them. He had his own pistol in hand in an instant, and snapped off a quick shot at the one on the left, wounding the Wraith and sending him to his knees. But that was all Ronon had time for. He could already hear the commander stirring behind him, and in a few seconds he'd have three very angry Wraith on him, and no cover whatsoever. That was a recipe for disaster.

So Ronon did the one thing Nekai had worked so hard to drill into him, the one thing that went against not only all his military training but against the very core of who he was.

He ran.

In four long paces he was hidden from immediate view. In eight even his motion was lost among the trees. In ten he had swung to the right, sliding between two tree trunks. Several more steps put him beside another tree a little further removed, and he caught a low branch and pulled himself up into its leaves. Then Ronon forced himself to take slow, deep breaths to stop his gasps and calm his racing heart, and he tried to listen past the thudding of his own blood.

The Wraith would be after him in seconds, he knew. With the tracking device, he couldn't hide no matter how good the cover. And though they had no aptitude for this terrain, there were three of them and they could communicate telepathically so they could coordinate without a sound. There was only one of him. He didn't have any other snares ready. He hadn't prepared any backup plans. And he had only the one gun and the one knife.

Ronon listened for pursuit, and grinned.

Time to improvise.

CHAPTER NINE

THERE was an old tree up ahead a ways, one that had rotted through and fallen at some point years past. The trunk had shattered when it fell, but large sections still survived, covered in moss and vines. Ronon had noticed it when he and Nekai had first arrived on this planet, and he'd used it for cover once during his training. Now he took a second to orient himself properly and then ran for it as fast as he could. The Wraith would be cautious, fearing a second ambush, but they would still be right behind him. He didn't have much time.

There was the little clearing the tree's fall had created, and there were the trunk segments. One of them was a little over eight feet long, almost completely hollowed out by rot and rain and insects, large portions of the top missing completely. Perfect. Ronon skidded to a stop just past it, deliberately took several more steps beyond that, and then carefully stepped to the side and retreated to the trunk, leaving no additional footprints to mark his change of course. That would give him an extra second or two, no more.

He studied the shattered trunk. Moss covered much of it, and vines had already crept around it as well. Rain had made the ground beneath it soft, and it had sunk in slightly. Perfect.

Squatting, he dug his fingers into the crumbly bark as far down as he could. Then, tensing his back and shoulders, he lifted. He felt his muscles pop with the strain as the ground resisted yielding its treasure, but after a few seconds something shifted under his hands. Then the trunk rose suddenly, as if the earth had surrendered all at once.

The ground beneath the trunk had been worn into a small crevice. It was damp and slimy and covered in grubs. Lovely. But Ronon didn't have time to be squeamish. Making sure his pistol was secure in its holster he stretched himself out in that narrow depression, all the while holding the trunk off with one stiffened arm. Then he slowly lowered it back into place. It didn't fit into the ground again, of course, but judging from the thin sliver of light along its side it should be close enough that only close scrutiny would reveal it had been moved.

He didn't intend to give them enough time to notice that.

Then he waited. It wouldn't be long, he knew. The Wraith were angry now, and the commander was intrigued as well. They would be after him as quickly as they could manage without blundering into another trap.

Too bad for them the trap was already waiting.

Ronon had his head to the side, the rough bark on the bottom of the trunk scraping his cheek, his arms folded and hands on either side of his head, palms flat against the tree. The air was musty and rich and dank, but it wasn't a bad smell, just earthy. Grubs squirmed under him but he did his best to ignore them and concentrate on the sounds beyond his makeshift hideout.

After a few seconds he was certain he could feel a faint vibration through the ground. Footsteps.

Then he heard them as well. Two sets, close by. As before, the commander's footfalls were silent.

Something crunched against the edge of the tree trunk, and the footsteps stopped. One of the warriors had nudged it with a booted toe. The sliver of light had vanished along most of one side. The Wraith were here. They were right overhead, Ronon knew. The tracking device showed he was here, but all they saw was a rotting tree trunk. So they assumed he was hiding within it, planning to ambush them.

Several energy discharges, matched an instant later by impacts on the trunk that shuddered through to his arms and face and body, confirmed Ronon's guess. The warriors had fired their weapons into the trunk, stunning the man lurking in that hollow.

Only he wasn't there.

He couldn't hear them — no doubt they were conversing in their heads — but Ronon could see the light shift to the side and he knew they were confused. They were wondering where he was, and whether the tracking device had been wrong somehow.

In a second they would back away and scan the area again.

Which meant he had to act — now.

With an enormous effort, Ronon put all his strength into his arms and legs — and heaved. The tree trunk, already dislodged, rocketed upward in a shower of shattered bark and tattered moss and rotted wood. It smashed full-force into all three Wraith, slamming them backward with its bulk.

Ronon was up in a sitting position the instant the trunk had cleared him, pistol flying from its holster. He put two shots into the chest of the warrior to the left, who dropped instantly, his breastplate smoking, the flesh beneath it destroyed, the Wraith heart within vaporized. A third shot took the other warrior under the right arm as he flung the trunk to the side, trying to clear it out of the way so he could raise his stun rifle. Then Ronon was rolling to the left, springing to his feet, and dashing across the clearing. Two energy blasts at his back told him the Wraith commander had been quicker to recover than his bodyguard, but both shots missed as he dove into leaves and vines and trunks, vanishing again from view.

Safely within the trees, Ronon grinned. One down, and one wounded. The odds were shifting.

Of course, next time the Wraith would be looking both high and low. He wouldn't be able to pull the same trick twice.

But that was fine. He had plenty of other tricks.

Ronon made his way carefully but quickly to the east, toward the one large water source they had found — a wide, quick stream that flowed out from under the hills, cascaded across several rocks, and then split into a series of rivulets that snaked their way among the trees. Some of those rivulets were clean and clear, flowing across rock and stone and tight-packed soil. Others grew muddier, traversing softer ground. And still others disappeared completely, absorbed into the earth around them. It was toward the last that Ronon turned his footsteps.

He had to be very careful here. Nekai had cautioned him of that when they had first arrived, and Ronon had discovered it for himself when he'd sunk up to his waist with a single wrong step. The ground here was thoroughly saturated, and though it looked solid it was little more than a wide bog. He was heavy enough that only a few spots could hold his weight.

But then, so were the Wraith.

Ronon made his way across the bog, wishing desperately that he could speed up but knowing to do so would spell his own death. He was only a third of the way across when a stun-bolt sizzled past his right shoulder, leaving it tingling from the near miss.

Out of time. He would have to hope he had gone far enough.

Turning, he spotted the Wraith commander and his remaining warrior. The warrior was the one who had fired — Ronon guessed he was too far away for the commander's stun-pistol, exactly as he'd hoped. And the warrior was having trouble holding his rifle, his right arm held at an awkward angle. The wound Ronon had just given him was throwing off his aim.

Perfect.

Crouching, Ronon raised his pistol and fired back. They were too far away for his shots to have any real effect, but they didn't know that, and both Wraith immediately dropped into defensive stances themselves. Then they began to creep across the field toward him, weapons raised.

They were paying full attention to him and his weapon. What they should have been watching were the ground beneath their feet.

The warrior stumbled first, of course — he was in front, and he was both heavier and clumsier than his master. He took a step and his foot sank into the ground, his weight parting the water-soaked earth like a curtain. The sudden shift caused him to pitch forward, and his elbow must have caught one of the more solid patches because his body tilted to the side like it had been shoved over. Then he had vanished beneath the bog's surface. The ground there rippled for a second before settling again. At a glance, no one would ever know the Wraith had disturbed it.

The Wraith commander was staring, aghast, at the spot where his warrior had been just seconds before. Ronon took advantage of that distraction to shift to the side several paces. He had deliberately kept what he thought was the edge of the bog close at hand, and now he felt the ground beneath him change in composition, becoming sturdier, dryer, and more solid. He was back on proper earth again. Which meant he could move normally without having to worry about falling through.

Too bad the Wraith commander couldn't say the same.

The remaining Wraith glanced up as Ronon sprinted toward him, eyes wide in shock. Surely he was wondering how anyone could move so quickly across ground that acted more like liquid than solid. That didn't stop the Wraith from raising his pistol and firing, but he was still badly shaken and misjudged Ronon's speed. The first shot was simply too far away, and the second crackled through the air more than a foot behind him.

Then Ronon was in range as well. He already had his own pistol in hand, and he fired once, twice, three times. Each shot struck true, hitting the Wraith in forehead, neck, and cheek. He toppled, thrusting out an arm to catch himself, and recoiled as his hand plunged into the bog. That instinctive revulsion saved him from sharing his warrior's fate, pulling the Wraith commander back and causing him to fall over backward instead. Fortunately for him, he landed on solid ground, right where his feet had been an instant before. Unfortunately, Ronon's attack had already done its work. The Wraith commander was barely alive when Ronon slowed to a stop beside him.

"Well . . . played, Runner," the Wraith gasped out as Ronon peered down at him, careful to keep just beyond its? reach. He knew all too well about the Wraith's feeding capabilities — one step too close and the commander could latch onto him, drawing from his life force and healing the damage. He wouldn't let that happen.

"You . . . gave me . . . a good . . . challenge," the commander continued, his voice growing weaker with each word. Already his eyes were starting to lose focus. "Glory to . . . the one who . . . captures . . . you." The last word was barely a whisper, and the commander slumped, his eyes glazing over. He was dead.

"No glory, then," Ronon told his fallen adversary grimly. "Because no one's going to capture me. Not ever." He stared at the body a moment more, then crouched beside it. Other Wraith could already be on their way, so he had to work fast. He took the Wraith's stun-pistol — it always paid to have a backup weapon — and stripped off the creature's long leather coat as well. Then he rolled the body over and forward and let the bog claim it. Once it had vanished Ronon rose and made his way back toward the cave where he knew Nekai would be waiting.

"It's me," Ronon called softly, coming to a breathless halt just shy of the cave. He didn't know how deeply his mentor was dug in, whether the Retemite could see him, but he did know better than to approach unannounced. "It's over."

After a few seconds, Nekai emerged, stun-pistol in hand. He studied Ronon, taking in his battered, mud-spattered appearance. "What happened?"

Ronon held up the leather coat. "They died. I didn't." He glanced up at the sky. "We should go."

"Absolutely," Nekai agreed. He disappeared again, but reemerged a few seconds later, his pack slung over his shoulder. "Congratulations," he said, offering his hand once he was close enough. "How does it feel?"

Ronon returned the handclasp and grinned. "Like a good start."

"Excellent!" Nekai clapped him on the back. "Now you're ready."

"Ready?" Ronon frowned as they disengaged. "Ready for what?"

But his mentor only smiled. "You'll see."

Nekai turned and led the way out of the foothills without another word. Ronon had no choice but to follow. No, that wasn't true—he did have a choice. Nekai had given him that. He could turn away, make his own course, and hunt the Wraith on his own. He had the skills now. But they'd be after him soon, and without Nekai to cancel out his tracking device he'd be an easy target. So perhaps it wasn't much of a choice at all.

Besides, Ronon admitted to himself as they walked, he was curious. All this time, Nekai had only concentrated on his training. But now, the way he'd said "you're ready," made it sound as if he had something bigger in mind.

Ronon had learned to trust the other man. Nekai had saved him from the Wraith, and in a way from himself. He was willing to see where the man would lead him next.

"Okay, so you learned hunting from Ranger Rick, the crazy version," Rodney commented, stretching and then biting back a curse as he bumped an elbow against the low ceiling. "That's swell, and very touching. What does that have to do with our current predicament?" He was being testy and he knew it, but he was tired and sore and he hated being stuck here in this little tiny alcove of a cave!

"I'm getting to that," Ronon assured him, taking a swig from his canteen. He offered it to Rodney, who accepted it and drank, though not before wiping the lip with his shirt cuff. He could hear his companion's smirk even in the near darkness.

The water was warm, and flat, and had that particular tang that came from being stored in a canteen too long. But it eased the dryness in his throat, and Rodney swallowed gratefully before handing it back. "So this guy who trained you," he continued after a few seconds, "this Nekai, he's the one we're dealing with?"

"Maybe."

"Maybe?" Rodney groaned. "If you're not even sure it's him, why are we doing Happy Story Hour?"

"If it's not him, it's one of the others." Rodney heard the growl in Ronon's voice and knew the big Satedan was just shy of losing his temper. As usual.

"Okay, okay." Rodney shifted and tried to make himself more comfortable, which of course just meant exposing other parts of his body to unfamiliar aches and pains. "Please continue."

Ronon glared at him for a minute, and it seemed like he might decide not to, just out of spite. But finally he picked up the tale again. "He led me out of the foothills," he explained, eyes and voice looking back into the distant past once more, "and straight to the planet's ancestral ring. I'd more or less expected that. It was what happened next that took me by surprise. . . ."

CHAPTER TEN

RONON studied the ancestral ring as they approached it, every sense on high alert. He kept expecting the massive circular arch to activate and a Wraith Dart to emerge from its depths, weapons firing down upon them before they could scramble to safety. And this ring, like all the others he'd seen, was set in a small clearing, so if danger did pour from it they would be easy targets.

"You learned how to activate the ring entirely on your own?" he asked Nekai as the other man made his way to the altar-like console and began tapping the broad square panels in some sort of sequence. Back on Sateda only a handful of elders and military commanders had mastered the secrets of the ring, and the techniques for opening and closing gateways to other worlds was carefully guarded — Ronon had been through rings several times, but a high-ranking officer had always been on hand to open the connection. Nekai had claimed he'd figured out the process himself, but what he was doing now seemed too careful and planned for Ronon to completely believe that.

"Not entirely," Nekai admitted over his shoulder, his hands still moving. "There were people on my world who knew how to operate it, and I had seen them at work enough times to have some sense of the procedure." He finished and glanced up. "When I went on the run I had no choice but to experiment firsthand." Then he grinned. "I'm still not entirely sure what I'm doing."

"So we could walk into the middle of a sun?" Ronon asked as the air within the ring began to shimmer and thicken. It rippled like water, then a plume burst forth from its center, quickly subsiding back and leaving a glistening surface stretched between the ring's edges.

"I doubt it," his mentor assured him. "They didn't put rings in suns, as far as we know." Not that anyone really knew much about the Ancestors or their activities — who was to say they hadn't been able to walk the surface of a star as easily as a man might stroll through a grassy plain? "But don't worry — this time we're going someplace specific."

Ronon was intrigued. Up until now he was sure they had selected locations entirely at random — that way if any Wraith were tracking them they wouldn't leave a discernible pattern. But now Nekai had a destination in mind?

"Lead the way," Ronon instructed, gesturing toward the ring. His companion chuckled but took the lead, walking confidently toward the ring and then stepped into it. The shimmering field parted around him, and he disappeared within its glowing surface.

With a sigh, Ronon followed, but he kept his hand on his pistol. He hated this part.

There was that second of disorientation, that sensation of being stretched and pulled and condensed, combined with the sudden rush of rapid motion. Everything blurred around him, his eyes only registering streaks of light and color, his ears filled with a dull rush as if they were trapped within a waterfall. He couldn't tell which way was up, what was forward, but his foot was still half-raised and so he set it down in front of him and then raised the other foot, trusting his body to complete the familiar motion.

Then he was through to the other side. The rushing faded, the colors resolved into a small, stark clearing surrounded by rocks and cliffs, his sense of balance returned. Ronon wasted no time shifting to one side of the ring and scanning the area. Nekai was doing the same.

There was no one else here, no sign that anyone else had been here, and after a second they both straightened. The air within the ring swirled in on itself, the shimmer vanishing into a tiny central vortex, and then with a faint popping sound that disappeared, leaving nothing but empty air behind. The ring had closed. Then Nekai made his way to the console nearby, a twin for the one they had left behind, attached a small dark square he'd pulled from a jacket pocket, and pushed a sequence of panels. There was a spark from the other object, which leaped to the console and produced an answering arc of electricity.

"Can they follow us here?" Ronon asked, relaxing only slightly. He relaxed a bit more when Nekai shook his head.

"Not a chance," the Retemite assured him, removing and pocketing the square. "I've scrambled the record of that last connection."

Ronon studied him. There was definitely something the stocky man wasn't saying. "How do you know?" he demanded. "We're here, they're there. How can you be sure?"

"Because I've been here before," Nekai answered easily, "and I've even used the same ring to reach this place twice in a row. I know how to recall the last destination entered, and when I tried it I got nothing. So I know scrambling it works."

Ronon nodded. That made sense. And it fit with Nekai's sense of caution. Of course he'd go back to a world he'd just come from, to make sure he'd removed all traces of his previous passage. "What was that little square thing?" he asked. "Is that what did it?" He'd never heard of anything that could affect an ancestral ring or its console, but his education in that area was admittedly limited.

"Just something I picked up in some old ruins a while back," Nekai answered. "Come on." He was already leaving the clearing and Ronon caught up to him in two long strides. The other man had his stun-pistol tucked in his belt but Ronon kept his own weapon drawn. He believed Nekai that the Wraith couldn't follow them here through the ring, but that didn't mean they hadn't found some other way to track them. Or that there weren't other threats nearby.

They seemed to be high up, he noticed as they half-walked, half-climbed. The air was thin and cold, and he almost considered putting on the Wraith leather coat he'd so recently acquired. But the idea of something from the Wraith touching his skin made him shiver worse than the cool breeze, so he kept the garment wadded in his other hand instead. He wasn't even entirely sure why he was keeping it, since he wouldn't ever wear it, but something in him had wanted a trophy. And perhaps he'd find some other use for the garment some day.

The ground was rough here, all rock and stone with only whatever dirt the wind had carried to them, and soon Ronon had to holster his pistol and tie the coat around his waist so he could free his hands for climbing. Nekai didn't speak and so Ronon didn't either, concentrating instead upon finding handholds and footholds through the crevices and up the cliffs and along the ledges that formed their current path.

Finally, after several hours of difficult travel, Nekai crested a small rise and nodded. Joining him, Ronon saw a small valley nestled into the rocks just below them — and something filling that space. Something large.

A spaceship.

"You keep this hidden here?" Ronon asked as he followed the Retemite down a narrow trail to the valley and up to the ship. He was impressed — he knew Nekai was resourceful, but stashing an entire ship here just for emergencies? That was something!

"There aren't any ancestral rings where we're going," Nekai responded, pulling a gray-brown tarp from the small ship and keying a code into the panel beside the airlock. The lights on the panel shifted to green and the door hissed as it slid open. He stepped inside, carrying the bundled-up tarp with him, and Ronon quickly followed.

It was a simple vessel, not unlike ones Ronon had traveled

in or even flown during his military days. Bare bones, no frills but good sturdy construction, decent shields but only a single gun and that only for last-ditch efforts — firing the weapon would probably drain the ship's power completely. This thing wasn't built for long-range travel, or for combat. It was strictly a shuttle.

Ronon scanned the sky through the viewport as Nekai slid into the pilot's seat and began powering up the engines. "We heading to that moon?" he asked, pointing at a faint crescent high in the sky.

Nekai hid it quickly, but Ronon saw the other man's eyes widen for a second. "How did you know?" he demanded.

"Just figured," Ronon answered with a shrug. He hid his grin and dropped into the co-pilot chair. Nice to know that even after these months of training he could still surprise the Retemite.

"Not bad," his mentor admitted, shaking his head. "I knew I was right about you." He didn't say anything further, but hit the thrusters. The ship groaned as power surged through it, then shuddered slightly as it lifted off the ground. It hovered for a second, adjusting its fields, and then shot into the sky with enough force that Ronon was pressed back into his seat. Seconds later the pressure eased as the planet's atmosphere fell away behind them, and they were out among the stars.

Ronon had always enjoyed space travel. There was something very freeing about floating through the galaxy, untethered by gravity, surrounded by the welcoming dark of space and the comforting twinkling of the many stars and other bodies it contained. It was beautiful up here, and soothing. This was the first time Ronon had been in space since his capture — or at least the first time he had been able to see it, since during his captivity he'd been held deep within a Hive somewhere — and he released a deep breath and let some of the tension ease out of him. Sometimes he thought he could simply stay up here forever.

It never lasted, though, and this trip was no exception. Already Nekai was turning the shuttle, curving its path around the planet and angling toward the moon that floated there, just out of reach. It was a small moon, blue-gray in color though its surface sparkled where the sun's rays struck it. Judging from their trajectory, Nekai was bringing them toward its dark side, out of sight of both sun and planet.

"What, you have a secret base up there?" Ronon asked idly, studying the moon as it drew quickly closer.

"Something like that," his companion replied. He didn't say any more, and Ronon decided not to press it. He'd find out soon enough.

Nekai proved to be a competent pilot if not a good one, and the shuttle jolted a bit as it came in for a landing on the pitted surface of the moon. Ronon pressed back into his chair, letting it absorb most of the impact, but was still tossed about as the shuttle set down. At least there wasn't a tearing sound coming from the underside, so he didn't think Nekai's fumbling had ruptured the hull. If it had, they'd know soon enough.

When the ship had halted its motion, groaning to a stop, Nekai shut everything down. "Suit up," he instructed, tossing a light atmospheric suit at Ronon and grabbing another himself off the rack occupying the shuttle's side wall. Ronon did so quickly — the suit was a standard one, much like the ones he had used as a Specialist, and was easily donned, sealed, and activated. He noticed as he did so that the rack still held six suits. Were they just spares, or was Nekai not the only one who used this shuttle — or this moon?

Once they both had their helmets on and oxygen pumping through, Nekai opened the airlock and hopped out. Ronon was right behind him. The moon had very little gravity, so his first step outside carried him several meters away in a slow arc.

He'd have to be careful about that. It had been a while since he'd had to move in microgravity.

With the shuttle shut up tight again, Nekai motioned for Ronon to stay close. Then he crouched and sprang, his momentum carrying him halfway to a cluster of nearby ridges, their shapes perfectly conical without an atmosphere to deform them. Ronon took off after the shorter man, his longer legs propelling him quickly, and he caught up in two strides, just in time to avoid slamming into those precipices. They were shorter than he'd first thought, perhaps fifty meters tall, and Nekai's next bound carried him straight up — he grabbed the closest cone near its top and hung there, waiting for Ronon to join him.

When Ronon was hanging from one of the crags as well, Nekai gestured ahead of them and down toward the ground. Ronon followed his motion — and stared. He had been half-expecting the secret base he'd joked about, so the sight of a deep crater just behind the peaks was not completely a surprise. It was exactly the terrain he would choose for a hideout: close to a flat plain where the shuttle could land, concealed behind these peaks, and deep in shadow.

But that didn't mean he'd expected the domed base he saw below him.

This was no mere hideout, Ronon realized as Nekai released his grip and let the moon's weak gravity tug him gently groundward again. He studied the dome more carefully as he followed his mentor down. It had been textured to match the moon's surface, he noticed, so it would be hard to spot unless you were practically on top of it. And it was big. Far too big for the needs of just one man.

His feet touched the ground and he bent his knees to absorb the impact, rather than be flung skyward again. By the time he straightened up there were two guns in his face.

That explained the extra atmosphere suits.

Ronon raised his hands slowly, palms outward, fingers extended, to show he wasn't about to try anything. The strangers weren't worried about Nekai at all, and when the Retemite motioned they lowered their weapons and stepped back, though they didn't holster them. Fair enough. Ronon would have done exactly the same in their position. For now he'd have to trust Nekai, and the fact that the man had spent far too much time training him to just lead him into a trap. The fact that these two clearly trusted Nekai as well was hopefully a good thing.

Nekai had already moved past their welcoming committee. Now he stepped up to the dome and pressed his hand flat against its surface. A quick swipe and part of that covering slid aside, revealing a door panel, which Nekai quickly accessed. Seconds later a portal opened behind the covering, which Ronon could see now was like a curtain over the dome itself. Nekai was already ducking through, and Ronon followed, his two temporary guards bringing up the rear.

Inside, the dome was equipped much like a military camp, with tents and folding chairs and crates of equipment. Three other people were sitting around a smokeless fire and stared as they entered. The dome's door was a full airlock with an inner door that had cycled open only once the outer door had closed again, so the trio weren't wearing atmosphere suits. Their clothes looked rugged and a bit worn, clearly meant for durability and comfort rather than fashion, and all three had pistols at their sides — he'd seen them reach for the weapons when they saw him, but then relax when they noticed Nekai and realized he was still flanked by his guards.

"Nekai! You're back!" One of the strangers — a short, slender woman with close-cropped white hair and large, slanting green eyes — hopped up from her crate and rushed over. She hugged him quickly, then stepped back, frowning. "Where've you been? We thought maybe you'd been taken."

"Sorry," Nekai told her as he pulled his helmet off. "No way to get word once we'd begun." He gestured for Ronon to remove his helmet as well, then addressed the others. "Everyone, gather round." The two left by the fire quickly joined them. "Meet Ronon Dex, former Specialist of the Satedan military. Now a Runner. Just like us."

That made Ronon start, and he studied each of these strangers in turn. They were all Runners?

They were studying him just as closely, and he could see the suspicion on their faces. And the caution that came only from hard experience. It was an expression he knew he carried himself. Yes, they were Runners. He'd never imagined there could be so many of them, much less that they might all be in one place. He would have wondered how each of them had managed to survive, but suspected he already knew the answer to that one. Clearly there was more to Nekai — and his plans — than he had realized.

"Ronon," Nekai continued, "this is Turen" — the woman who had hugged Nekai nodded — "Adarr" — one of the two behind him, a lean man nearly as tall as he was with skin the color of bleached bone, spiky white hair, and arctic blue eyes — "Frayne" — a short man with broad shoulders, long arms, and a fuzz of orange hair across his head and cheeks and jaw — "Setien" — the other guard, who proved to be a tall, powerfully built woman with thick black hair and regal features — "and Banje" — the last to approach, a man of average height and build with weathered skin, dull brown hair, but sharp black eyes.

Ronon nodded to each of them, and most of them nodded back, though Adarr and Setien still hadn't holstered their weapons. "What is this place?" he asked Nekai, though the question was tossed out to all of them. Several of them frowned, and they all turned to the Retemite for his answer. Just as Ronon had thought — Nekai was their leader.

"This," Nekai answered, "is our home. Such as it is. We are

the V'rdai." He turned and clasped Ronon's hand. "And you are now one of us."

CHAPTER ELEVEN

THAT proclamation brought an instant wave of noise.

"What?" was the most obvious reply, shouted by several of the others at once. "Have you gone mad?" came from the raven-tressed warrior-woman, Setien. Banje was the only one not shouting. His scowl said more than enough all by itself.

"Hold on." Ronon held up his hands, both to ask for quiet and to protect himself in case any of them turned to violence. He left his pistol in its holster, though — no sense antagonizing them. Further. No one responded, so he raised his voice. "Hold on!" That shut them up, and they all turned toward him instead of Nekai.

"I appreciate being included," he told them and Nekai, "but I don't even know what's going on here. And it's clear you're a unit. I don't want to disrupt that." He'd figured it was a fair bet that most, if not all, of the others had military training like his own, and the shift he saw from several of them confirmed that. They knew military language, and recognized what he was saying — that he'd respect the chain of command, that he wasn't here to cause trouble or take over, that if he was included he'd play by the rules. That meant a lot.

Ronon remembered all too well when his unit back on Sateda had been assigned a new member. The newcomer had been cocky at first, brash and demanding, convinced he knew better than anyone else, including Ronon himself. As a result, he'd tried bucking the system, ignoring rules he didn't like, bending others, and both encouraging and even occasionally ordering the others to do the same. He'd acted like an outsider, and so they'd treated him like one. It had taken Ronon dragging him outside one morning and beating him almost to a pulp before the new addition had accepted that you had to know your place, and accept it. After that he'd lost a lot of his arrogance, and had discovered that the more experienced unit members knew a lot they could teach him. Tyre had eventually become a valued member of the unit, Ronon's right hand, but it had been neither a quick nor an easy process.

Ronon was determined not to repeat his lost friend's mistakes.

"You won't disrupt it," Nekai assured him, glaring at the others to make sure they got the message as well. "And you are one of us."

Ronon shook his head. Nekai was an expert hunter, and he said he'd been a warrior, but it was obvious he'd never been a soldier. Perhaps the Retem had had no fixed military, no standing army — Ronon had seen worlds like that, where everyone was trained to fight and came together in times of need, but still fought more or less alone. Good for learning to be self-sufficient, but bad for understanding how to build a unit and foster the close camaraderie needed in such a team. Ordering the others to accept him was not the way to win their approval.

Then again, neither was contradicting the commanding officer. Especially not right from the start.

"What is 'us'?" Ronon asked instead. "You said 'V'rdai' — I don't know that word."

As he'd hoped, one of the others answered. "It's short for 'V'rdai Nehar'lem,'" the white-haired woman — Turen, Ronon remembered — told him sharply. "Nekai taught it to us — it's a Retem phrase. It means 'when the hunted become the hunters.'" Her quick, vicious grin told him what she thought of that idea, and he caught approving nods from the others as well.

Ronon studied her. Slight build, short stature, white hair, slanting eyes, pert features — "You're Hiñati," he half-asked after a second.

Those large green eyes widened slightly. "You know of my people?"

"We had trade dealings with them," Ronon told her. "Our composite armors for your blades."

"We made beautiful blades," she agreed, her eyes unfocusing as she stared off into the past. "Elegant and deadly."

"I know — I had one," Ronon agreed. "A dagger, double-edged, long as my hand, with a horn grip. Perfectly balanced."

She was studying him in turn now. "Your people gave us our armor?" She took in his nod. "They were well-crafted — light but sturdy, durable, surprisingly flexible." Ronon felt a flush of pride. Sateda had been known for its armor. "Not that it stopped the Wraith," she added, almost as an accusation.

"Nor for us either," he agreed, biting back an angry reply about her people's blades being no more effective at saving either world. He was trying to build bridges, not burn them. "I'd gladly have it again, though — and I miss that dagger."

That earned him a small, quick smile from her. "I miss mine as well," she admitted softly. "Perhaps some day we'll find some of them again, my people's blades and your people's armor. They would serve us well now." Ronon noticed the "us," which could have been meant to include him along with the rest. One person at least conditionally willing to accept him.

The others were still unswayed, however. "There is no 'us,'" Setien insisted loudly. "We are V'rdai. He is a stranger." She leveled her gaze at him, gray eyes as hard as flint boring into him. "You are not welcome here. Go back whence you came."

"His world is gone," Nekai snapped at her. "Just like yours. And yours. And yours. Just like all of ours. They destroyed his world and made him a Runner. The same as they did to each of us." Hearing it stated so baldly struck Ronon like a physical blow, and he gritted his teeth as he fought to keep his legs from buckling beneath him. He knew Sateda was gone, of course — he had seen much of it destroyed before he was taken, including his beloved Melena. But hearing it described, its utter desolation described so matter-of-factly, stripped away any false hopes he might have still harbored. There really was no going back. He was the last Satedan alive. Or at least the last one alive and free.

"That's not our problem," the short orange-haired man — Frayne? — was saying. "I'm sorry for him, but he's not V'rdai. He's not one of us. We're a team." He glanced at Ronon, sympathy evident in his face. "What we do is dangerous, to ourselves and to those around us. You're better off on your own."

That produced a snort from Turen. "Better off on his own?" she scoffed. "That's ridiculous! If you don't want him here, say so, but you know as well as I do that being on his own would only get him killed, and fast!"

Nekai was wise enough to step in before the exchange grew more heated. "He knows what we do," he told the rest of them. "Or at least, how we do it. Where do you think I've been all this time? I've been training him."

That got stares from everyone, and Ronon made a mental note. There were two kinds of commanders — those who shared their plans and those who didn't. Nekai was clearly one of the latter. If the commander had his team's trust, such a relationship could work, but it meant following blindly and trusting him to know what he was doing. Ronon wasn't big on trust. Still, Nekai had yet to steer him wrong, and had saved his life and given him the skills he needed to pursue his goal of vengeance, so he would at least give the man the benefit of the doubt. For now.

"You trained him?" Banje asked. "To make him one of us?"

Nekai nodded. "I was out scouting when I saw the dot appear on my monitor," he explained. "I knew it wasn't one of you, which could only mean one thing — a new Runner. So I went to check him out." He grinned at Ronon. "He was howling his rage at the top of his lungs. Then he broke a limb off a tree — not a dead branch, a live limb — and prepared to club the first Wraith to get close." Several of the others chuckled, but all of them nodded slightly. Ronon guessed he wasn't the first to take such an aggressive course of action.

"Did he knock you out?" It was the tall one, Adarr. They were the first words he'd spoken directly to Ronon, and they were surprisingly friendly.

"Shot me," Ronon agreed. "In the back." The chuckles grew louder.

"Three times," Nekai added, which Ronon hadn't known. The chuckles changed to gasps. "It took three shots to take him down."

"Three?" Frayne was staring openly at Ronon. "That's insane! That's —"

" — as many as it would take to put down a Wraith," Nekai finished for him. "Yes."

"A Wraith — or one of their followers," Banje pointed out quietly. His voice was as sharp as his eyes, but soft at the same time. "How do we know he isn't one of them?"

But Nekai was already shaking his head. "He hates the Wraith as much as any of us," the Retemite assured them all. "I've seen his eyes when he faced them. Believe me — he'd rather die than submit to them." Ronon nodded fiercely, scowling back at Banje. Any man who claimed he was a Wraith follower would pay with his life for such an insult!

To his credit, Banje nodded and held up his hands. "Sorry," he told Ronon. "Just making sure." Ronon could hardly argue that one.

"So you've spent the past three months training him?" Turen asked, returning to the original conversation. Ronon was already starting to like her.

"Yes, and he's a natural," Nekai answered. "Once I convinced him that running away was sometimes the smartest move."

More chuckles, this time even from Setien — judging from her aggressive stance Ronon suspected she'd been just as uncomfortable with that thought as he had been. "He killed three Wraith just hours ago, all without my help." The glances this time were more appreciative, less hostile, and Ronon understood why Nekai had told him he was finally ready. It hadn't just been about making sure he'd mastered the skills — it was also about earning the trust of the other V'rdai.

"I was brought in six months ago," Adarr volunteered suddenly. "My people were the Fanash. When Nekai found me, I was trying to chip a piece of stone into a spearhead." He stepped forward, past the others, and extended a hand. "If Nekai says you are one of us, I welcome you."

Ronon met him halfway and clasped hands with him. "Thank you."

Turen was next to offer her hand, and she smiled as she welcomed him to the V'rdai. Frayne was less enthusiastic. "I guess we'll see how it goes," he muttered, but his handclasp was firm.

That left Setien and Banje — the most aggressive member and the one Ronon had already pegged as Nekai's second in command. It didn't surprise him that Banje was the one who acted first. As second, he had to back Nekai. Plus he had yet to be antagonistic, just cautious.

"It may take a while for you to fit in," he warned as he shook Ronon's hand. "But give it time." That quiet addition told Ronon that Banje wasn't worried — he was just cautioning him not to assume an instant bond with the others, or to assume he had their complete trust yet. Which was fair. Trust had to be earned.

Everyone turned to Setien, who was still standing behind Ronon, her pistol lowered but still in her hand. She was glaring at him, at Nekai, at all of them. Then she sighed. "Fine!" she announced, making a big display of holstering her weapon.

"You can stay. Unless you anger me, in which case I'll snap your neck!"

Adarr grinned. "She threatens everyone like that," he assured Ronon. "You'll get used to it."

Ronon nodded. "You're welcome to try," he told Setien, but he made sure he was grinning when he said it. He wanted her to see that he wasn't making a threat. Still, as tall and powerful as she was, he was still bigger, and he was an expert at barehanded combat. He had no intention of being a pushover. One of the most important tricks when joining a unit was establishing that you could hold your own, so that when you did give way they knew it was from respect and not from weakness.

Setien answered his grin with one of her own. "I'll take you up on that," she assured him, and Ronon didn't miss the looks of horror that flashed across most of the others' faces. Clearly they'd all sparred with her before. Only Banje was unswayed—he gave Ronon a quick nod, clearly understanding his move and approving of it. Already Ronon could see that Banje was the one to watch for cues on how to behave.

And he had a feeling he was going to need a lot of cues.

CHAPTER TWELVE

"YOU'LL bunk with me," Banje told him. He was giving Ronon a quick tour of the dome, which wasn't very hard considering it was perhaps a hundred meters across. Of course, that made sense given the tracking devices each of them bore — they'd want to stay close to at least one other at all times to blur the signal and keep them and their base undetected. "Adarr, you're with Frayne." The two other men nodded, as did Ronon. Nekai would have his own tent, of course, and clearly Banje put the newest man in his own tent where he could keep an eye on him. Adarr had been the most recent before Ronon, but now he'd proved himself and could bunk with Frayne instead.

That was fine. Ronon judged Frayne to be twitchy and a complainer, neither of which sat well with him. Adarr was friendly — maybe too friendly, the kind who wanted to sit up all night swapping stories and being buddies. Ronon didn't need that when he was trying to sleep. He had the feeling Banje would be quiet but not rude, and that was ideal in a tentmate. Especially if they were going to be getting into combat situations.

Because no one had told Ronon yet exactly what the V'rdai did. He got that the name spoke to some vengeance, and that was fine with him, but how exactly? What was their structure? What were their plans, their strategies? How did they intend to hurt the Wraith? He was itching to know, but figured this was a test, the first of many. They were waiting to see how long before his curiosity won out over his discipline and he started asking questions.

He was determined to wait them out.

"That's our tent," Banje continued, gesturing at the second of three that formed a neat row beyond the fire. "Frayne and Adarr are to the left, Turen and Setien to the right. Nekai's is over there." That was a fourth tent, a short distance away from and behind the others. The commander clearly liked his privacy. Or maybe the others just felt it was a mark of respect — Nekai hadn't seemed too concerned with distance when they were curled up in a cave hiding from the Wraith.

"We don't bother with a proper mess," Ronon's guide was saying. "Not enough of us to need one. We keep the fire going during the day and use that for any cooking, and we rotate chores. Can you cook?"

Ronon shrugged. "Well enough." They'd handled things the same way back in his unit, and he hadn't been the best at preparing meals but he hadn't been the worst, either.

"Fine. Stores are there" — another tent, this one much bigger — "and basic equipment's over there" — another large tent beside it. He eyed Ronon, specifically his attire — he was still wearing the loose shirt and drawstring pants the Wraith had given him upon his capture, now spattered with mud and blood and filth from the past three months. "We've got some clothes that'll probably fit you. Boots're a little tougher, but we'll see what we can do. Setien's a fair hand at cobbling, though you'd never know it — if we don't have anything that fits she can probably put something together."

Ronon and Nekai had shucked their atmospheric suits after the initial introductions, and now Banje eyed the leather coat around Ronon's waist, his bland features wrinkled in distaste. "You plan on wearing that?" was all he said, but the tone spoke volumes.

"No." Ronon didn't bother to explain further. Maybe by the time he figured out what he wanted to do with the trophy, he'd be comfortable enough with the others to feel like talking about it. Maybe.

"That's Nekai's pistol, isn't it?" Frayne asked from behind Ronon. He was gesturing to the weapon at Ronon's side.

"Not anymore," Ronon told him. He grinned, and the

smaller man backed away a step. Yes, definitely twitchy.

"How'd you get his gun?" Adarr wanted to know.

Ronon shrugged. "I asked." The answer apparently stunned the others into silence, and after a second the tour continued.

The dome was well laid-out, in proper military fashion. The space had been divided into quadrants. There were chemical latrines off in the far corner of one quadrant, showers in another, equipment and stores in a third, and the one airlock centered in the wall of the fourth. The fire was at the center, with the tents just behind it. The rest was open space. Plenty of room to train, to spar, to pace. The supplies, what Ronon saw of them, were a strange mixture. Some looked like military issue, no-nonsense and sturdy. Others were clearly handmade, though those ranged from crude to elegant, from barely lashed together to cunningly fitted. Then there was everything in between, most of which looked as if it had been purchased at some rural bazaar. Considering they had access to an ancestral ring, Ronon guessed that some of the materials had been purchased on various worlds, and others had been crafted here. It gave the dome a more eclectic feel, softening the military edge but not disguising it completely.

"Water's reclaimed from the air, and recycled from waste," Banje mentioned. "We ration it, both for drinking and for cleaning, so don't make a mess." They'd returned to the area around the fire. "Food's a mix of rations and whatever we can bring back from a hunt. Not a lot of frills here, but it's solid and safe." He turned to face Ronon. "Any questions?"

Ronon could almost hear Adarr and Frayne hold their breath, so he deliberately opened his mouth as if to speak — then shut it again. "Nope," he finally drawled before dropping to his haunches and then stretching out beside the fire. The other two men goggled at him.

"That's it?" Frayne couldn't help asking. "'Nope'? You're in this dome with five other Runners, you have no idea who we are or what we're doing, and you don't have any questions? None at all?"

Ronon shrugged, putting all the nonchalance he could into that gesture. "Figured you'd tell me anything I needed to know," he said slowly. Then he smiled.

"Ha!" Adarr crowed. The tall thin man slapped his leg. "He totally suckered you, Frayne! He didn't ask a single question — but you did! You owe me one week of dish-scraping duty!"

"Aw, man!" Frayne hung his head, but after a second he laughed, too. "Yeah, you got me good, I'll admit it. Nicely played, man." He dropped down across from Ronon and gave him a friendly nod. "Nice one."

"Thanks." Banje and Adarr settled down as well, though Ronon noticed Banje sat so he could keep an eye on the airlock. Setien and Turen had already been by the fire and had watched the whole exchange, barely hiding their laughter. "So, now that your wager's settled, somebody care to fill me in?"

Turen glanced toward Nekai's tent. The others all looked at Banje. Interesting. He nodded slightly but didn't say anything himself. After another second, Adarr cleared his throat.

"We're hunters," he offered hesitantly. "We hunt the Wraith instead of the other way round."

"That much I gathered," Ronon told him, but he was careful not to snap at the tall man — at least Adarr was trying to answer his question. "So, what, you hunt in teams? All together? You use this as a base and strike from here, or this is a bolt hole and only gets used between hunts? You target Darts and Hives, or places you know the Wraith will be, or one of you plays bait and the rest set an ambush? You've got weapons stashed away, or it's strictly gun and knife work?"

Frayne, Turen, and Adarr stared. Setien grinned. Banje's only reaction was a slight smile and a quick dip of his chin.

"Ancestors, you thought of all that just now?" Frayne asked finally. "Where'd you learn all that stuff?"

"You were a Specialist, right?" Banje asked softly. It wasn't really a question, but Ronon nodded anyway. "You had your own unit." He glanced around at the others. "So did I. Adarr and Frayne were soldiers — they never had to worry about mapping out a mission, just following orders." His matter-of-fact tone prevented them from taking insult — it wasn't a slight on their ability, just a statement about their lack of strategic training. "Turen's people didn't have a standing military — when they had to fight they did, but it was more individualistic. Setien — well, she's a special case." Off to the side, Setien straightened, shoulders back, chest forward — proud, not angry. "She was a specialist of a different sort. She pulled solo missions." That meant an assassin, Ronon translated in his head. Or a saboteur. Or a spy. No wonder she was so confident — she was used to fighting without any backup at all.

"These are the kind of questions a good commander asks when given a mission," Banje continued, now more to the others than to Ronon. "Finding out the mission parameters so you can plan accordingly for you and your team." His eyes held a new measure of respect. "They're exactly the questions I asked when Nekai first recruited me." The gasp Frayne and Adarr were unable to hide only confirmed the awe they held for Banje. Nekai might be their overall leader, the man with the plan and the vision, but Banje was their unit commander, the one who actually held them together and took charge of the missions. Winning his trust and respect were imperative if Ronon wanted to stay here.

Fortunately, it looked like he was off to an excellent start.

"Missions vary in length, size, and number," Banje was now talking directly to Ronon. "We never work from here — this location has to remain secure at all times. We take the shuttles — we have two others besides the one you and Nekai used, one up here and one down there — to the planet below and then jump from there. Typically we work in three- to six-man teams, though obviously we'll be able to go up to seven now." Another mark of a good commander — even though Ronon didn't have his full trust yet, Banje was already planning how to include him in their missions. He wasn't about to leave a valuable resource untapped. "Most often we jump together to a random world, scout a location well away from any settlements, dig in, and send one of us out as bait. When the Wraith show up we ambush them instead. Weapons are what you see here." He gestured at his own side, and all around them. "We don't have anything strong enough to take out a Dart, much less a Hive." A quick, wolfish grin flickered across his lips. "But we're working on it."

Ronon nodded. A good, thorough briefing. He only had one more question. "When do we start?"

A few of the others grinned, but Banje shook his head. "Not yet," he replied. "At least, not you." Neither his voice nor his eyes held any malice. "Sorry."

"I get it," Ronon assured him. "You want to make sure I can be trusted first. And you need to see how I handle myself as part of a team. That's fair."

The answering nod from Banje was well worth the effort Ronon had made to rein in his own impatience. "Figured you'd understand," was all the black-eyed man said, but those three words conveyed a hidden level of praise. Ronon knew Banje wouldn't have expected any of the others to appreciate his decision as easily or with as little explanation — he'd probably had to explain it in detail to each one in turn, when they were the new recruits. Ronon wondered about the timeline of this unit — who had come first? Who had been second? He knew Adarr has been the most recent before him, but that was as far as his knowledge went. Clearly he'd have to learn more about the V'rdai, both the individuals and the team. That would come with time.

Off which, right now, he had a surprising abundance. Only a few months before he'd been alone in the woods on a strange planet, unarmed and barely clothed, wounded and grief-stricken and enraged, ready to throw his own life away against the first Wraith he saw. Now he had weapons, allies, new skills, and a clear purpose: kill as many Wraith as possible. If that took him years, that was fine. He could wait. His grief was still there, raw and hot and threatening to overwhelm him at any second, but having a purpose helped. He could distract himself by planning, by training, by fighting. The grief became something he could use, something to help motivate him.

It was strangely comforting to know, glancing around at these other men and women as they sat joking and laughing, that he was among people who understood. Each of them were Runners like him. Each of them was the last member of their respective races. Each of them had suffered a loss as extreme as his own. And each of them had survived it, had been found by Nekai, and had come together to form this unit, the V'rdai.

It was like finding a second home.

And Ronon discovered he was determined to make his place among them.

CHAPTER THIRTEEN

OVER the next week, Ronon did exactly that. He did his share of the chores, he sat with the others around the fire, he checked and cleaned weapons, he slept, he traded stories.

Some of the V'rdai were more closemouthed than others. Setien, he learned, had a hundred tales of missions she'd gone on, foes she'd defeated, enemies she'd crushed single-handedly. To hear her tell of it, she had been a one-woman army, and had helped her people, the Mahoiran, defeat many other worlds where many of her peers had failed and where whole armadas had lost before. If not for the way she moved, with the reflexes of a natural warrior, Ronon would have assumed she was exaggerating. As it was, he was half-convinced, or at least he believed half of what she said about herself might be true.

Adarr was equally talkative, but not about himself. When asked, he always claimed he hadn't been anything special, just another Fenabian warrior, and that he had no idea why the Wraith had let him live when the rest of his people had been slaughtered or enslaved. What he lacked in self-confidence however he made up for in good nature, and he was happy to talk about his people, his family, old legends, boyhood exploits, and anything else that came to mind. After only a day Ronon was doubly glad he hadn't been asked to bunk with the tall, pale man — he'd never have gotten a second's sleep.

Turen was friendly and willing to talk, but though she held up her end of any conversation she rarely said anything about herself or her people. Frayne was even more close-lipped — of all the V'rdai he was the one who made it clear he still didn't trust Ronon or completely accept him, though he was starting to relax that mistrust a bit. Ronon didn't blame him. Given what they had all been through as Runners, they should be cautious. And if Frayne's caution bordered on paranoia, well, better to be safe than to be tricked by anyone.

Banje rarely spoke at all, though it didn't seem to be anything against Ronon — he was just as quiet with the others. Most of his responses were a few words, and only when asked a direct question. The rest of the time he simply sat back, watched, and listened.

Nekai only joined them occasionally. When he did, the Retemite was a little more relaxed than he had been when it had just been him and Ronon. Which made sense. That had been out in the wild, with the threat of Wraith attacks at any moment — and with a half-trained Satedan barely containing his desire to hurl himself at even the chance of facing a Wraith. Here he was back in his element, in the base he had obviously built, surrounded by people he had trained. Even so, Nekai never relaxed completely. There was always an air of distance around him, as if he were holding himself slightly aloof. A lot of military commanders behaved that way, refusing to let themselves become one with their men in order to better maintain their authority. Ronon hadn't been one of them — for him it was about earning his unit's trust and respect rather than reminding them he was a higher rank, and he'd been happy to laugh and drink and joke with them between missions and even during quiet moments on them. But each commander was different, and Nekai clearly felt he needed to remain in command, even during times of quiet.

When they weren't talking, the V'rdai were doing chores, though there were few enough of those. Or they were sleeping. Or playing cards. Or exercising. Or Ronon's favorite — they were fighting. Each other. Only for practice, of course. But it was better than nothing. And sparring gave him a much better idea of each of his new teammate's capabilities, as well as more insight into their personality.

It was only his second day when he had his first sparring

match. And there had never been any question as to who would be his first opponent.

"Time to show me what you've got, big man," Setien said the first time as they stepped into the chalked-off circle the V'rdai used for combat exercises. "Let's see if you're half as good as you think you are."

"Let's see if you are," Ronon taunted her, making a show of stretching and flexing. As he'd suspected she might, the warrior-woman chose the moment his arms were behind his back to hurl herself upon him, both hands coming down fast and straight-edged on either side of his neck.

Ronon had been expecting something like that, however, and he snapped his own arms forward even as he flung himself backward — her hands stopped short of his new position, missing him entirely, while his own palms slammed into her sides and pounded the air from her lungs in a single explosive breath.

He twisted to the side then, keeping his feet as she hurtled toward the ground. Her body didn't hit the rough floor, however — instead her hands pushed down and she vaulted forward, twisting in mid-air to land on her feet a few paces away from him.

"Not bad," Setien admitted, gasping to restore air to her lungs. "Good feint."

"Thanks." Ronon waited, knowing patience wasn't her strong suit and determined to make her come to him. It took less than a second before her fist snaked out, punching hard toward his face. He knocked the blow aside, responding with one of his own, even as his other hand blocked a straight-fingered thrust toward his gut with her second hand.

They traded blows for a few seconds before disengaging and stepping back. Neither of them had been able to land a solid blow, though they'd each had their fists glance off flesh a few times.

"You're good," Setien acknowledged. "Better than any of them." Her nod took in the other V'rdai, who were all crowded around the ring, watching closely. Her eyes never left Ronon, however.

"You're no slouch yourself," Ronon told her. In truth, he hadn't faced an opponent like her since his unarmed instructor, back in training. That man had been short and slight but lightning-fast, able to strike like a serpent while you were still blinking. Setien was almost as fast, and considerably stronger. Fortunately, she lacked his old instructor's tactical sense. She was too aggressive to wait for the perfect opening.

As if to prove his point, she suddenly spun in, launching a vicious side kick that could have shattered at least one rib. If it had connected. But Ronon had seen her pivot on the one foot and, knowing what that meant, he stepped forward himself, moving into her arc so that the back of her knee struck his side instead of her foot. Then he wrapped one arm around her leg, trapping it there, and pounded her across the jaw with the other hand.

Setien stumbled from the impact, but it wasn't enough to stun her. He felt her body coil in his grip. Then she kicked up with her free leg, scissoring both legs together as she spun parallel to the ground, before lashing out to clip Ronon in the jaw with her unencumbered foot. He staggered and stepped back, releasing her leg, and she completed the move by slamming both knees into his chest, knocking him to the ground. The second her feet touched the ground again she was launching herself forward, flipping over and landing hard on his stomach to drive the air from his body just as he'd done to her before.

Only this time he was pinned beneath her, and she was squeezing with her thighs and knees enough to make his ribs cry out in protest.

"Yield," she crowed down at him, one hand moving to his throat, the other cocking back for a knockout punch. "Yield or it's lights out."

Ronon managed to wheeze out a laugh. "What, already?" he gasped. "It's still early yet." He ignored her hands and instead slammed both fists forward — directly into her impressive chest. Setien's eyes flew open at the impact on such a sensitive area, and she cried out involuntarily, both hands going instinctively to protect her chest from further assault. She recovered almost instantly, but it was too late — Ronon had used her distraction to drive his hands between himself and her legs. Now he hooked a hand around each thigh and had heaved upward. Setien went flying off him, and he rolled to the side and then to his feet. He took advantage of the time it took her to recover to catch his breath again.

"How dare you!" she spat at him once she was on her own feet again. She stalked toward him like a great angry cat, her eyes flashing — if she'd had a tail it would have been lashing left to right in a frenzy. "I will not be manhandled!"

He shrugged. "All's fair in a fight," he pointed out. Then he had to stop talking — all of his attention was on fending off her latest barrage of kicks, punches, slaps, and jabs. A few got through, and Ronon was even more bruised and winded when he managed to push her away again a minute later. She'd been aggressive before, but now she was actually enraged, and if her blows were a bit more wild and a bit more loose, they had even more power behind them. Each one that connected felt like he'd been kicked by a mule.

"Okay," he said finally, holding up both hands. "I yield. I yield!"

"Really?" Setien paused in mid-stride, one hand still raised behind her. "You yield?"

"Yes." Ronon dropped to his butt on the hard ground, wincing a little, and leaned back on his hands. It was a vulnerable position — he wouldn't be able to defend himself properly like this, with his weight on his arms — and he'd chosen it deliberately. "You win. This time."

He'd hoped she'd be gracious in victory, but he couldn't prevent himself from tensing as she lowered her hand and crossed the distance to him. She stared down at him for a second, hands on her hips. Then she favored him with a wide grin and extended a hand to help him to his feet.

"Well fought!" she said, laughing as she hauled him up without effort. Then she hugged him, which surprised Ronon completely — and apparently shocked the others, given the wordless exclamations he heard all around him. "You almost had me several times there!"

"Just wait till next time," Ronon assured her, giving her a quick squeeze back before pulling away. He didn't want her or anyone else getting the wrong idea — including his own body. Right now his blood was singing from the recent combat, senses alive and pulse pounding — it would be all too easy to give in to the adrenaline. But his grief for Melena was still far too raw. "I won't give in so quickly."

She slapped him on the back. "Good!" she said, and he could see that she meant it. "It's nice to have a proper opponent again!" For a second he saw sadness in her eyes, before she banished it deliberately. "Only a few of my own people could ever come close to matching me, and I've met no one since who could last more than a few seconds."

"She's right," Adarr volunteered as Frayne led the way back to the fire. "Setien's amazing in a fight. It's a wonder you lasted as long as you did."

Privately, Ronon disagreed. He hadn't been beaten, though there was no guarantee he wouldn't have been — Setien really was good. But so was he. He'd felt it was wise to let her win this first match, though. He didn't want any bad blood between them, or with any of the other V'rdai. Next time he promised himself he'd keep going until one of them was actually unable to continue.

Of course, the way his ribs protested when he sank down

onto a crate by the fire, that could easily be him.

Either way, it would be one hell of a match. And he was happy to know his fighting skills wouldn't suffer any. Sparring with Setien would definitely force him to stay sharp.

Ronon had fully expected Setien to be a strong combatant, given her size, physique, grace, and attitude. Likewise, he was unsurprised to discover over the next two weeks that Adarr and Frayne were both solid but unexceptional fighters, though Frayne did have impressive reach and strength for a man his size. One of the other V'rdai, however, proved to be a revelation in the training ring.

"I don't want to hurt you." Ronon gazed down at Turen, frowning. He was nearly twice her height! And he probably weighed twice what she did, as well.

But the tiny white-haired Hiñati just smiled at him, those slanted green eyes twinkling. "Don't worry—you won't," she assured him.

Ronon glanced around. As with his match against Setien, the others were gathered at the edge of the training circle, watching intensely. He couldn't really blame them—judging by what he'd seen so far, between missions there was little else to do but train, sleep, talk, play cards, and eat. And watching a fight was more entertaining than playing cards any day.

He caught Banje's eye, and the other man—Ronon had learned he was Desedan, but little more—gave him a slight nod. Well, if Banje felt it was all right to spar with Turen he'd have to accept that. Still, Ronon resolved to go easy on her. One solid hit could break her into pieces!

He gave her a slight bow, really little more than a dip of the head, eyes on her the whole time. Concerned didn't equal stupid and he knew better than to take his eyes off an opponent, even one as unassuming as his current foe. Then, without any windup, he swung at her, a powerful backhand that would knock her to one side and send her flying from the ring. One step beyond its boundary and you forfeited the match. A quick and easy end, and nobody got seriously hurt.

Except that Turen wasn't there. She slipped under his blow, stepped into his space, and hit him once, twice, three times in the stomach. The blows weren't hard but they were fast and perfectly aimed, and Ronon doubled over, exhaling in a great whoosh of air despite himself. His arm was still extended but he chopped down with the other one, aiming for the juncture between neck and shoulder. Turen sidestepped it, but at least it gave him the second he needed to regain his balance and back away again.

His stomach ached from her blows, and he was gasping to refill his lungs. She wasn't even breathing hard, and her smile was just a little bit sharper.

"Okay," Ronon muttered, "I guess I don't have to worry about hurting you, then." Apparently Turen's ears were as sharp as her smile, because her grin widened.

This time Ronon was careful not to overcommit. When he closed the distance again, he thrust forward with both hands at once, intending to grapple Turen. Once he had a solid grip he'd simply fling her out of the ring and be done with it.

That didn't work, of course. Fast as a whip she ducked under one hand, hitting him on the wrist with the edge of her hand instead. She found a nerve there and Ronon felt his fingers go limp. Damn! He wasn't able to make a fist but he still snapped his hand back toward her — the back of it caught her shoulder and the force of the blow staggered her, though she recovered almost at once. Hells, she was fast!

Clever, too. She knew he had only one good hand now, and she was clearly determined to take advantage of that as long as it lasted. She was already weaving her way toward him, shifting from side to side so he couldn't get a clear shot at her, and staying on his weak side to protect herself further.

But Ronon had some tricks of his own. He spun away slightly, then back again, and at the same time lashed out not with his numb hand but with the elbow. It caught Turen on the chin, and this time she did lose her balance, though she managed to jab him in the forearm as she went down.

Ronon threw himself after her without a second's pause. By the time she hit the ground he was in mid-air, and though Turen twisted to one side she wasn't able to evade him completely. He hit the ground hard on both knees, but his bruised forearm was across her neck, and he put just enough pressure there to let her know how easily he could crush her throat. She stopped struggling immediately.

"I yield," she gasped against the pressure, and Ronon sat back at once, releasing her. Then he rose to his feet and offered her a hand — his good one — back up.

"Ancestors, you're fast!" he told her once they were both back on their feet. His fingers were starting to tingle back to life again, and he rubbed at them absently.

"So are you," Turen admitted, brushing herself off. "I'm impressed — most non-Hiñati can't even touch me."

"I believe it." Ronon shook his head. "I thought you had me there for a minute."

She grinned at him, a friendly smile but one filled with clear pride — and perhaps a little longing. "You should see me with blades in my hand," she assured him quietly.

"It's true," Adarr agreed from the sideline. "When we hunt Turen prefers blades to guns, and once you see her in action you'll know why. They're like flickers of light!"

Ronon studied the tiny woman with new respect. He'd heard stories of the Hiñati fighters and their speed and skill with swords and knives, but he'd never met one in person. Because of her size and looks he hadn't taken Turen for a true warrior, but of course it made sense that the Wraith would have kept one of the finest of the Hiñati to turn into a Runner. He'd certainly know better than to underestimate her again!

"We'll have to spar with blades next time," he told her. Then he added, "I have a feeling I could learn a lot from you."

That was exactly the right thing to say — Turen's grin widened into a beaming smile, and her cheeks flushed slightly. "Any time," she assured him.

"Any time except now," Nekai corrected. He'd approached while they were still talking in the ring, or at least Ronon assumed so — he hadn't seen the V'rdai leader during the match itself, though admittedly he'd been a little distracted. "Right now we have more important things to do."

Ronon glanced at the Retemite but didn't ask the obvious question. It had only been two weeks, and demanding answers from Nekai would only make him look insubordinate. That was no way to win the others' trust.

Fortunately, in this group he didn't have to say a word. "Are we going hunting?" Adarr asked.

Nekai nodded. "Everyone suit up." He met Ronon's eye and gave him a quick, predatory grin, a look Ronon had come to know well during his training. "Everyone."

Ronon took it as a good sign that no one protested once Nekai's meaning sank in. Frayne scowled for a second, but then shrugged. Banje nodded. Setien grinned, and Turen smiled. Adarr was the most effusive, but Ronon had already realized that the tall thin man was the most outgoing of the unit.

"Your first hunt with us!" He told Ronon as they all trooped over toward the airlock and the rack of atmosphere suits beside it. "This is going to be great!"

Ronon nodded. He didn't trust himself to speak at the moment. He hadn't dared expect that he'd be included in this mission. But he was thrilled that he was. His involvement was a clear message from Nekai to the others, saying that he was truly one of them and that he had Nekai's full trust. The fact that the others had more or less accepted that decision meant they were starting to trust him as well.

But far more importantly, Ronon was tired of sitting around waiting. He had spent three months training with Nekai, and then two weeks here in this dome, waiting. Now, finally, they were going to hunt. They were going after the Wraith.

And Ronon fully intended to return with the blood of at least one more Wraith on his hands.

Not that one was enough. Not by a long shot. But it would do for a start.

CHAPTER FOURTEEN

"I HOPE wherever it is we're going has fruit trees." Setien licked her lips. "It's been far too long since we've had fresh fruit."

"You and your fruit fetish," Frayne said, laughing as he dodged her lazy backhanded swipe. "I swear, you like fruit better than you like men!"

"Fruit doesn't disappoint," she retorted, laughing in turn as Frayne blushed bright red. "Find me a man who can hold up and I'll consider changing my priorities." Her gaze swept Ronon, bold and daring, but he refused to react. Setien was an interesting woman, and certainly striking, but he wasn't interested. It was far too soon for him to even consider another relationship.

Instead he watched the front, where Nekai and Turen had taken the pilot and co-pilot chairs. The rest of them were hanging onto the grips spaced along the sides, just like in a military drop. The handholds were too high for Turen to reach comfortably, which was presumably why the diminutive Hiñati was sitting up front instead and Banje was back here with them.

Nekai aimed the shuttle for what looked like the valley where he and Ronon had found it. As they drew close Ronon scanned the immediate area, looking for signs of a similar craft, but he didn't see one.

Not surprisingly, Banje noticed his search and guessed the reason behind it. "Twenty kilometers to the southwest," he answered softly. "It's got a tarp over it, just like this one had — you wouldn't be able to spot it from the air."

Ronon nodded, mentally mapping out probable locations. Twenty kilometers made sense — they were ten to fifteen from the ancestral ring, which put it roughly between the two shuttle locations but kept them far enough apart that anyone searching for one would never stumble across the other.

"One stays by the dome at all times?" he guessed out loud, and Banje nodded. That was exactly how he'd have done it, too — keep one ship close at hand for an emergency escape. With three shuttles you could do that, have one on the planet at all times in case it was needed, and have one at either location as necessary. But that begged another question. "How'd you get your hands on three shuttles?"

"It wasn't easy," Adarr answered, his chuckle threatening to turn into a giggle. His fingers were even whiter than the rest of him where they gripped the handhold. Apparently the thin man was a nervous flier. "They had two before I joined, but I helped them get the third one — it might have been this one, I can't really tell them apart all that well. But we were on this one planet, it had the most glorious trees, I remember their leaves were like sunbeams, all slender and golden, and we — "

"Enough yammering!" Frayne told his bunkmate sharply, giving him a glare to accompany the harsh words. "Just because you can't handle flying doesn't mean the rest of us should have to listen to you going on and on!"

"He asked," Adarr mumbled, but his cheeks were flaming and he looked down at his feet. "I was just trying to tell him — "

"We scrounged them," Setien cut in, clearly hoping to shut down an argument in the making. "Most of the time we wind up on an uninhabited world, but sometimes we find one with actual settlements. And occasionally" — her eyes flashed — "it's someplace the Wraith have destroyed. They don't bother with the tech — no reason to, when theirs is better — so they leave everything behind." She rapped one hand against the hull beside her. "This one we scavenged from a dead world. The body was intact but the systems were dead. Adarr found parts from others to fix it. He's very good with machines."

The tall man brightened. "I don't like to fly them, but I can repair them," he agreed, happy for the praise. He was like a big puppy, Ronon thought, all long limbs and enthusiasm. Yet again he wondered why the Wraith had chosen him to survive as a Runner—and just how long he would have survived without Nekai's intervention. Probably as long as he would have, he admitted privately to himself, which meant he had no room to criticize the other man.

There was something that still didn't make sense to him, though. "You were able to find and repair a shuttle but couldn't get any weapons beyond pistols and rifles?" he asked. "And no armor either?"

This time it was Banje who answered. "The Wraith transport most of their victims," he reminded sharply. "Weapons and armor, too. Anyone they've killed—" he shrugged, but for once Ronon saw a flicker of emotion on the other man's face: pain. "The bodies are too badly damaged to salvage anything, including their gear."

Clearly the Desedan had suffered a horrible loss, just as they all had. From what he'd said Ronon guessed that someone close to the man had been among the "too badly damaged." He didn't press the issue. Banje had answered his question.

Their landing was just as rough as the one on the moon had been, and all of them clung to their handholds as they were jostled about. "Let me pilot next time!" Frayne complained as he struggled to his feet again, wincing slightly—the little man's arms were long enough to reach the grip without a problem but stretching that far put him off-balance and he'd wound up dangling from it when the ship had tilted and scraped its way to a stop.

"Frayne's a really good pilot," Adarr whispered to Ronon as they waited for Nekai to power down and open the airlock. "He had a fighter of his own, back on his world."

That explained a lot about the little man, Ronon thought as they stepped back out into the valley and covered the shuttle with the tarp again—judging from the marks on the ground Nekai had gotten within a few meters of the ship's earlier position, which was actually fairly good. Frayne must come from one of the few worlds beside Sateda advanced enough to actually have fliers. He was fast enough and alert enough to have been a good fighter pilot, and his twitchiness would actually be an advantage in the air where he'd need to fire upon foes before they could target him back. Perhaps the orange-haired man had given the Wraith such competition in the air that they'd assumed he'd be just as effective on the ground, and that's why they'd opted to turn him into a Runner.

Or perhaps it had amused them to see someone so talented in the air be so clueless on the ground. It was hard to say.

The team continued to banter as they made their way to the ancestral ring, but once there Banje motioned them to silence. There was no telling what world they'd wind up on once Nekai opened a portal, or whether there might be settlements nearby. Or Wraith. Adarr whispered to Ronon that once they'd stumbled through a gate, only to find a squad of Wraith warriors standing guard there. Only the fact that the Wraith clearly hadn't been expecting them, and Turen and Banje's fast reflexes, had allowed them to kill the closest and scatter the rest while the portal closed and Nekai quickly dialed a new location. They'd barely made it through the new portal in time, and then they'd had to hide until they were sure the Wraith hadn't followed them.

"How does Nekai know what to dial?" Ronon asked softly, as much to himself as to the others, but Turen heard him.

"We found something on one of the Wraith we killed, a while back," she explained softly. "A little plaque with line after line of symbols. The same symbols as that console." She gestured toward Nekai with her chin. "It was a list of places. So far, every one Nekai's tried has been a proper world."

Handy, Ronon thought. Nekai must have been consulting

that list somehow when the two of them had used the rings, or he'd learned a few of the numbers by heart. Ronon certainly wasn't complaining. He remembered hearing tales of rings that floated in outer space, or stood deep beneath seas or even ice or dirt. Good to know they wouldn't be walking into one of those!

Nekai worked his magic on the console while Banje and the others stood to the far side of the ring, weapons at the ready. Ronon was still unaccustomed enough to the rings that he started slightly when its surface plumed outward, earning him a few chuckles and snorts from the others, but that was fair enough. The new recruit always got picked on a bit, and he'd been surprised so far how little of that he'd had to put up with. The fact that he was a Runner like the rest of them had certainly made some difference, since they knew exactly what he'd been through and respected the fact that the grief and pain were still very raw for him, and Nekai's personal training and invitation had most likely helped as well, but still Ronon had expected a few more pranks and jokes at his expense. Perhaps his sparring with Setien first had also done away with those, he thought as they stepped through the portal one at a time. The others had seen he was not to be trifled with, and so had left well enough alone.

Ronon found the trip through the ring disorienting but forced himself to keep moving, staggering after Turen as the team marched quickly across the small clearing and into the bushes beyond. There was no sign of Wraith presence yet, so Banje and Nekai allowed them a few minutes to get their bearings.

The trees they took cover under proved to be heavy with native fruit. There were both something that looked like perfectly spherical green grapes but proved to be utterly inedible — eliciting a cry of outrage from Setien and a "Never disappoints, hm?" from Frayne — and something like an apple but blue-black and juicy-sweet like a plum. After Banje used a small chemical tester to make sure the fruits were safe to eat — though Setien had already demonstrated that by shoving a whole one in her mouth, chewing, and swallowing triumphantly — they all devoured as many as they could stomach of the second kind, and harvested great handfuls more to secret in various pockets and bring back with them. Once their hunger was sated, Banje had them form up again and they moved out.

They trekked for an hour, perhaps a little more, before Nekai returned from scouting ahead and signaled that he'd found a suitable spot. The others followed him to a small copse of trees in the middle of a denser forest. The copse had enough space for Ronon to stretch out both arms and not graze a tree at all, but the branches overhead still filtered some of the sunlight, creating a soft dappled haze instead of a harsh glare. Just beyond the copse the trees were older, taller, thicker, and set more closely together, providing more shade and cover but allowing less room to maneuver. They were perfectly placed to provide shelter when setting an ambush.

"Turen, you're up," Banje told the tiny Hiñati, who nodded and took off at a run in the direction Nekai pointed. "Everyone else, fan out within the trees. Keep to within two meters of each other, though, otherwise your devices will show on the monitors."

Ronon obediently took to the shade, scaling a low-hanging branch and swinging himself up into the canopy it and its siblings offered. He couldn't help asking, though, "Why Turen? She's the smallest of us — she can't run as fast or cover as much ground."

"She's fast enough," Nekai told him from a spot between two thick protruding roots a few trees over. All the foliage muffled his voice oddly, but it was just loud enough to reach Ronon if he strained to hear. "And she's the most agile of us. Plus she's not as good in an ambush, so she's better for bait."

Ronon mused on that as he settled in to wait. Not as good in an ambush — that must be because of what Adarr had said back in the dome, about how Turen preferred blades to guns. They wouldn't be much use at range, but she'd be able to strike fast if a Wraith got in too close — like trying to feed off a Runner it thought was helpless.

The area grew quiet as their various rustlings and creakings faded away, and Ronon closed his eyes, determined to be as patient as he could manage. There was no telling how far Turen would run before turning back — she wanted to get far enough away that the Wraith wouldn't start from here, but close enough that she could get back to this spot easily and could reach it before they found her. Ronon assumed she knew the right distance from previous hunts, and he figured she could take care of herself regardless. His biggest concern right now was remembering what Nekai had taught him about being still — he didn't want his growing impatience to manifest as shifting restlessly on his perch, because the sound and motion could give all of them away.

So he waited.

Ronon wasn't sure how long he'd rested — he'd slipped into a light doze, conserving energy and resting but still alert enough that he could wake at any time — before something woke him. He blinked once, twice, careful not to stretch or yawn as he glanced around. He could just make out Nekai between the roots but the V'rdai leader didn't move a muscle. Between them Adarr was up in the branches of another tree, and he was so still Ronon thought at first he was looking at a collection of sun-bleached sticks. Frayne was on Ronon's other side, as were Banje and Setien, and he didn't dare turn his head to look at them but he guessed none of them had made the noise he'd heard through his sleep. Which meant it was probably Turen.

And that meant she was coming their way. And hopefully leading the Wraith behind her.

After a few seconds Ronon heard a sound again, followed quickly by another. Footsteps. Someone running — and the gait was rapid, meaning someone with short legs moving quickly. Definitely Turen. Then he picked up other noises behind those, slower and heavier. More footsteps, larger and longer and less hurried.

Wraith.

Moving slowly and carefully to avoid making any noise, Ronon eased his pistol from its holster. He raised it in one smooth arc, keeping it close to the tree trunk he was nestled against so its barrel wouldn't gleam or protrude. The copse was right before him, and he would have a clear line of sight on anyone moving into or through it. He held his breath and tensed his trigger finger as the footsteps drew closer.

A second later a slight figure burst into the copse, white hair gleaming in the comparatively bright light. Turen. She got a little more than halfway across the space before she stumbled and dropped to one knee. But Ronon wasn't fooled. Not after sparring with her. He couldn't imagine the agile little woman tripping on anything.

But her pursuers didn't know that. They came into view a few seconds later, slowing as they spotted their prey apparently downed by a stray root or rock. There were three of them again, one commander and two warriors, as before — Ronon suspected that was their standard configuration, at least when hunting. He sighted down his barrel, targeting the commander's head. Then he waited, tracking the Wraith as it moved in for the kill. Shooting now would risk them turning and fleeing back into the forest if they didn't go down with the first barrage. Better to wait until they were dead center, then gun them all down.

Of course, that meant the Wraith were getting closer to Turen. She was still on the ground, hunched over, hands against her stomach, as if she'd injured herself when she fell. Ronon couldn't see the Wraith warriors' faces through their masks, but the commander was openly gloating.

"Well, well," he was saying softly, his words a snakelike hiss through his pointed teeth. "Turen Masaglia of the Hiñati. We've been hunting for you for quite some time, my dear. You've certainly led us on a merry chase. But it ends now." He extended one hand, the life-sucking organ in his palm clearly visible and took another step closer. He was almost near enough to reach her now.

"Yes, it does," Ronon heard Turen say quietly. Then she had turned, rising to her feet as she moved, her blades flashing out and around and down. They were little more than a flicker in the light, but the Wraith commander stumbled backward, a cry on his lips as he stared at the bloody stump where his hand had been.

Before he could voice that cry, Ronon shot him. The red bolt struck the Wraith in the right temple just as another shot caught him in the throat, and the commander convulsed as his body fell backward, a third shot striking him even as he toppled. He was dead before he hit the ground.

The others had opened fire on the two warriors, and Ronon quickly switched to them as well. It was difficult to tell who hit whom, but within seconds both warriors were also dead, and Turen was standing alone in the copse.

She knelt quickly and checked all three bodies before nodding. The others emerged from their cover and converged on her and on their fallen prey.

"You all right?" Nekai asked her, and Turen nodded quickly. She wiped her blades — two long, wicked-looking daggers — on the commander's torso before replacing them in sheaths strapped to her thighs. Then she flashed Ronon a brilliant smile as if to say "See? Told you you should see me with blades in my hands."

Banje had dropped to a crouch beside the commander and

was checking not his body but his wrist, the one that still had a hand attached. "Damn," he muttered quietly, holding up the limb for the others to see. "Shattered. Must have caught a stray bolt."

There was a device on the dead Wraith's wrist, a familiar-looking screen though this one was cracked and blackened and smoking. A tracking monitor.

"We only have two," Banje explained to Ronon, rising to his feet again after appropriating the commander's stun-pistol. "Nekai has one and I have the other." He raised his right arm to show the tracking monitor strapped there. "They tend to damage easily, and we haven't been able to recover any others intact."

Out of the corner of his eye Ronon saw Nekai's brow furrow and his mouth turn down at the edges. When he glanced over, however, the Retemite was as stone-faced as ever. Odd. He'd seemed displeased about Banje's statement. But was it because they hadn't been able to acquire more than two of the monitors — or because someone besides him had one?

The others had checked over the warriors' bodies, and collected their stun rifles and knives. "We should get moving," Nekai instructed. "Best not to linger by the bodies. Back to base." He nodded at Ronon. "Good job on your first mission. You fit in just fine."

Setien clapped Ronon on the back, staggering him slightly from the force of the blow. "Absolutely!" she agreed cheerfully. "You are now truly one of us!"

Turen and Adarr both smiled their assent, and Banje nodded. Even Frayne grunted what might have been approval, or at least wary acceptance. Ronon allowed himself to smile as well. He felt like one of them, to be honest, and it was a good feeling. It had been too long since he had been part of a team, with comrades he could count on. Not that he was ready to trust them completely yet, but that would come in time. For now it was good to know someone else had his back in a fight — and to know they trusted him to have theirs.

They had almost reached the ancestral ring when Banje motioned the others to stop. They did at once, freezing as the Desedan cocked his head to one side, listening intently. Then he gestured to the sides and they all dove for cover.

"What is it?" Frayne whispered as they wriggled behind trees and rocks and bushes. "More hunters?"

Banje shook his head and gestured up toward the canopy and beyond. Then Ronon heard it. A faint droning sound that quickly grew to a high-pitched scream that made his head pound.

A ship.

And he recognized that particular pitch, which cut into his thoughts and his ears alike. This wasn't just any ship.

It was a Wraith Dart.

"Is it after us?" Adarr asked from behind a tree trunk. "Are they hunting us with ships now?"

"Unlikely," Nekai answered softly, almost invisible within a scraggly bush. "It's probably just on its way to somewhere else."

Ronon considered that for only a second. "Does it have a tracking monitor?" he asked, his words little more than a whisper through clenched teeth.

"It might," Nekai admitted. "We don't know — so far we've only seen hunters with them, and they've all been on foot. Why?"

Ronon was thinking fast. "If it doesn't have one, it won't know about us," he answered. "But it may know about the hunters we just killed. And it may realize they're dead."

"It may," Banje agreed. "They're telepathic, and if it knows other Wraith are on this world it may call out to them as a matter of course." The scream had faded now, and Ronon found he could think straight again. The Dart had moved on.

"Which means it may track them down when they don't answer," Ronon continued his thought. He rose from his crouch.

"Where are you going?" Nekai demanded sharply, half-rising as well.

Ronon glanced at him but didn't stop. "To kill a Dart," he replied as he passed. "Anyone care to join me?"

To his credit, Nekai considered for only a second before abandoning his cover completely. "You're insane," he pointed out as he closed the distance between himself and Ronon. "We don't have anything that can take down a Dart." But he was grinning as he said it.

"We don't need to take out the Dart," Ronon replied, a plan already forming in his head. "We just need to take out the pilot. The rest will take care of itself." He glanced around, gauging the distance back to the copse. "But we have to hurry—if he gets there before we do, we're sunk."

Nekai nodded at Banje, who immediately popped to his feet. "Back to the copse," the Desedan ordered. "Fast as you can! Move!"

And then they were off at a run. Ronon let his body settle into a long, loping stride, his legs covering the ground swiftly, his blood singing through his veins. He didn't care if the others were with him or not at this point. All he cared about was the lone Wraith approaching that clearing. The three they'd just killed, it had been impossible to tell who had fired the killing shot. But not this time.

This one was all his.

CHAPTER FIFTEEN

"SO WHAT'S the plan?" Nekai asked, sprinting to catch up to Ronon as they ducked through the woods.

"We wait until the Dart reaches the bodies," Ronon replied between gasps. He was pushing himself as fast as he could through the foliage — any faster and he'd trip over a root and go flying — and he was impressed but not completely surprised that the shorter Retemite was keeping up. "The pilot sees the dead bodies, leaves the Dart to investigate, and we take him out while he's on the ground and vulnerable."

"Won't work," Banje told him from his other side. The Desedan wasn't even breathing hard as far as Ronon could tell, but somehow he was keeping up without having to run at all. "Dart pilots don't leave their ships except inside a Hive."

"He'll have to in order to check the bodies," Ronon argued.

"No, he won't," Nekai said. "He'll just beam them up."

Ronon almost slammed into a tree as he turned to stare at the V'rdai leader. "Beam them up? What're you talking about?"

"How'd they catch you?" Adarr asked from just over his shoulder. "Didn't they beam you up in a Dart?"

Ronon shook his head, trying to keep up his pace, avoid trees, and follow this conversation all at the same time. "They blew up a hospital," he said, trying to tamp down the pain before it could overwhelm him again. "I was in it with — with someone. The blast knocked me back, and then the Wraith entered. I fought, they knocked me out, and I woke up in a Hive, strapped to a table." He forced himself to focus on the table, on the procedure, on the Wraith leaning over him leering. That way he didn't have to think about Melena, or about seeing her outlined in the blast for an instant before it vaporized her.

It almost worked.

"The Darts have transport systems," Adarr was explaining. "They dematerialize you and beam you up into some sort of storage cell within them. Then when they get back to the Hive they rematerialize you in one of their holding pens. You're stunned for a bit, so you can't put up a fight." The tall man shuddered, clearly remembering the experience firsthand.

"So the pilot won't bother to check the bodies on the ground," Nekai finished. "He'll beam them up into his Dart and bring them back to the Hive that way. If they were alive when he reached them, they'll still be alive when they're rematerialized. If they were dead, it doesn't much matter."

Ronon nodded. Okay, plan number one shot down. Time to come up with a plan number two. "What if one of us plays dead among the corpses?" he suggested, taking a short hop over a protruding tree root as high as his knee. "Once inside we overpower the pilot and take over the Dart."

The others were all shaking their heads. "It doesn't work like that," Nekai told him. "They don't beam you up into a passenger seat or a cage, there's no room for that in a Dart. You're just a collection of excited atoms, floating in a little cylinder or something somewhere, until they put you back together again."

Something about what he'd just said struck a chord somewhere within Ronon's brain. He tried to focus on it. They were almost back to the copse now. No sign of the Dart yet, so that was good, anyway — it meant they might have a few minutes left to figure out a proper plan.

"Excited atoms," he repeated. Yes, that had been it. "Whatever they beam up is just a bunch of excited atoms floating around in a tube somewhere inside the Dart."

"Exactly." They were within sight of the copse, just shy of their previous ambush positions, and Nekai slowed to a stop and turned to study Ronon. "You have an idea?"

Ronon nodded. He beckoned Adarr closer, and then grabbed one of the Wraith stun-rifles the tall man was carrying, souvenirs from the recent hunt. "These things," he said, turning it over in his hands. "They've got energy packs." He glanced up at Adarr. "Can you overload them?"

Adarr scratched his nose and studied the other rifle, which he was still carrying. "I think so," he said after a second. "Yes, I think so. But what good'll that do? They'll just explode the second someone tries to use them again."

"Right — or the second the energy is removed from its casing," Banje stated, catching on. He nodded at Ronon, a slight grin on his face. "Nice."

Nekai had figured it out as well. "You want to overload these two rifles and put them back on the Wraith," he stated out loud, probably as much for himself as for the others who had now joined them. "When the pilot beams them onto the Dart the energy from the rifles will be released. They'll already be primed to explode, and with nothing else to contain the energy that's what'll happen. They'll blow up the Dart from the inside."

Ronon nodded. "I hope so. If it doesn't work, all we've lost is two stun-rifles. The pilot won't even know we were here."

Nekai nodded to Adarr. "Do it."

The tall man immediately crouched down, his long, deft fingers removing a panel on the first stun-rifle to reveal the energy compartments within. Turen joined him, taking the other rifle from Ronon — she lacked Adarr's training or way with machines but she had quick fingers and sharp eyes, and mimicked what he did. Within a minute they were standing again, the two weapons held gingerly before them. Ronon noticed that the glowing spheres on the sides of the rifles were now throbbing dangerously.

"Put them on the bodies," Nekai instructed, and Adarr and Turen hurried to do so. They had just ducked back under the cover of the trees when they all heard that distinctive scream somewhere up above. It was growing louder by the second. "Everybody down!"

Ronon crouched behind a thick set of exposed roots. The others found similar hiding places. There was no time to climb among the branches, but it shouldn't be necessary. The Dart pilot wasn't looking for them, and wouldn't be able to go below the tree canopy regardless. They were safe here. For now.

The scream grew in intensity, once again making Ronon's ears ache and his head throb, and then a long, pointed shape appeared in the sparse foliage above the copse. Long and pointed and narrow, he'd always thought the Darts looked more like predators than vessels, almost like the head of a vicious bird-beast with its long sharp beak and the curving jaws to either side and the bony ridges above and in back. The cockpit was a single dark bubble like a deformed black teardrop down the middle, and it stood out against the pale bone-like hull. The whole ship seemed organic, but that was because it was — Wraith vessels were grown rather than built.

And this one was now hovering over the copse just beyond them. Its engine noise was now so piercing Ronon had to clap his hands to his ears to keep from screaming himself at the pain. He caught glimpses of the others doing likewise. It was a good thing they were hidden, because none of them would be able to draw a weapon, much less fire it, if the Dart were to come after them.

Fortunately, the Dart pilot had other things on his mind. Like the three dead Wraith crumpled on the ground below it. After a few seconds a greenish-white beam shot from the belly of the ship, enveloping all three bodies. Squinting hard, Ronon thought he could still make out the throbbing dots of the rifle energy packs through the overall glow. Then the beam's light intensified, and the bodies vanished within it. He watched closely as the beam withdrew, recoiling back into the Dart. It winked out, and the ship pivoted, its long nose turning back in the direction of the ancestral ring.

The scream grew louder. The Dart was getting ready to return home.

And then it exploded.

Ronon threw himself down as the blast flattened the trees around them, chunks of organic metal flung every which way like jagged missiles. The Dart had released a tremendous burst of energy as well, green-white like its transport beam, and that wave incinerated the first row of trees and blackened the next, the ones Ronon and the others had hidden behind. He felt it singe the hairs on his head and on his outflung arms, and his entire body tingled from the heat. Then it dissipated, and he glanced up and around.

The copse was now a charred circle in the forest, the very ground there torn apart and in some places melted to glass from the force of the explosion. The trees they had used for shelter were bent and bowed away from the impact, and many of them were charred and still smoldering, their leaves burned away. He held his breath as he looked for signs of the other V'rdai, releasing it slowly as he saw heads and shoulders and limbs rise into view.

"Everyone okay?" Nekai called out, his voice a little shaky. The V'rdai leader rose to his feet from behind what had been a sturdy tree and was now a hollowed-out, smoking piece of trunk.

"Barely," Frayne grumbled, but the orange-haired man looked intact when he stood up a short distance away. "Damn near lost my eyebrows!"

"That would have been a good look for you," Setien told him, springing up from behind a small cluster of rocks. She looked completely unfazed, her cheeks flushed and her eyes dancing even though she was covered in dirt and grass and bits of burnt bark. "That was glorious!"

Adarr was wiping himself off. "I'm fine," he acknowledged. Then he grinned at Ronon. "Looks like it worked."

"Definitely." Banje looked exactly as he had — if he'd gotten covered in debris it didn't show. "Nice idea."

Turen was fine as well, and crouched to pull a piece of shattered Dart from a nearby tree. "Strange material," she murmured, running her fingers along it. "Like metal, but not quite."

Ronon noticed a piece near him as well, and tugged it from the ground where it had lodged. It was long and narrow and pointy, possible the tip of the Dart's nose. Held in one hand, it was almost like a naked blade, though one without a handle or hilt. He waved it about a little, considering the heft, a new idea forming.

"Think you could make something out of this?" he asked Turen, showing her his find.

The little Hiñati woman examined it, then nodded. "It's strong and sharp," she said, "and sturdy enough to withstand deep space. I don't have all the proper tools, but I could manage to do something with it, yes." She grinned up at him. "You want a sword."

"I do, yes." Ronon's people carried swords and knives as well as guns, and he missed the familiar weight of a blade in his hand. "I bet this stuff could cut through Wraith armor, too."

"Probably," she agreed. She began scanning the area, retrieving a few other likely pieces, and Nekai let that continue for a minute before he called them all together again. He had something in his hand as well, and several of them gasped in surprise when they saw what it was. It looked a lot like the consoles that stood beside each ancestral ring, only significantly smaller.

"This must be how the Dart opens a ring," Nekai explained, holding it up for them to see better. "I'm thinking it could come in handy."

"Definitely." Adarr was clearly itching to study it. "I could wire it into one of our shuttles and we could fly through rings just like they do! Or we could rig a handle for it, and use it to open them before we reach the clearing, so we can just jump through! Or —"

"There are a lot of possibilities," Nekai agreed, cutting him off, "but we'll worry about that later. Right now we need to get moving. Killing a trio of hunters is one thing. Destroying a Dart is another. The Wraith will definitely notice that, and they'll send more Darts to investigate." He clapped Ronon on the shoulder. "It was an excellent idea, and I'm sure we'll use it again, but not today. Time to return to base."

Ronon nodded and fell in line with the others as they prepared to move out. But he kept the Dart fragment clutched in his hand, and there was a small smile on his face. Shattering that Dart had been his idea, his plan. His kill. Something the V'rdai had never managed to do before.

Something he fully intended to do again. And again.

The Wraith would learn to fear him. To fear the V'rdai.

And then they would die.

CHAPTER SIXTEEN

"WOW."

Ronon nodded. Adarr's unusually short statement more than summed up what he suspected they were all feeling. "Wow," indeed.

They stood there, staring down at the devastation that stretched out before them. Ronon had been with the V'rdai, had been part of them, for almost eight months now. They had killed Wraith by the dozens, possibly by the scores, even with Nekai's caution about making themselves too visible and Banje's concerns about letting the Wraith track them too long or come too close to their base. He'd gotten used to the ancestral rings, or at least able to walk through one without being disoriented more than a few seconds and capable of approaching one with only a slight shiver. But this was the first time they'd traveled through to any place larger than a small village.

This was the first time they'd seen a city after the Wraith had finished with it.

The first time, for Ronon, since Sateda itself.

He gaped unashamedly at the ruins below. The ring had been placed on a short, wide, flat-topped hill, almost a plateau save for its tough blue-green grass and the tiny yellow and white flowers dotted among it. The city was less than a hundred meters away, obviously built close enough to take full advantage of the ring and its possibilities.

No doubt that had made them a clear target for the Wraith.

There was no telling how long it had been, but there was no smoke, no fire. Everything had long since burned out. The buildings were blackened wrecks, what remained of them, and the streets were littered with rubble where those same buildings had been shattered. If there were bodies, Ronon couldn't see them from here. That, at least, was a blessing.

Banje reacted first, as usual. Ronon had long since learned that the quiet Desedan was never fazed for long by anything. "Change of plans," he announced. "Scavenging parties."

The others nodded, including Nekai. That was something else Ronon had gotten used to. Nekai led the V'rdai, but more often than not when they were actually on the ground it was Banje who gave the orders. Still, that wasn't unusual. Ronon had seen similar situations plenty of times before, back on Sateda. Nekai was a commander, a leader, the man with the grand plans and the long-range strategies. Banje was a lieutenant, practical and hard-nosed and good at the minute details and the immediate concerns. And Nekai knew that. He respected Banje enough not to contradict him, and Banje respected him enough not to counter any of Nekai's plans, or to argue with him in front of the others. It was a good, solid system, and obviously it had served the V'rdai well long before Ronon had arrived. It still worked nicely now.

They split into three teams: Nekai and Turen, Ronon and Frayne, Banje and Setien and Adarr. Again, smart. Each team had a heavy-hitter: Nekai was a good enough hunter to count, even if he didn't have the same physical combat skills as Ronon or Setien. Something they'd proven in the ring, Ronon remembered with a grin, thinking back to one of the few times they'd been able to coax the Retemite into joining their sparring matches. He was good, but Ronon had put him on the ground almost immediately. And he and Setien were still a dead match for best hand-to-hand combatant in the unit.

Each team also had a spotter, since Turen had the best eyes in the V'rdai, with Banje, Frayne, Adarr, and Ronon himself not far behind. Adarr was their only real mechanic, but Frayne knew enough to fake it, especially around anything with an engine. Plus Banje was the only one who could really keep

Setien in line, and Turen would sulk if she didn't get paired with Nekai — the little Hiñati had it bad for their leader, though she was careful to keep things professional. No romance among Runners. It produced too many entanglements, clouded judgment, dulled reflexes, contradicted survival instincts — all of which could be fatal.

"Move out," Banje ordered, and the teams scurried down the hill, splitting off only once they'd reached the edges of the city proper. Two-man teams meant their tracking devices would still overlap signals, but it wasn't as secure as three or more, so they had to move fast. Scout the city, look for anything worth salvaging, regroup, and get out again.

They'd done this many times over Ronon's tenure with the V'rdai. But always before it had been a village or town, where they could grab food and maybe some clothes. They had enough weapons, at least in terms of personal armaments, and those places were too small and too primitive to have any decent armor or heavier equipment, so food and clothing were about it.

This was different.

Ronon could tell that this had once been a major city. He was guessing a million inhabitants, possibly more. A few buildings still rose as much as ten stories into the air, and their jagged tops proclaimed that once they had reached far higher, daring to graze the clouds themselves. The streets were broad and straight, the city laid out in a neat grid broken here and there by circles — those might have been for traffic, or for use as parks and gathering places, or perhaps both. They were covered in dust and debris now, of course.

But a city this size had possessed advanced technology, on a par with the cities of his own world. They'd probably had some sort of security force, both for internal conflicts and for potential invasions through the ancestral ring. Those guards would have possessed body armor, maybe energy rifles, possibly even explosives.

Things they could definitely use.

"Come on, come on," Frayne urged as they scouted down one of the streets. "Let's go! The sooner we snatch and grab, the sooner we're back."

Ronon laughed at the smaller man's impatience. "What's your hurry?" he asked. "You that eager to get your butt whipped in the ring again?" Setien and Frayne had been sparring when Nekai had announced it was time for another mission. Not surprisingly, the orange-haired Yadonite had been losing. Badly.

"I don't like places like this," Frayne grumbled in reply, shrugging off Ronon's dig. "Remind me too much of home."

That one Ronon couldn't argue, and so saw no need to comment. He'd learned a lot about the other V'rdai over the past eight months, and he was comfortable with all of them now, just as they were comfortable with him. Ever since that first hunt, when he'd led them to taking down their first Dart, he'd been fully accepted as part of the team. Even Frayne had never doubted him again. That didn't stop the shorter man from griping about Ronon occasionally, but that was just Frayne. He wasn't happy unless he had something to complain about. And if there wasn't anything? He would invent something. Ronon was fairly certain it was just a pose, and that it amused Frayne to come across as a constant complainer. Fairly certain.

In this case, though, Ronon knew the concern was genuine. Frayne's homeworld, Yadon, had been one of the few worlds the Wraith had allowed to advance technologically, a place of vast oceans and towering cities. The people there flew from place to place because there was no other way — the waters were too turbulent to allow for sea travel, and land was sparse enough that it was completely covered by the metropolises that housed the many Yadonites. That was why Frayne was such a good pilot. As with all his people, he had learned early, and practiced often. Ever since his world's destruction, however, he had been uncomfortable in anything more populous than their own dome. Even small villages made him jumpy.

Being in a large city like this, especially one this badly damaged, had him jumping at shadows and starting at the slightest breeze.

"Been a little while, at least," Ronon commented, kicking a pile of cloth and bones out of his path. "That's a good thing." It was, too. Clearly this city had been hit some time ago, long enough that the bodies had all disintegrated down to the bones. He shuddered to think of walking this giant mass tomb a few months or years earlier, when the corpses were still rotting. "Means no fresh food, though."

His companion grunted. "Not likely to find anything like that here, anyway," he pointed out, his eyes still restlessly scanning ahead of them. "Everything'd be processed."

"Right." Ronon hadn't thought about that. It had been so long since he'd been in a proper city, and even then he'd been in the military. All of their food had taken the form of hard, long-lasting rations. Whenever he'd been on leave Melena had made salads and other meals with fresh meat and fruit, so he'd simply assumed that was what civilians ate all the time. But of course they hadn't. He felt a sudden, sharp pang of renewed sorrow. She'd saved the good stuff for when he'd visited.

"Might be able to find some decent gear, if we can locate a security station," Ronon pointed out, forcing his thoughts back to the present. "Body armor, weapons — boots."

That got a laugh from Frayne. "What, Setien's work not to your liking?" the little man teased.

Ronon frowned down at his feet. "She's good," he answered. "Not her fault she didn't have much to work with." He'd been able to get clean clothes, good and sturdy, from the stores the V'rdai had collected. But they hadn't possessed any footwear large enough to accommodate him — Adarr had small feet for a man his height, and Setien's were large for a woman but not for a man, so the team had never had a need to collect bigger shoes or boots. Setien was good with leatherworking — her father had taught her, she'd revealed during one of the rare times she'd talked about the family she'd lost long before the Wraith had appeared — and she had cobbled together a pair of sandals for him at first, so he'd at least have something to protect his soles from rough terrain. Later she'd found enough leather scraps to put together a pair of patchwork boots. They were the right size, and as solid as she could make them, but none of the scraps had been bigger than his fist so there was as much stitching as material protecting his feet. And nowhere near enough cushioning.

Every chance they'd had since then, Ronon had searched for a proper pair of boots. And every time he did, Frayne had needled him about it.

But never within Setien's hearing.

Still, the orange-haired Yadonite had brought more than one pair of boots to Ronon's attention. None of them had fit, but the smaller man was trying. That made up for all the teasing.

They reached one of the circles in the road, and Ronon saw that both his guesses had been correct. The road swept around the space, linking to another road that cut across and creating a wide intersection, but in the center was an area that had clearly been grass and bushes and possibly small benches. Both decorative and functional, restful and productive. Ronon glanced around again, this time noticing how the architecture was handsome and smooth and attractive without being garish or purely ornamental. Whoever these people had been, they had built well.

But their very prosperity had no doubt attracted the Wraith's attention. And led to their demise.

Down the way, Ronon spotted Banje, Setien, and Adarr. They had reached a similar intersection level with his own.

"Find anything?" Setien shouted over to him.

Ronon shook his head. "Nothing so far."

"Neither have we." She waved. "First one to find the fruit gets first dibs!" Then she and her teammates were off again.

Ronon shook his head, laughing. Setien and her fruit! He hadn't really believed her the time she'd threatened to beat him for the last fig they'd found on one world — until she'd tackled him and wrestled it from his grip. Now he knew to give her a wide berth when anything like that was involved.

"We'd better keep up," Frayne said, and Ronon nodded and followed him further down the road. They both kept their eyes peeled, but so far there was nothing. The buildings all seemed to have been workplaces, not factories or homes, and the ones they did search had nothing in them but rubble and shattered desks and chairs and what must have been monitors of some sort. All completely useless to them.

"Let's hope the others are having better luck," Ronon muttered as they exited enough of the dust-coated offices. "It may be that all the homes and markets were on the other end of the city. And we may not have enough time to reach them before Banje orders a retreat."

"Fine by me," Frayne replied. He shuddered. "Being closed in by all this death gives me the creeps."

A sudden flicker of movement caught Ronon's eye, and he spun, dropping to a crouch even as his pistol cleared its holster and came up, targeting what he was seeing. Then he lowered it again as his brain caught up, resolving the motion into Adarr racing toward them.

"Come quick!" the tall Fenabian gasped as soon as he was close enough. "We found something!"

"Something good or something bad?" Ronon asked as he and Frayne closed the distance to their teammate, who spun and headed back the way he'd come, with them right behind him. He figured whatever they'd found wasn't a threat or he'd hear gunfire. Unless it was something too big for the three of them to handle in which case Adarr would have cautioned them to quiet. Right now the pale, lanky mechanic seemed far more interested in speed than stealth.

"Good," Adarr replied. "Maybe. We need Frayne." Ronon and Frayne exchanged a quick glance, both of them feeling a rising excitement. Frayne was far and away the best pilot they had—he'd proven that when Nekai had finally let him handle the shuttle on the way to one mission, and he'd set it down so gently they hadn't even known he'd landed until he powered the engines down. If Banje wanted him specifically, it could only mean one thing—they'd found a ship!

Ronon had already heard the stories behind the V'rdai's three existing shuttles. Nekai had found one himself, before meeting any of the others. It had been intact and abandoned, and he had simply taken it and left before anyone could come looking for it. He and Turen and Banje—they had been the first two he'd recruited, at least among the surviving V'rdai—had discovered the second outside a small village by a lake some-where, a hole through its front and a dead man in the pilot's chair. The village had contained nothing but bodies, clearly the victims of a Wraith attack. They had managed to repair the damage enough to get the craft spaceworthy again.

The third one had been discovered only a few months before Ronon's arrival. Adarr was part of the V'rdai by then, and when the team had happened upon a small spaceport he'd been able to rebuild a working shuttle from the wreckage of the five different ships that had been unlucky enough to be sitting there when the Wraith had struck.

But if it was a question of checking to see if a craft still worked, they'd want Adarr. So why send for Frayne? Unless they had something they thought could fly, and didn't know how it worked. If anyone could figure out a spaceship's con-trols, it would be Frayne.

Sure enough, after another ten minutes of running, Adarr led them into a wide, open area to one side of the city. There were a few low buildings here, each one with a pair of wide doors across the front. Hangars. Wreckage littered what had clearly been a landing strip of some kind, and Banje and Setien were checking out a shape that looked surprisingly intact.

A shuttle. Or at least a small spaceship of some sort. Even from here Ronon could tell that much.

"We think it might still work," Banje told them as they slowed and walked the last few feet to join him. "But we have no idea how it works, or what it's capable of."

Frayne nodded, his eyes already working their way over the hull. "Spaceworthy, definitely," he announced absently, studying it — his usual grumpiness disappeared completely as he considered the puzzle before them. "Not interstellar, though — not with those engine ports." He circled it. "Limited shields, no significant weapons. Another shuttle, definitely, but strictly short-range. It'd fit through the ring, though. We could use it to get back and forth to the base, if we could bring it there, but that's about it. And that's assuming I can figure out the controls once we get it open." He didn't sound too worried about that, though, and neither was anyone else. If it could fly, Frayne could fly it.

Banje shook his head, clearly frustrated. "Three is all we need for that," he said. "Any more and we risk drawing attention to ourselves. Looks like we leave it."

He turned to walk away, but Ronon held up a hand to stop him. "This thing can fly?"

It was Adarr who answered him. "I think so — I'd have to go over its systems more carefully, but I'm pretty sure I can get it to power up, and the engines themselves are undamaged." He glanced around. "If necessary I can probably replace anything I can't repair."

"What're you thinking?" Banje asked Ronon quietly. The two of them had established a strong rapport over the past eight months. They thought a lot alike, though Banje was more cautious and Ronon took more risks. Never stupid risks, though, and the Desedan knew that. He also knew that Ronon was always looking for new ways to kill more Wraith.

"I'm thinking we could use this thing after all," Ronon replied, still playing with ideas as they formed. "Not for us, though. Just as bait."

"Bait?" Setien laughed. "It's an old shuttle in a burned-out spaceport on the edge of a ruined city. Who're we going to lure here with that?"

"Nobody." Ronon grinned at her. "But it won't be here. Good bait has to be somewhere the prey can see it."

Frayne groaned. "Why do I get the feeling I've just been volunteered for something I really won't like?" But Ronon saw how the Yadonite's eyes kept straying back to the shuttle. Frayne loved to fly, and did so any chance he got. And this was a new ship, one he'd never tested before.

"Don't worry," Ronon assured him. "You'll have the easy part." He looked at the others. "Adarr, I'll need your help. I can handle the rest myself."

Banje studied him, then shook his head. But all he said was, "Setien, go find Nekai. Tell him Ronon's having another one of his crazy plans."

Setien nodded. "Don't kill anything until I get back!" she demanded, taking off at a dead run. Within seconds she had vanished among the buildings.

Ronon had already pulled Adarr over to the shuttle, and gestured at its engines. "How stable are these things?"

Adarr frowned. "I'd have to go over them carefully," he replied after a second. "But probably not very."

"Good." Ronon laughed at the other man's surprise. "Now, how easy would it be to push them past their limit?"

CHAPTER SEVENTEEN

"THIS is crazy — you know this is crazy." Frayne didn't bother to look over at Ronon, but he didn't have to — the two of them were the only ones in the new shuttle, and his voice carried easily.

"Maybe so," Ronon agreed absently. "But it'll work. And it's better than leaving this wreck back at that city — or trudging through yet another forest, waiting to get jumped."

The orange-haired pilot shook his head, then stopped and shrugged. "Maybe you're right," he admitted after a second. "If I've got to go, I'd rather it was out here in space than down there on the ground. Quicker up here."

Ronon leaned forward — this shuttle didn't have a copilot seat, so he'd settled for the perch right behind Frayne's pilot chair — and clasped the other man on the shoulder. "You're not dying today," he assured his friend. "And with any luck, neither am I." He grinned to himself. "But the Wraith are."

Something beeped on one of the nested consoles, and Frayne hit a few switches and tugged back on the controls. Ronon felt the ship slow, shedding its velocity as it fired reverse thrusters to counter the momentum. Everything shuddered for a few seconds, then stilled completely.

"We're here," Frayne announced, flicking a few toggles. He swiveled his chair around and stood. "Didn't handle too badly, after all that. Not as tight on the axis as our others, though."

"You did great," Ronon assured him. And he had. The little Yadonite had figured out the strange shuttle's controls in less than an hour, and had piloted it here from the planet without incident. Of course, that had been the easy part.

Another beep, and Frayne scanned the displays. "Incoming," he announced. They both stared out the viewport, looking for any sign of an approaching ship, and after a second Ronon noticed a dull star that was growing larger.

"There," he said, pointing it out, and Frayne nodded. Together they watched the shape expand, growing from a tiny dot to a small blob to a small triangular shape. After a few more seconds they could see a darker band across the front, which then resolved into a viewscreen as the shape itself became clearly a shuttle. One headed right toward them.

"Let's hope Nekai knows what he's doing with that thing," Frayne muttered, "or he'll ram right into us and then we'll all go up." Privately, Ronon agreed. The V'rdai leader was a competent pilot but not a great one, and this required a very delicate hand. That's why the plan had been for him to bring their other shuttle close and then let Frayne cross in an atmosphere suit and pilot it the rest of the way.

But Nekai wasn't always that good at following others' directions. Ronon suspected it was because he'd been a leader for too long — he was used to giving commands, not taking them. It had been enough of a struggle getting him to go back and retrieve the other shuttle.

"No, it's too risky," he'd said when Ronon had outlined his barely formed plan. "Not just for you, but for us. We could lose the shuttle, we could lead the Wraith right back to our base, we could all get recaptured. This isn't what I've trained the V'rdai for."

"Maybe not," Ronon had replied, tamping down his anger and impatience, "but it's what a lot of us were trained for. Just not by you. I had a whole life as a soldier before the Wraith caught me. So did Banje. So did Setien and Adarr and Frayne. We can do this. And we can take our fight with the Wraith to a whole new level."

Nekai had still shaken his head. "I won't risk leading them back to our base."

"You won't be. Take two or three of the others with you. That way they can't follow your signal. Adarr, Frayne, and whoever else you leave behind will stay here with me. When you bring the shuttle back through with that device we salvaged from the Dart, the rest of them can join you. Frayne and I will pilot this heap, and you can follow us. Simple."

Nekai had looked up at him, one eyebrow arched in question. "What makes you think I can find this world again through the ring?"

That had gotten a snort from Ronon. "I know you memorize each combination," he'd replied too low for anyone else to hear. "You may dial them at random but you never dial the same one twice. You can find it again." He deliberately didn't mention the list Turen had told him about — he'd never seen it and decided that if Nekai didn't want to tell him about that himself, he wouldn't let on that he knew. Not that it changed anything — it just meant Nekai was memorizing the next address on the list before they left the dome, because he never consulted anything when dialing and Ronon suspected the list was safely back at their base.

They'd locked gazes for a moment, but finally the Retemite had nodded. "All right. We'll try this crazy plan of yours. But if you get blown to bits, don't come crying to me."

"Fair enough."

That part had gone without a hitch, and a few hours later Nekai and the others had returned with one of their regular shuttles and the Dart's ring-dialing device. Adarr and Setien had joined him — Adarr had stayed behind to work on the engines and Setien to stand guard — and they'd lifted off again almost immediately. Frayne had been right behind them. It had been a mark of the little Yadonite's skill that he'd passed the other V'rdai on the way and led them to this spot instead of the other way around. They'd decided not to try taking the shuttles through a ring again, just in case the Wraith had some way to monitor when their devices were used, and had simply flown to a a patch of space within view of the ruined city's planet instead.

Now they watched as the other shuttle slowed and finally stopped perhaps ten meters away. "Cutting it close," Frayne muttered. He was already in his atmosphere suit, as was Ronon, but Ronon stayed in place as Frayne moved to the airlock. "Sure you don't want to just come back with me and forget all this?" The smaller man asked as he cycled the portal open.

"No. This will work." Ronon gestured toward their waiting teammates. "Go on. Bring them in."

Frayne shrugged once and raised a hand in farewell. Then he was gone, floating out into space. He moved easily, bridging the distance between the two shuttles just as the other ship's airlock also opened and Setien leaned out. She caught Frayne's outstretched arm on the first attempt and hauled him in, then sealed the airlock again behind her. Ronon did the same on his ship.

After a minute he felt a faint shudder and saw the engines of the other shuttle light again. The ship pulled away, and accelerated smoothly — within a minute it had disappeared behind a nearby moon.

Ronon sank down onto the pilot's chair. Now there was nothing to do but wait.

It felt strange, sitting here in a barely functional shuttle, no shields or weapons, no defenses, no place to hide. After all these months with the V'rdai, he'd gotten used to having them around — because of the tracking devices they were never more than five meters from at least one teammate at all times, and being all alone on this ship made him realize how much he missed that constant company. Even Frayne's complaints or Adarr's chatter or Setien's boasts would be welcome.

But having the others nearby brought a degree of security, of safety. As long as they were together, the Wraith couldn't track them.

And right now he needed them to track him.

His whole plan depended upon it.

Time passed. Ronon leaned back, stretched out his legs, and shut his eyes. No sense staring out at space, starting at every star that flickered. Far better to get some rest. He'd need it once things started happening.

A muted beeping woke him from his doze, and he sat up quickly, blinking as he stared out of the viewport. Was that a ship approaching? Yes. But what ship?

He rose to a crouch, his hand going to his pistol where he'd belted it outside his atmosphere suit. But he relaxed when the ship drew closer and he recognized its forward profile. The other V'rdai were back.

The shuttle grew larger so quickly Ronon had a moment's concern that it might smash into him and through him, leaving a trail of twisted metal and bloody flesh in its wake. But it slowed when it was less than a hundred meters away, its thrusters firing in controlled bursts even as the ship's angle shifted downward. It pivoted on its central axis as it dropped, rotating lengthwise, and slid up beside his stationary ship. With Frayne at the controls, the V'rdai shuttle brushed his ship so gently the hull barely rocked, and then eased to a stop directly beneath him. A second later, a short, sharp rap reverberated through the floor.

Ronon stamped once in reply. They didn't have short-range communicators in their suits, and wouldn't have risked using them even if they did, so for now stomping would have to suffice. That was fine, though. They didn't need to communicate too much. The fact that the others had returned meant they'd detected an approaching ship. And out here, in the middle of nowhere, with a dead planet below? There was only one race that would bother to send a ship anywhere near this area.

The Wraith.

Which meant they weren't here for the planet. They already

knew it was dead — after all, they'd killed it.

No, they were here for him.

Of course, right now they'd be a little confused. Their tracking monitors had shown his device, clear as day, and they'd followed the signal out here to empty space. But now it had vanished again, courtesy of the other V'rdai separated from him by two metal hulls.

So the Wraith would be studying the area with their more conventional scanners. And they'd pick up this ship. Just sitting here, apparently dead in space.

Only it was two ships. One directly below the other. Nestled too close to be distinguished by anything but a close-up visual.

Which meant it was time for the second half of the plan.

Ronon stepped over to the console. Adarr had shown him what to push, and now he repeated the motions the tall mechanic had demonstrated, pulling this lever here and pushing this button there, then dialing this switch all the way to one side. The shuttle shuddered beneath his feet as its engines roared back to life, but he hadn't released any of the building pressure yet. He hadn't given the ship a direction or tapped into that thrust. It was all still potential, waiting for release.

He intended to release it. Just not in the way someone might expect.

Glancing over everything again to make sure he'd done it right, Ronon nodded and stomped once more before stepping to the airlock. He cycled it open and slid through, closing it again behind him. Then, using handholds Adarr had attached alongside while they'd waited back on the planet, he moved down to the bottom of the shuttle. The V'rdai ship was waiting there, its own engines quiet to avoid detection, its airlock open. Setien grinned at him as she crouched and reached down. Ronon caught her hand and allowed himself to be pulled inside.

"All set?" Banje asked as the airlock shut and Ronon was reunited with the rest of the team.

"Set," he confirmed. He straightened slowly, letting his body adjust to the sudden change in orientation — what had been down for him in the other shuttle was now up here. "Where are they?"

"Less than four hundred meters, and closing fast," Frayne answered from the controls. "Not a Dart, either. Way too big for that, though not nearly large enough for a Hive. Looks like a cruiser."

Several of them shuddered at that, Ronon included. He'd seen cruisers over Sateda, during the battle. The Wraith used them to escort their Hive-ships — and to transport human prisoners, storing them for easy feeding. Whoever had detected his signal must have commandeered one to go after him. He hoped there were a lot of Wraith on board.

"Should be within visual range right about — now," Frayne commented, and the others all started looking for signs of the approaching foe. Not surprisingly, Turen spotted it first, and pointed it out to the others. It had looked like a rock, dull and dark gray and lumpy, but it was definitely on an intercept course, and growing quickly.

"This had better work," Nekai muttered to Ronon. "There's no way we can take a cruiser otherwise."

"It'll work," Ronon assured him, then glanced at Adarr for confirmation. The lanky man nodded. "It'll work."

They stayed where they were, no one daring to speak or move, as the Wraith ship slowed just above them. It was shaped like a Dart but much, much larger, with a wider body and broader wings and an expanded bridge section. Cruisers were capable of carrying Darts, but since it hadn't released any Ronon hoped this one had flown in with an empty hangar. After all, the Wraith in charge was expecting a lone Runner on a stalled shuttle.

Too bad that wasn't what was waiting for him.

"Time to go," Banje whispered as the Wraith ship came to a stop. It was alongside the other shuttle, its forward airlock only a few meters away. Frayne nodded and nudged the controls, easing their ship down and away from the others, gliding to the side so the very shuttle they'd been hiding beneath concealed his departure. Within seconds they were a dozen meters away, and that distance increased rapidly.

Ronon looked at Nekai, who nodded his permission. "Now," Ronon commanded. Frayne hit a control on his console, and they all heard the squawk as the shuttle transmitted a signal to the ship Ronon had just abandoned. Then Frayne was gunning their engines, putting as much distance as possible between them and the two remaining ships.

They were perhaps two hundred meters away when the shuttle exploded.

The shock waves buffeted them about, but Frayne kept a tight grip on the controls and kept them pointed well away.

Which was a good thing, because two seconds later the cruiser detonated as well.

That impact put the shuttle into a spin, throwing everyone against walls and ceiling and floor as it spiraled out of control. But only for a moment. Frayne soon had the ship stabilized again, and pivoted it around so they could admire the sight of debris being flung in every direction right where they had waited just a minute before.

"Beautiful!" Setien judged, slapping Ronon on the back hard enough to make him take a quick half-step forward. "Absolutely brilliant!"

"Nicely done," Banje agreed. The others all nodded and added their congratulations and enthusiasm.

Ronon smiled and accepted it all. He was pleased. Everything had gone exactly as he'd hoped — better, even. The Wraith had detected his signal and then lost it but found the shuttle. They'd approached incautiously, assuming they had nothing to fear, and so hadn't bothered to put up any shields. Adarr had rigged the engines to overload once they were activated, and then wired in the communications system so a message on the right frequency would trigger that activation. The shuttle had gone up, and clearly its destruction had damaged something within the cruiser enough that the Wraith ship had exploded right behind it. There was no way anything had survived that.

"Smart," Nekai admitted, clapping Ronon on the shoulder and clasping his arm. "Our biggest victory yet. But let's not try this too often, hm? I don't know where we'd get more shuttles." He was grinning when he said it, and Ronon grinned back. It felt good to have struck such a major blow.

And he vowed that it wouldn't be the last. Or the most severe.

The Wraith wouldn't know who had caused the explosion. But they might figure out a Runner had been involved. And eventually, they would learn to fear the Runners.

To fear him.

Because he was going to give them good reason to be afraid.

"Ronon Dex, conqueror of the Wraith," Rodney declared, though not loudly — even at a whisper the sound echoed around them until it made his head ring. "So why didn't you and your buddies simply slaughter every last Wraith? Would have saved us a lot of trouble, that's for sure."

"We tried," Ronon growled. "We took out plenty of them. Not as many as Atlantis, but there were only seven of us, with barely any gear."

"Sure, sure, you got notches in your bedpost and written commendations and merit badges, the works," Rodney agreed. "Sounds perfect. If you like killing."

"It was. And I do." That last was said with deliberate menace, but Rodney waved it off.

"You didn't go to all this trouble to keep me alive just to kill me," he pointed out.

"No, I went to all this trouble to keep you alive so you can repair the Jumper and get us out of here. It's Sheppard and Teyla I'm worried about."

Rodney nodded. He was trying not to think about their two friends, and what might be happening to them right now. He was safe, if a little bruised, and sitting in a cave listening to Ronon's equivalent of a campfire story. They'd been captured and were probably being beaten, maybe tortured — or worse.

"Okay, so we have the perfect killing team," he said, forcing his attention back to Ronon's tale. "A true hunter's paradise. Why aren't you still there with them?"

"Because nothing lasts forever," Ronon answered after a minute. There was something different in his voice, and it took Rodney a second to place it. Regret. But more than that — grief. He'd only heard Ronon sound this way once before, when he'd talked about his wife and their homeworld, Sateda.

"Something happened, didn't it?" Rodney asked. "What?" He was genuinely curious.

"We were at war with the Wraith," Ronon reminded him, his voice dropping even lower. "And every war has casualties." He didn't say anything for a minute, and Rodney waited, not rushing him. He could tell this was something Ronon actually wanted to talk about, maybe even needed to.

Sure enough, after that minute of silence had stretched into two, Ronon picked up his tale again. "Sometimes it doesn't take much to bring everything crashing down," he started. "It can be something tiny. Or it can be something huge. Or it can be both at once. That's what happened to us. . . ."

CHAPTER EIGHTEEN

"HOW'RE the boots?"

"Shhh!" Ronon motioned Adarr to quiet, looking around quickly to make sure no one had heard them. Not that there was anyone to hear except Setien, and she was out in front as always. After a few seconds he decided it was safer to answer than to risk his other teammate's asking again. "They're good. Thanks."

The lanky Fenabian smiled. Adarr had been the one who'd found the boots on their last salvage mission, and he'd been as thrilled as a puppy when he'd presented them to Ronon. They'd discovered stashed clothing and even footwear a few times before, but these were the first that were large enough to accommodate Ronon's big feet. For the first time in well over a year, he was wearing proper boots instead of something Setien had cobbled together from scraps. He could definitely feel the difference, and his feet and legs thanked him for it every day.

Now wasn't the time to think about that, however. They were on a new world, on the hunt once again, and this time Nekai had broken them into slightly different teams: the Retemite had paired himself with Frayne, put Turen with Banje, and then grouped Ronon, Adarr, and Setien. "We're getting too comfortable in our ways," he'd told them all. "We should each be able to work with anyone else in the unit."

He was right, of course. And Adarr was easy enough to handle, other than having to tell him to keep quiet every ten seconds. Setien was an entirely different matter. She'd been with the V'rdai longer than Ronon, and she was used to doing things her own way and without being too encumbered by teammates. Plus, Nekai had left the situation nebulous — Banje was the V'rdai second-in-command, so obviously he had authority over Turen, but there was no clear command structure after that. Ronon had command experience and Setien didn't, which might mean he was in charge of their trio, but try telling Setien that!

Ronon shook his head, though he couldn't help smiling a little. Setien was certainly something. Over the past nineteen months, he and the aggressive Mahoiran had grown close. Very close. Neither of them was looking for a relationship, of course. Ronon was still grieving for Melena, and Setien never talked about anyone back home but he suspected, due to the nature of her occupation, she'd never wanted attachments in general. And that was fine. They were still Runners, which meant they still faced the possibility of having to disappear at any time — not exactly a healthy way to start a relationship. But that didn't mean they couldn't find comfort in another's company — or that they couldn't enjoy certain physical activities together as well.

Of course, with Setien that often meant sparring. Before or after. Or during.

But she certainly kept things interesting.

As if on cue, she let out a squawk of delight up ahead. "Pears!" she announced, throwing any stealth to the wind and straightening up to stare up at one of the trees around them. Nekai had a knack for finding them heavily forested worlds, which certainly made hunting and ambushing Wraith easier but also increased the risk of a distracted Setien. Just like now. She'd caught sight of the fruits, dangling well out of her reach, and was utterly transfixed.

"Not now," Ronon warned, catching up to her and putting a hand on her arm. She shook him off, though not meanly, but didn't look away from the object of her desire. "Besides," he reasoned, "it's out of our reach. We may find others closer to hand."

That at least got her moving again. "Fine," she said, shouldering past him and resuming her forward position. "But I get them first!"

"Who'd dare to get in your way?" Adarr muttered at her back, and Ronon stifled a laugh. The pale man was right—all the V'rdai knew the danger of getting between Setien and fresh fruit. She'd nearly trampled Frayne a few months back when the little orange-haired man had discovered a batch of wild strawberries.

They kept moving, eyes peeled. Ronon was stalking along in his typical hunter's crouch. Adarr was alternating between imitating him and bouncing along like a little kid, oblivious to any danger. And Setien was moving with her usual confident stride, no stealth at all but still completely alert to any danger.

Something nagged at the back of Ronon's head as they walked, but he couldn't figure out what. They'd seen no signs of anyone else around, no hint of any nearby settlements, and no evidence of Wraith visitation. The trees were tall and broad and solid, their branches low enough for him to reach if he stretched but high enough that he could stand up straight and not worry about banging his head, the canopy thick enough to block most of the two suns' light but sparse enough to allow some dappled beams to dance down and illuminate the forest floor. The temperature was pleasant, cool and brisk, and there were birds somewhere, along with an occasional chittering or scraping that suggested other woodland creatures. That was always a good sign—animals instinctively feared the Wraith, and would disappear at the first hint of the lifesuckers.

But something still felt wrong.

Ronon was trying to puzzle it out when he heard Setien give a triumphant cry. "There!" she shouted, and for a second Ronon expected to see Wraith up ahead. But instead she was pointing up slightly, toward another tree a short distance in front of her—and a thick cluster of pears that hung within easy reach.

"They're mine!" And she charged forward to claim them.

Which is when Ronon realized what had been bothering him. All of the fruit they'd seen had been out of reach. But there were plenty of branches within reach. They'd just all been stripped bare. And that meant either very industrious critters who didn't like heights — or people. People harvesting the fruit.

And why would those people leave a single clump of pears where anyone could get them? They wouldn't —

— unless it was a trap.

"Setien, no!" Ronon sprinted toward her, but she was ahead of him and moving just as fast to reach her prize. He was still several feet from her when she reached up, plucked one of the ripe, golden fruits —

— and vanished upward in a whoosh of air and leaves and bark.

"Setien!" Ronon skidded to a stop where she'd been standing and craned his neck, peering up into the thick foliage. There! He caught a patch of darker black against the shadows — that had to be her hair. "Setien, are you all right?"

"Unhh," came a weak groan from up above. A few seconds later it was followed by a string of curses, each one louder and more depraved, and Ronon relaxed slightly. If she was well enough to curse, she couldn't be too badly injured.

"What happened?" Adarr demanded, finally catching up. The lanky mechanic might have legs almost as long as Ronon's but he flailed too much for them to build up much speed, plus his lean frame lacked heavy muscle.

"Setien triggered a snare," Ronon explained quickly, studying the offending branch itself. He could see now where a notch had been cut into the wood to hold the rope or vine or whatever had been used. "The pears were bait, and she fell for it."

"Who traps fruit?" Setien demanded from somewhere overhead. "That's insane!"

"They caught you, didn't they?" Ronon retorted, frustration and concern lending an edge to his voice.

"Is it Wraith?" Adarr asked, pulling his pistol and swinging around wildly. Ronon had to stop him and hold him in place before the other man shot one or both of them by accident.

"It's not Wraith," he assured the other man quietly. "They don't set traps like this."

"Oh. Right." Adarr calmed down slightly. Unfortunately, that also meant he started talking again. "I guess that makes sense. I mean, we've never seen them set traps like that before, why start now? And why would they think anyone would just happen along on a random planet and grab that particular bunch of pears, anyway? Kinda weird." He scratched at his chin. "So who did set it, then?"

"Hunters," Ronon growled, one hand on his pistol as he studied the shadows all around them. "Probably meant it for a big cat or a small bear or something." He risked a quick glance up at where he knew Setien had to be. "Looks like they got one."

"I heard that!" Setien shouted down at him. "Just wait until I get out of this thing, I'll —"

"Can you?" Ronon cut her off.

"Can I what?"

"Can you get out?"

"Don't you think I would have by now?" she demanded. Which was a fair point — she was hardly one to sit around waiting for someone else to rescue her. "No! It's got me wound all around like a holiday present! I can't reach my gun, my knife, or anything!"

"Probably for the best, really," Adarr pointed out softly to Ronon. "If she could she'd have shot the vine or rope or whatever it is holding her up there. Then she'd have plummeted straight down." He squinted up. "I'm guessing she's at least twenty meters up, maybe more. That's a hell of a drop, even for her."

Ronon stared at him, a chill racing down his spine. It took him a second to find his voice. "Go get Nekai. Get all the others. Hurry."

"What? But —" The other man saw the look on his face and nodded, shutting his mouth quickly. "I'm on it." Then he was gone in a flurry of limbs.

"What're you doing?" Setien asked. "Why'd you send Adarr away? Just climb up here and cut me down and we can get moving again!"

"I'm working on it," Ronon assured her, holstering his gun and grabbing the branch with both hands. He jumped and hauled himself up, then stood carefully, one hand against the trunk for balance, and studied his surroundings. No sign of the snare's other end at this level, though that didn't mean it wasn't here — whoever had set this trap knew their woodcraft, and there was plenty of bark and leaves and branches to use for cover. "But we're on a time limit."

She understood at once. "How high am I?" There was no fear in her voice, but the outrage was gone as well. Now she was all business.

"At least twenty meters."

"Oh." He thought he heard her sigh, though he couldn't be sure from this distance — it might have been a breeze rustling through some leaves. "I can't even reach my gun. Or raise my fist."

"I know." He felt around the trunk carefully but didn't find anything. So he wrapped his arms around it instead and shimmied up to the next branch to repeat the process.

Each climb took him closer to Setien, and even if he couldn't locate the rest of the snare, if he could get close enough, he could try to swing her over to him, then cut her loose.

The problem was, she was well beyond the overlap range of the tracking device. Which meant she'd become fully exposed the second she'd been trapped. And every minute Ronon couldn't reach her meant another minute the Wraith might notice her signal and lock onto it.

They'd gone from being the hunters to being the hunted again. Only this time Setien was bound and helpless. Ronon tried not to think about what would happen if he couldn't get her free in time.

It felt like hours had passed before Adarr returned, though Ronon knew it had to be less than that. If for no other reason than that he hadn't managed to make much progress in climbing. Adarr had clearly filled the others in on the situation, and Banje immediately called up to them as they all gathered around the base of the tree.

"Ronon, come down," he said. "Turen's on her way up."

Ronon considered arguing for a minute, then nodded. He had height and reach and muscle over Turen, but the higher he climbed the thinner the branches became. He'd already had to climb past several because they wouldn't support his weight. Once he got much higher the trunk might not be willing to hold him either. Turen was small and light and fast — she'd be able to get a lot farther than he could.

He passed her on the way, and she gave him a quick smile. "I'll get her," she assured him, but Ronon knew she was just trying to cheer him up. They had no idea how high Setien really was, or how difficult it might be to disarm the snare. They had to face the possibility that she was stuck up there until the original hunters returned to claim their prize — or until the Wraith beat them to it.

Back on the ground, Banje was conferring with Nekai. Ronon joined them. "This is my fault," he told them at once. "I should have seen the snare. I should have stopped her."

"You had no reason to look for traps here," Nekai argued. "None of us did. We haven't seen any signs of settlement anywhere — as far as we knew, this whole world was uninhabited."

"It might still be," Banje pointed out. "They may be using the ring to come through and hunt here, then return to their own world. That would explain why we haven't seen any settlements anywhere."

"If that's the case, it could be a while before they return," Frayne offered from behind them. "So that's good, anyway." The fact that he was trying to be hopeful only underscored the gravity of the situation.

"The Wraith won't be as patient," Ronon pointed out. "She's been up there almost an hour, maybe more. No way they haven't picked up on her signal by now."

"If Turen can't cut Setien down right away, she'll get close enough to fog the signal again," Nekai assured him. "We'll hide and ambush any Wraith who show up. Then we can get her down at our leisure."

Ronon nodded. But he still paced impatiently for the next half hour, waiting for word.

Finally, Turen called down, "I'm as close as I can get, I think."

"How close is that?" Nekai shouted up.

"Ten, maybe twelve meters," she answered. "No sign of the rest of the snare — whoever set this is really good. They've got the vine supported by upper limbs from three different trees, which is why it can handle her weight."

"Hey!" Setien screeched at that, but she didn't add anything further.

"If it's ten meters, she might be okay," Banje pointed out quietly. "If it's twelve, though, they're both exposed." He looked at Nekai, who shook his head.

"We can't risk both of them," the V'rdai leader decided, his voice rough. "We need to get ready. Turen!" he called up. "Come back down!"

"I might be able to get a little higher — " she offered, but Nekai cut her off.

"Come down right now!"

"Go," Setien agreed. "They'll be on their way. You don't want to be up here when they arrive."

"I can't just leave you hanging here!" Turen argued.

"You can, and you must," Setien told her. "Go down now. You can come back up after the Wraith are dead." But even from down below Ronon could hear the dull cast to her voice, so unlike her. Setien was already preparing herself for the fact that she might not survive this situation.

"We've got to do something!" Ronon told Nekai angrily. "We can fashion a net, string it across the trees below her, and then cut the vine!"

"We will," Nekai agreed. "As soon as we can. But we don't have a net. And the Wraith will be coming. We need to deal with them first. Take cover." Ronon didn't move. "Now, Ronon!"

"He's right, Ronon," Setien shouted down to him. "I'm already bait — no sense in offering them more."

Ronon growled but finally took shelter behind a tree. He had his pistol in hand already, fingers tight around the butt, and he drew his sword as well, keeping the blade low so it wouldn't flash in the filtered sunlight. It had taken him and Turen weeks to fashion the jagged Dart fragment into a proper blade, and longer for him to find something he felt was suitable for the rest of the weapon. He had finally settled on using only Wraith trophies. A Wraith jaw-bone formed the hilt and handle. A braid of Wraith hair wrapped around that for the grip, and the leather coat he'd taken from the first commander he'd killed formed the scabbard. The sword served not only as a weapon but as a symbol of his hatred for the Wraith, and now he focused on that, trying to push his fear for Setien aside. He'd kill anyone who came for her. Then they would get her loose and all head back to their base together.

It seemed far too soon before they began hearing sounds in the forest, coming from the direction of the ancestral ring.

"Wraith," Banje whispered, alerting the rest of them, and Ronon strained to pick up what the Desedan's sharp ears had noticed. But he didn't hear anything.

At least, not at first. After another minute he picked up a faint rustling. It could have been the wind, but then he heard it again. And again. It was too regular to be a breeze. They were footsteps.

But soft ones, not the heavy warrior's tread he was used to. He glanced at Banje, who caught his eye and then shrugged. He was puzzled as well.

Ronon peeked out from behind his tree — and froze, knowing that to move again might draw attention. He had seen a flash of white among the browns and greens and golds up ahead. Then another. And another. Even with so quick a glimpse, he recognized the shading. Wraith hair and flesh. Three of them.

But not warriors. The warriors wore those helmets to protect their heads, and those covered their hair and faces completely. These Wraith were bareheaded.

Which meant they were commanders. That explained why they were so quiet — the commanders were more graceful, more stealthy then the warriors they used for brute force.

But three commanders at once? Hunting together? The Wraith had never done that before!

The others had noticed now as well, and Ronon saw each of them tense in turn as they realized the same thing he had. The Wraith had changed their hunting tactics. And going up against three commanders was very different from taking out one commander and two warriors.

Especially without Setien.

Ronon started to raise his pistol, but a hand on his wrist stopped him. Nekai. The V'rdai leader had closed the distance between them so quietly Ronon hadn't even noticed.

"Not yet," Nekai whispered. "Wait until they stop beneath her. Then we'll take them."

Ronon hesitated, then nodded. It was the smart thing to do. They'd be more exposed that way, and they'd be stationary. He just didn't like letting them get that close to Setien.

But he knew if she was down here she'd have agreed. They had to take out all three Wraith at once, to prevent them from summoning help, and this was the best way to do it.

He relaxed his arm slightly, and Nekai removed his hand. Then the Retemite slid away again, stopping a few feet to the side where he could take refuge behind another tree.

And they waited.

Within minutes the Wraith had reached the site of the snare. They moved silently, eyes wary, weapons drawn. These three would not be taken by surprise. When they stopped, they put their backs to each other, so that they had all sides covered. Only then did one of them glance up, and then only quickly.

"What have we here?" it called out, its words hissing from between its pointed teeth. "Setien D'onbach of the Mahoir? Quite the prize!"

"An odd place to find yourself," one of the others commented, clearly speaking out loud for her benefit. "So high and so defenseless. Almost like a gift!"

"But who would make us such an offering?" the third pondered. "Not that we can refuse, of course." Even from here Ronon could see its sharp grin.

"The question becomes, how to retrieve our present?" the first one asked. "We dislike climbing, especially when other dangers could lurk nearby."

"Cut me loose and I'll come down to you," Setien offered, which made all three Wraith laugh.

"That is a good plan," one agreed after their chuckling had ceased. "Yes, perhaps we should cut you down."

Then they all raised their pistols as one, and began firing—straight up.

"No!" Ronon gave up all pretense of hiding and burst from

his cover, charging the Wraith. He was already shooting at them as he ran, sword raised high to cut them down as soon as he was close enough. Behind him he heard commotion as the others followed, and more gunfire whizzed past him, targeting the three commanders.

But the Wraith had clearly been ready for any threat. They split up at once, diving behind nearby trees, and returned fire,, continuing to shoot up into the branches every few seconds. And apparently their pistols had multiple settings like Ronon's because he could hear the crackle of leaves and wood burning up above. Those were no stun-bolts!

He had winged one of the commanders before they could duck away, and now he targeted that one, circling the tree it was using for cover. They traded shots back and forth before Ronon was able to swing around the other side and lash out with his sword. The blade bit deep through Wraith leather and flesh, and he heard the commander gasp in pain as he dropped to his knees. Ronon was pivoting back around the trunk again in an instant, sword flashing as it leapt forward to strike the Wraith's head from his shoulders.

One down, two to go.

But those two were firmly entrenched now, and the other V'rdai hadn't been able to get the drop on them yet. Nor could Ronon, not without running right into their weapons fire.

"We need to go!" Nekai shouted, aiming at one Wraith but just missing him and striking the tree instead. Chunks of bark and wood flew.

"Not without Setien!" Ronon insisted. He looked for a way to get behind the Wraith but didn't see one.

"They'll have reinforcements on the way!" Nekai insisted. "We'll all get killed — or captured!" The thought made Ronon shiver. But he wouldn't abandon her. He couldn't!

One of the two remaining Wraith fired upward again, and Ronon heard something snap up among the leaves. Then he heard what sounded like a strong wind — but it was coming straight down.

"Look out!" Banje yelled, ducking back behind a tree. The others followed his lead, except for Ronon — the Wraith were taking refuge as well, and he used the opportunity to cross the space to one of them. The Wraith commander had just enough time to glance up when Ronon's shadow fell across him, sword blade and pistol bolt right behind it and both centered on his head.

The Wraith's body dropped, Ronon turned —

— and leaped backward to avoid being crushed by a large shape as it crashed to the ground right beside him.

It was only when he picked himself up again that he realized it was Setien. The last shot must have struck one of the branches supporting her, and the others couldn't hold her weight alone. Or it had severed the vine itself. Either way, she had plummeted more than twenty meters — for a second he berated himself for not trying to catch her, then admitted that was ridiculous. Falling from that height, she would have crushed him, and then they would both be dead.

For there was no question as to whether she'd survive. Not anymore. Ronon dropped to his knees beside her, trying not to notice the way her limbs were bent in every direction, or where bone poked through flesh. He ignored the blood seeping into the ground all around him, soaking his pants where his knees touched, and reached for her head. She was still alive, her eyes still blinking, though they were already glazing over and blood was trickling from her nose and mouth and ears.

"Always . . . knew . . . fruit would be . . . the death . . . of me," she whispered thickly, and Ronon tried to smile. Behind him the remaining Wraith stirred — Setien's impact had stunned him — then cried out and thrashed and stilled as five V'rdai shot him at once. But Ronon ignored them all.

"You can't die," he told Setien. "Who's going to whip my

ass in the ring?"

She managed a weak smile, though one side of her face didn't respond. "Next . . . time," she managed. Then her whole body convulsed and went slack, and the light faded from her eyes. She was gone.

Ronon didn't know how long he sat like that, her head cradled in his hands, before he felt a hand on his shoulder. "We have to go," Banje told him, his voice even softer than usual.

"I know." Ronon laid her on the ground as gently as he could and allowed the other man to help him to his feet. He also knew they couldn't bring Setien back with them. Not with the tracking device still imbedded in her back. She'd lead the Wraith right to their base the first time the rest of the team went out on a mission. And she wouldn't have wanted that.

Turen stepped up beside Ronon and handed him something without a word. It was a pear, one of the ones from the trap, slightly bruised now but still fresh. Ronon nodded his thanks and placed it in Setien's shattered hands, then clasped them around the fruit. If there was an afterlife, she wouldn't arrive empty-handed.

Then he turned and let the others lead him back toward the ancestral ring. None of them spoke, not even Adarr. Ronon knew there had been other V'rdai before him, but not many of them, and not for a long time. Setien had been part of the unit for years. Things would never be the same without her.

They had a second nasty surprise when they got within sight of the ring. There were Wraith troops stationed around it, and several Darts whizzing overhead. Obviously the Wraith were finally taking them seriously, but now was exactly the wrong time for them to have to fight their way home.

Fortunately, someone must have discovered the three dead commanders soon after they left the scene. Within minutes of reaching the ring Ronon and the others saw the Darts take off, heading in the direction of the trap. Half of the troops followed.

Only a handful remained to defend the ring, and they seemed to think they were safe from attack in the middle of a clearing. The V'rdai cut them down quickly, then sprinted to the ring as Nekai worked the controls, dialing open a portal and setting it to scramble the signal once they'd passed through.

A minute later, the gate closed behind them. They took two more jumps before returning to the shuttle, just to make sure no one had followed them.

Ronon barely remembered any of it.

CHAPTER NINETEEN

"NEKAI'S back!"

Adarr's shout startled the rest into motion, Ronon included. It had been almost two months since Setien's death, and over three weeks since their leader had taken a shuttle and disappeared. Ronon had thought at first that it was simply a reaction to Setien's death, but the others had told him that Nekai had done this a few times before—and the last two times it had been to recruit first Adarr and then Ronon himself. So none of them were too surprised a few minutes later when they saw four people step in through the dome's airlock: Frayne and Banje, who had gone to escort the new arrivals in once their systems had detected the approaching shuttle, Nekai, and one other.

Female, Ronon determined as he and Adarr and Turen joined the others. Average height, narrow build, the same loping gait he and Nekai and Banje possessed. Turen had an even more fluid walk, graceful and quick and quiet despite her shorter legs, and neither Frayne nor Adarr had ever fully mastered the hunter's stride. But this woman clearly had.

"You're back!' As when he'd first arrived, Ronon noticed that Turen approached Nekai rapidly, fast enough and with enough enthusiasm that he thought the little Hiñati woman would throw herself on the stocky Retemite, but at the last minute she slowed down and gave him a quick, awkward embrace instead. Frayne caught Ronon's gaze and rolled his eyes. As bunkmates, the two of them had plenty of time to sit and talk at night, and more than once the conversation had turned to Turen's obvious obsession with Nekai. Ronon had judged it equal parts hero worship, physical desire, and genuine affection. Frayne, being less kind, had ignored the third possibility and insisted it was entirely because Nekai had saved her and so was now this magnificent but untouchable figure in her eyes. Certainly the "untouchable" part seemed true — the rest of them all knew about her interest but if Nekai ever noticed he never acknowledged it, and Turen had never once acted on it.

This time was proving to be no exception.

Except that the newcomer's reaction was interesting. She'd stepped closer to Nekai when Turen had approached, almost but not quite putting herself in the shorter woman's way. And the minute Turen disengaged and stepped back the new woman slid even closer, her arm brushing against Nekai's side. Possessive, Ronon recognized. The woman was staking her claim. And Nekai didn't react one way or another — he didn't reciprocate but he didn't move away either.

Judging by Turen's scowl, she had seen it as well.

"Welcome back," Ronon told Nekai, edging past Turen to offer Nekai his hand once the Retemite had pulled off his helmet. "Glad you're okay."

"I'm fine," Nekai assured him and all of them, exchanging greetings with the others as well. "Everything here okay?"

"Fine," Banje answered, having already shucked his suit as well, but the one-word answer was even more flat than usual for the terse Desedan. Of course none of them were fine. There was still a large, Setien-shaped hole in their midst. It was impossible not to notice it — when they were eating, when they were parceling out chores, when they were training, when they were sparring. Especially when they were sparring. Banje and Turen had taken to double-teaming Ronon, and the pair worked together extremely well, his skill and experience coupled with her speed and agility, but it wasn't the same. So yes, they were fine: they were healthy, they'd kept up their practice and training, they were eating and exercising and even sleeping.

But they weren't well. Not by a long shot.

The newcomer had removed her helmet now, revealing a narrow face with sharp, angular features, dark brown hair pulled back in a severe bun, and black eyes that flickered constantly across them all. "Everyone, meet Lanara," Nekai introduced her, and Ronon saw Turen bristle at the obvious pride in his voice. "The newest member of the V'rdai."

"I'm Adarr." Of course the tall Fenabian was the first to welcome her. He offered a hand but pulled it back after she didn't clasp it, accepting her curt nod instead.

"Ronon." He got a similar nod. So she wasn't a touchy-feely type. She was still standing awfully close to Nekai, though. Ronon had seen enough body language back in the Satedan military to be fairly sure the two had slept together, and more than once. That was going to make matters . . . complicated.

Frayne and Banje introduced themselves as well, and finally Turen gave the new woman a grudging nod. "Turen," she muttered, shooting daggers at Nekai and barely sparing Lanara a glance. Oh yes, definitely complicated.

"Lanara is Kadrean," Nekai told them. "Her people are some of the finest hunters in the galaxy, and Lanara is one of the best they've ever produced. That's why I was able to return so quickly — she's already a better hunter than I'll ever be. We just needed to adapt her skills to hunting Wraith."

"They're a lot slower than alca-beasts," Lanara announced, her thin lips pulling back in a vicious smile. "And less dangerous close up." Her voice matched the rest of her, clear and sharp. Ronon wondered if she'd always been like this, or if becoming a Runner had stripped away any calmer emotions she might have possessed. He'd probably been just as brusque when he'd first arrived, but he'd still had some sense of humor buried deep inside. Of course, for him it had been three months since his capture. For her, assuming Nekai had found her as quickly, it had been only a few weeks. He couldn't fault her for still being raw. He just wondered if that would ease with time.

"Have you been out since I left?" Nekai was asking Banje, and frowned when the Desedan shook his head. "Well, we need to fix that. I know we're all still upset about Setien's death, but sitting here doesn't do her memory any honor. We need to remember her the way she'd want most, by laughing in the face of danger and killing as many Wraith as possible."

"And eating fresh fruit whenever we find it," Frayne muttered, which brought a smile to everyone's faces. Everyone except Lanara and Turen, who were now busy glaring at each other.

Nekai had smiled along with the rest of them, but now that glimpse of humor vanished. "It's time we got serious," he informed them gravely. "We've been taking the fight to the Wraith when we can, yes — and sometimes even when we probably shouldn't." That last had been accompanied by a quick glance at Ronon, but he only grinned in reply. "But now we have to do more. We need to manufacture situations to draw them in, set bigger traps, lure more Wraith to their death. Ronon's scheme with the dead shuttle worked beautifully, and took out an entire cruiser! We have to set more snares like that. Maybe even find a way to trap the ancestral rings themselves, so we can take out a Dart as it passes through."

He was pacing now, and the others watched him intently, knowing there was more their leader wished to say. Lanara had been forced to back away to give him room as he moved, and Ronon didn't miss the victorious smirk Turen sent her way. If Nekai thought the two women were going to bunk together, someone would have to disabuse him of that notion, and quickly. Otherwise Lanara wouldn't last a week — she might be an excellent hunter, but up close no one could match Turen with a blade.

But Nekai was speaking again. "We also need to accept the fact that sometimes, the Wraith may not be our only targets." That pronouncement met with stunned silence, and he stopped moving and looked at each of them in turn before nodding. "Yes, you heard me right. There are people out there, despicable people, who not only do not stand against the Wraith but who actively help them."

Beside him, Lanara's face twisted into an ugly scowl of pure hate. "My people fell," she declared, "because one of our elders struck a deal with the Wraith. She gave up our patrol patterns and shut down our security grid in exchange for a guarantee of personal safety." Her words emerged like blows, each one expelled by bitterness. "My whole world gone, just so she could save her own skin."

Nekai nodded. "It's people like that we may run up against from time to time," he warned. "Especially since we've been making a mark on the Wraith. There's a reason they changed their hunting patterns, and that's because they're scared. Of us." He gave them a few seconds to appreciate that fact. "But that means they've put the word out as well. They don't know much about us, since we don't leave any of them alive to talk, but they must know by now that we're a band of Runners and that we're hunting them in turn. They'll have warned every planet under their control, and there will be standing orders to bring us in if we're found." He frowned. "Some people would do so only to protect their own people, and I can't entirely fault them for that. But others would turn us in to save themselves alone, or to curry favor with the Wraith." He scowled. "And those people are no better than the Wraith themselves. Which means we must treat them the same way."

"You want us to hunt them?" Adarr asked. "How?"

"No, not hunt them," Nekai corrected. "We're still hunting Wraith and Wraith alone. But if we run across those who willingly help the Wraith, we must treat them as enemies. And deal with them accordingly."

Ronon nodded. This was war, after all. Anyone who chose to side with the enemy became the enemy. He knew that, and knew he'd have no problem pulling the trigger on such a person. Neither would Banje or, judging from her expression,

Lanara. He wasn't sure how Frayne or Adarr or Turen would
handle such a situation.

With any luck, they wouldn't ever have to find out.

They spent the next two weeks together in the dome, the
V'rdai now back up to seven. Ostensibly they were waiting
for Nekai to regain his bearings and work out a new plan of
attack against the more alert and organized Wraith hunting
parties, but everyone knew the truth — they were taking the
time to get used to their newest member.

And Lanara definitely took some getting used to.

She was fine at sparring, fast and wiry with sharp reflexes
and excellent balance. Her melee skills were solid, though
Turen delighted in trouncing her new rival several times in a
row, until Lanara acknowledged that she'd never be as good
with blades. What she lacked in close-in fighting, however, she
made up for at distance. It turned out that Lanara was phe-
nomenal at ranged combat — she had the best aim Ronon had
ever seen, and could place bullet, arrow, or knife perfectly on
target time after time from a hundred paces, whether standing, running, or dodging and rolling. After watching her shoot
and throw and after sparring with her several times in the
ring, Ronon knew he wouldn't have to worry about whether
she could handle herself on a hunt.

The problem wasn't with her skills. It was with her personality. Lanara, the rest of the V'rdai discovered, was not an easy
woman to get along with. She was short-tempered and sharp-
tongued, had a vicious sense of humor, thought very highly
of herself, and expected people to jump every time she issued
an order. Her possessive attitude toward Nekai had instantly
earned her Turen's dislike, and the two had survived as bunkmates less than a night before Turen kicked Lanara out and
threatened to gut her if she ever returned. The fact that Lanara
then stalked off to Nekai's tent and spent the night there didn't

help matters. He and Banje cleared out one of the supply tents the next day, and gave the new space to Lanara, but the damage had already been done. Ronon knew Turen well enough by now to know that she would do what she was told, and that she would hunt and fight alongside Lanara when necessary. But the two women would never be friends, and if it ever came down to going the extra distance for the prickly Kadrean, Ronon suspected Turen would find an excuse to come up short.

Frayne didn't like her much better. The short Yadonite didn't take well to arrogance, and had tolerated Setien's over-confidence only because her boasts were so amusing and so shameless. Lanara was just a little more conniving, a little more manipulative, a little more aware of her own behavior, and that put Frayne on edge.

Adarr was the most easy-going of the V'rdai, and he did his best to be friendly with Lanara. But she wasn't much interested in friends, and all his attempts to entertain her or engage her in conversation fell flat. Eventually he just left her alone.

Ronon didn't care for the newcomer much either. She was a poor substitute for Setien in every way except hunting, and they already had hunters. He was civil with her, but didn't even bother trying to be her friend. That actually seemed to suit Lanara fine, and Ronon was surprised when Banje pointed out one night that he probably got along with her better than anyone else outside Nekai himself.

Banje, for his part, recognized Lanara as a potential rebel and was quick to squash that. On her second day he made it very clear to her, in his quiet way, that he was Nekai's second-in-command and that she would follow his orders or leave at once. To her credit, Lanara agreed and abided by it. She never once refused a direct order, and never directly challenged Banje's authority, though her arch comments and barbed remarks made it clear she thought she could do a better job.

If Nekai noticed any of this, he didn't try to intervene. Which was probably for the best. Every good commander knew you had to let the troops sort themselves out, and that's exactly what Nekai was doing.

As it was, when he declared two weeks later that they were going hunting, the V'rdai were ready. They were just as dangerous as they had been with Setien — in some ways more so, because Lanara was less of a loose cannon and more of a hunter. If the team wasn't as relaxed together, and didn't joke and laugh as much on the way to the mission, no one was about to let that get in the way of killing Wraith.

But as they left the dome and made their way to the shuttle, Ronon realized that for the first time in over a year he felt as if the V'rdai were a team and only a team. They no longer felt like a family.

"So you just got up and left?"

Rodney could just see Ronon shaking his head, and felt the breeze caused by his braids. "Not quite."

"Well, you said it didn't feel like a family anymore."

"It didn't. It wasn't. But it was still a team. A good team. And we still had a job to do, a purpose. I wasn't going to walk away from that." Rodney thought he caught a glimpse of a smile, but if so it was a small, sad one. "Besides, I didn't have anywhere else to go."

"Okay, what happened?" Rodney was eager to find out. "Was it the new girl, Lanara? Did she do something that made it impossible to stay."

"No." Ronon sighed. "I wish she had. That would have been easier to handle. But it wasn't her. It was Nekai."

"What'd he do?"

"We were on another mission," Ronon explained. "some planet I've never seen before, all sun and sand. . . ."

CHAPTER TWENTY

"SHHH! I hear something!"

Banje's whispered comment froze the rest of them. They were crouched down, waiting behind rocks — for once they'd wound up on a world of sand and stone rather than trees and dirt, and they were all feeling the lack of shade even as they appreciated the increased security of stone cover over wood and bark. Turen at least had been smart enough to position herself so the shadow from one of the surrounding boulders fell across her — if she was going to have to play bait the least she could do was wait in the shade.

Now her head came up, green eyes narrowed in concentration, head tilting slightly. She had apparently heard Banje, or had picked up on a noise herself. Either way, she was ready. And so were the rest of them, Ronon thought, tensing.

It had been two months since Lanara had joined them. She was now fully a member of the V'rdai, at least when they were on missions. Back at the dome was another story. She still didn't mesh well with the others. But they could all live with that. It had been a miracle the original group had gotten along so well, and you didn't expect miracles to repeat themselves.

Ronon brought his attention back to the matter at hand, sliding his pistol from its holster and readying it. He had a few new weapons, flash grenades Banje and Adarr had managed to cobble together from some supplies they'd located after the last salvage run, but he only had two of those and didn't want to waste them. His pistol would probably be enough, and if not his sword was ready across his back as well. He'd caught sounds now as well: a skitter of loose rocks, what might have been a footfall, something else clanking or jingling. It didn't quite sound like Wraith — they were usually quieter than that—but they could be wearing new armor or carrying different weapons. It could also be people from one of the villages they'd spotted in the valleys below, though, so Ronon watched and listened for more details.

After a minute the sounds grew clearer. Definitely footsteps, a bunch of them, and metal against metal or leather or wood or even flesh, and something else as well. Something he wasn't used to. Voices. Whoever was approaching was talking, and there were definitely several of them.

He relaxed slightly, and noticed Turen doing the same, though she stayed in her huddle. It could be a Wraith trick, but so far at least that hadn't been their style. They were all about intimidation and stealth (when hunting), not deception. More likely these were people from some of those villages. Which meant they were simply a distraction.

If whoever it was stumbled upon them, however, it could ruin the hunt. They'd have to get rid of the strangers before the Wraith arrived.

Ronon started to stand, reholstering his pistol, but Nekai gave him a curt gesture to return to his cover. "Why?" Ronon whispered across to the Retemite. "They're not Wraith—they're natives."

"We don't know that," Nekai replied sharply. "And even if they are, they could still be working with the Wraith. Don't let your guard down!"

Ronon shrugged and ducked back down behind his rock, but he didn't draw his pistol. There was no point. He understood why Nekai was being cautious, and appreciated that, but whoever was approaching was making no effort to hide their location. They weren't a threat. Ronon was sure of it.

Sure enough, the voices and footsteps and jangling increased in volume, and then a group of people came into view. They stopped when they saw Turen, then rushed toward her.

"Ancestors!" one of them swore, his hand going to a waterskin at his side. "Are you all right?"

"Did you fall?" Another asked, also moving closer. "Are you hurt?"

There were five of them in all, Ronon saw. They wore loose shirts and thin baggy pants and sturdy studded sandals that laced up their legs, with cloths over their heads and necks and faces to protect them from the sun. The jangling had come from the packs they wore, from which hung a variety of small metal and wood and what looked like bone items. Ronon spotted cups, bowls, serving spoons, small lanterns, and other household items. These men were merchants, or peddlers. He guessed they moved from village to village, selling or trading items they'd made and repairing others.

Each of them had a sword, long and thin and curved, stuck through the sash they wore for belts, plus a long knife and a pistol. But none of them were reaching for those, or even turning to check the area for possible dangers. They were clearly not trained for combat, and not expecting any trouble. They saw in Turen only a woman in trouble, and their first impulse was to help.

Ronon started to rise again, knowing he was right and determined to move these men along before the Wraith spotted them and saw through the planned ambush.

He was halfway out from behind his boulder when a pistol shot sizzled through the air. It took the first peddler through the throat. He crumpled, surprise registering just before his face went slack. The waterskin fell to the ground with a dull clatter, water spilling out across the rock.

Stunned, Ronon turned and glanced behind him. Nekai's pistol was still extended, and he was switching his focus to one of the other men, who were now starting to cry out as they realized their friend was dead.

"Take them down!" Nekai shouted. Turen rose from her stooped position, knives flashing out and forward and across, and the second man dropped with a gurgling shriek, thin cloth and flesh alike sliced clean through. His blood mingled with the water as his body joined the first on the ground.

Then the other V'rdai were shooting as well. The three remaining peddlers never had a chance. One of them had shown enough presence of mind to drop down, but Nekai had chosen this ambush site well and Lanara caught the man through the throat, his ducking motion becoming a stumble and then a facedown splat upon the rough terrain. The other two had simply frozen at the sudden violence, and were picked off just as easily.

Within seconds the only people standing were Turen and Ronon. She was wiping her blades clean and returning them to their sheaths. Ronon thought he saw her hands shake slightly, but wasn't sure. He was too busy turning to glare at Nekai, who was finally rising and stepping toward the carnage as well.

"Let's get out of here," Nekai said, finally lowering his own pistol. "This hunt's ruined."

"Ruined?" Ronon stared at him. "The hunt? What about them?" He gestured at the bodies.

"What about them?" Nekai squinted up at the sun. "Scavengers will find them soon enough. The sun will finish whatever they don't. But no way the Wraith won't notice the stench, or the blood. We'll have to retreat, try again another time."

"Never mind the hunt," Ronon shouted, stepping closer to the other man. "You just murdered five people!"

Nekai met his glare, the Retemite's scowl showing he was starting to grow angry as well. "'You'?" he repeated softly. "We're a team, Ronon. A unit. You're one of us. Don't go thinking you're not."

Ronon brushed the distinction aside. "Fine — we just murdered five people!"

"We did what we had to do," Nekai answered. "That's all.

Now let's go."

He turned away, but Ronon wasn't finished. "We didn't have to do this!" he insisted. "They weren't a threat to us!"

"Of course they were," Nekai replied. "They interrupted our hunt. They could have attacked Turen." The look of gratitude and hero worship she shot him almost turned Ronon's stomach, especially after the violence he'd just witnessed. War was one thing, but slaughter was another. And this hadn't been war.

"They didn't draw a single weapon," he pointed out. "They were offering her water! They were asking if she was hurt!"

"You're going soft," Lanara sneered, stepping close to Nekai. Turen's happiness vanished instantly, replaced by the scowl she often wore these days. "They're sympathizers. Sympathizers deserve to die."

"Sympathizers?" Ronon glanced around at the others. Frayne and Adarr wouldn't meet his eyes. Banje did, but his expression was unreadable. Turen was still scowling, as were Lanara and Nekai — he thought Turen was more annoyed at Lanara than at him but it was hard to tell. "What did you see that could possibly suggest they were sympathizers? They didn't mention the Wraith, they aren't carrying Wraith weapons, and they didn't look like they were trying to hurt or capture Turen. They were going to help her! How does that make them sympathizers?"

"It doesn't matter," Nekai answered brusquely. "They weren't part of this unit. That makes them the enemy."

Ronon couldn't believe what he was hearing. "What?"

"Look," his mentor said, stepping a little closer to him. "You know the Wraith as well as I do. You know what they can do. They can get to anyone. They could turn them, or torture them, or simply bribe them. The point is, if we'd let them live, the Wraith could have used them to get information about us — and that would put all of us at risk. It would put our mission at risk." He laid a hand on Ronon's shoulder. "We couldn't trust them not to turn on us, or to be turned against us. We can't trust anyone except ourselves. It's us against the Wraith, and with their influence that means we have to treat it as us against the rest of the galaxy. Everyone else has to be considered hostile. It's the only way we can survive. The only way we can continue our hunt."

Ronon shrugged free of Nekai's grip. "I don't believe that," he responded. "Treat anyone we don't know as a potential threat, yes, but actively hostile? What, do you just want us to kill anyone who crosses our path, no matter what?" He glared at their leader, but the glare turned to a stare of disbelief when the Retemite didn't even try to deny the accusation. "You would!" Ronon said softly, the words hissing between clenched teeth. "You want us to wage war on the entire galaxy, and everyone in it."

"We're already at war," Nekai shot back. "I want us to win."

"We're at war with the Wraith," Ronon corrected. "Not everyone else. They're not involved. They're not soldiers. If we start killing them, we're just murderers, not warriors. And that makes us no better than the Wraith!"

Lanara's gasp warned him just in time as she lunged for him, a knife already in her hand. "How dare you?" she cried, slashing at his throat. He blocked the thrust and trapped her arm to keep her from trying again, but the look she gave him was almost sharp enough to kill all on its own. "How dare you compare us to them? They're monsters!"

"So are we," Ronon told her, taking the knife away and then pushing her back, not hard but forcefully enough that she couldn't prevent it. "If we start killing innocents, we're just as bad as they are." He shook his head. "Worse. The Wraith kill to survive. You want us to kill just because it's less complicated—killing everyone takes less effort than figuring out who we can trust."

He turned and looked at the others. His teammates. His friends. "Are you all okay with this?" he demanded of them. "Are you fine with being told to murder people who've never done anything to you? Really?"

Turen was the first to reply. "If Nekai says we have to," she asserted, raising her chin defiantly, "then that's what we'll do." The approving nod Nekai gave her would have set her tail to wagging if she'd been a dog.

"I don't have anything against those poor fellows," Frayne admitted, gesturing toward the dead peddlers. "But if it's them or us, I'm gonna go with us every time. What's wrong with that?"

"It's not my place to figure out who we do or don't fight," Adarr said. "I just do what I'm told."

That left Banje. "Come on," Ronon urged him. "You must see this is wrong. You commanded a unit, just like I did. You know what it means to give orders, and to have to live up to that responsibility. Some orders are just wrong. We're not murderers. We're soldiers — but that means only fighting other soldiers, not helpless civilians."

Banje didn't answer for a moment. When he did, however, he shook his head. "I don't know," he admitted so quietly Ronon had to strain to hear him. "Maybe we shouldn't have killed them. But what's done is done. And Nekai is right — everyone is a potential threat. We have to treat everyone outside our unit as a possible hostile, at least at first. It may be the only way for us to stay alive."

"If you shoot to kill at first sight, there won't be anything beyond 'at first,'" Ronon replied bitterly. His shock at Nekai's actions had faded, to be replaced by disappointment at the way his friends had simply accepted their leader's skewed perspective as their own. He wished Setien was here, then realized that perhaps he didn't. She wouldn't have approved of killing bystanders, but she also would have thrown the decision back in Nekai's face — she'd never known how to back down, and it might have led to violence among the V'rdai itself. Besides, she'd believed in their mission just as much as he had. Seeing it tarnished and twisted like this might have destroyed her.

Nekai was speaking again, and Ronon realized he'd tuned the other man out at first. "— changing," he was saying, "and we have to adapt if we're going to survive. They've expanded their activities, increased their hunts, enlisted allies and scouts and spies. We have to be even more vigilant and even more careful as a result. We can't risk waiting to see if someone is a friend or a foe — by the time we ask them and get a clear answer it could be too late. We'll have to assume everyone is an enemy unless we already know otherwise." The other V'rdai were nodding, though only Lanara showed any enthusiasm. The others were just accepting Nekai's lead as usual.

"We aren't looking for trouble, or for other people," Nekai added, focusing his attention on Ronon. "But if we run across them, we can't leave them behind to possibly go to the Wraith. We'll have to take them out first." His eyes bored into Ronon. "I need to know I can count on each and every one of you to do what's necessary without a moment's hesitation."

The others all nodded and agreed, though some a little more quickly than others. But Ronon shook his head.

"I'll do what's necessary, yes," he answered. "But this wasn't. And I won't kill innocent people just because you think the Wraith could draw information out of them."

"That's not good enough," Nekai told him bluntly. "If you go around second-guessing me on a mission, it could get all of us killed. You've got to be with us completely."

"I won't follow blindly," Ronon insisted. "I'm not a drone. None of us are."

"No, we're a team," Nekai replied. "We're the V'rdai. And you're either one of us — or you're not."

Ronon didn't like where this was heading. He glanced

around quickly, noticing that the others had formed a loose circle around him, and took a step back from Nekai, half-raising his hands in front of him. "I am V'rdai," he insisted. "But that doesn't mean I'll agree to mindless slaughter."

"If you won't follow orders, you're not one of us," Nekai said coldly. "And if you're not one of us" — suddenly his pistol was up, and pointing straight at Ronon's chest — "you're one of them. You're a threat to our existence."

"Hold on!" Adarr exclaimed, reaching out and trying to push Nekai's arm back down. Nekai shoved him away, never taking his eyes off Ronon. "This is crazy! He is one of us! You know that. Ancestors, you trained him! This is getting out of hand."

"We can't trust him," Lanara snapped, her words almost a snarl. "He would have saved those men if he could have. Next time he might side with them over us — or with the Wraith instead!"

"You're insane," Turen told her, hatred making each word razor-sharp. "I trust Ronon with my life — and I trust him a lot more than I trust you."

"Let's all just calm down," Frayne suggested, holding both hands out to show he at least wasn't reaching for a gun. "Let's talk about this. It's just a misunderstanding."

"It isn't," Ronon told his bunkmate sadly, though he was still watching Nekai and that pistol. "Things have changed. Nekai has changed. And he wants us to change with him. But I can't do that. I can't be a cold-blooded killer. Of Wraith, yes — I'll happily kill every last one of them. But not of people who never did anything to us. That's just not right. It's not who we are. And it's not who we want to become."

"There must be some middle ground," Adarr insisted, trying to put himself between Nekai and Ronon. "We all still want the same thing."

"Maybe," Ronon agreed. "But not the same way." He watched

for the opening he knew was coming, and when Nekai's attention wandered just long enough for him to sidestep Adarr, Ronon was ready. His hand reached to his belt and pulled free one of the two rough metal cylinders hanging there. By the time Nekai had a clear line of fire again, Ronon had the object in his hand, which was down at his side and slightly in back, just out of Nekai's view.

"I don't want to shoot you," Nekai told him. "But I will if it's the only way."

"The only way to what?" Ronon demanded. "To get blind obedience? To turn our war on the Wraith into a war against every living creature in the galaxy? If that's what you want, then yes, it is the only way." He stalked forward, looming over Nekai. "Go ahead. Shoot me. Because I won't become some mindless killer for you."

"Back off," Nekai warned, but Ronon ignored him and took another step. The gun was almost against his chest now. "I will kill you, Ronon."

"I know you will," Ronon admitted. And it was true—he could see it in his mentor's eyes. "You'd kill any of us. Killing is all you have left." He'd admired Nekai, and respected him. But now he saw that the years of hunting, and of watching others die, had eaten away at the V'rdai leader. Losing Setien had probably been the last straw.

"Maybe so," Nekai agreed softly. "But at least it's something."

Ronon edged forward a little bit more, closing the last of the distance, and felt the pistol barrel poking into him. "Do it, then," he urged. "Kill me. Kill me!"

His sudden aggression unnerved Nekai, who reflexively took a step back, trying to free his pistol again. And that was the second opening Ronon needed.

His free hand lashed out, catching Nekai's wrist and shoving it hard to the side so Nekai's shot went wide. At the same time, he hurled the cylinder behind the other man, then spun on one foot, maintaining his grip so Nekai pivoted with him.

The flash grenade detonated with a sharp hiss and a quick bang, and a brilliant burst of light lit the small clearing. Ronon had turned his head away and squeezed his eyes shut tight, but none of the others had been that lucky. They all stood clutching at their eyes, blinded and half-dazed.

Nekai had been facing the grenade when it went off, his eyes still wide from the shock of Ronon's sudden move, and his body went rigid from shock. Ronon released the other man's wrist and let him crumple to the ground, then leaped over and past him, through the gap that had created. In two quick bounds he was back past the rock he had recently used for shelter, and then he was running for his life. It wouldn't take the others long to recover, and once they did he knew they'd pursue him. His only hope was to make it to the ancestral ring before they caught up with him, and hope he could figure out how to open a portal and run somewhere they couldn't find him.

Of course, the minute he passed out of range from the other V'rdai, his tracking device would become visible to the Wraith again. Which meant he was about to have two groups hunting him instead of just one.

Well, thought Ronon as he ran along a narrow ledge and leaped over a small ravine, I never did like things to be too easy.

He just hoped this wasn't more than he could handle.

CHAPTER TWENTY-ONE

RODNEY stared at the pale blob, all he could make out of his companion in the trickle of light filtering into their cramped hiding place. "How — how did you escape?" he asked finally, his voice hoarse from disuse. He had sat, spellbound and silent, through the last portion of the Satedan's story. "You get the Stargate to open?"

He felt more than saw Ronon's nod. "Through sheer luck," the big Satedan admitted. "Nekai worked out a way to lock down a gate, but it wasn't completely reliable yet and so he didn't always use it. That time, he hadn't, which was good — if he had, I'd have been sunk. Instead I banged on the console a bunch, and somehow I activated it. I was sure the other V'rdai were right behind me by then, so I dove through. Then I just ran as fast as I could. I knew the gate would close almost immediately, so if they weren't right behind me they'd have to reopen it — Nekai had said he could recall the last location dialed but by that point I wasn't sure I believed him. Either way, the more distance I could put between them and me, the better."

"And they didn't come after you?"

He thought Ronon shrugged. "I have no idea," was the answer. "The world I found had a few villages, one decent-sized city — and a tiny spaceport. I stole a ship and took off. Ditched it on the next inhabitable planet I could find, located a Stargate, and managed to activate it. After that I just kept moving."

"So you never saw them again?" Rodney asked.

"Never."

"And you're sure this is them now?"

Again he felt the air shift as his companion nodded. "Positive."

"Because of the shuttle?" The fact that Ronon had come up with that idea didn't surprise him — the Satedan had proven over their time together that he was very good at thinking on his feet, at adapting materials, and at causing mayhem. The shuttle setup was a perfect combination of those three traits. Though clearly these V'rdai had refined the technique over the years. There hadn't been a second ship lurking nearby, and the shuttle had clearly been rigged to explode when activated or when it registered a certain amount of energy nearby. Like from their Jumper powering up to leave.

"The shuttle," Ronon agreed, "and the way they went after Sheppard and Teyla. They knew if they only wounded whatever ship approached the shuttle, it would have to set down here. That's why they were waiting here. They've probably got traps set up all around the area. Sheppard and Teyla must have tripped one of them."

"But you're sure they're still alive?" Rodney pressed.

"Pretty sure," was the less-than-inspiring reply. "They know there're more than two of us. They'll be cautious, careful, prepared for the worst — and that means assuming whoever's left is dangerous. Killing them means two fewer enemies to worry about, but it also means they don't have any leverage, or any lures. Keeping them captive is a better bet. That way they can draw us in and kill all of us together."

"Great. That's something to look forward to," Rodney muttered. He was still thinking about Ronon's story. "So you were with them for almost two years?"

"That's right." Beside him Ronon shifted, probably trying to make himself a little more comfortable in their rocky prison.

"And then you were on your own for five years after that?"

"Yep."

Rodney was having trouble processing that. "How the hell

did you survive that long?" he finally blurted out. Well, he wasn't known for beating around the bush. "I mean, those first two years you had a whole team with you, and your signals cancelled each other out. But the last five it was just you, and nothing to shield you from the Wraith!"

"I was lucky," Ronon told him bluntly. But after a second he added, "and well-trained. All those skills Nekai taught me? They kept me alive."

"I assume the Wraith came after you?"

"All the time," Ronon answered. "They had my tracking device visible on their monitors now, but even so they were cautious. For two years, every time they found a Runner a pack of hunters wound up dead. That helped me — it meant they didn't just charge in. They took their time. And that gave me time to notice them coming, and set up a proper welcome." Rodney saw a flash of lesser darkness in the shadows, and realized Ronon had grinned. He shuddered. He'd seen that grin far too many times, always right before Ronon shot something. Or someone.

Something else was bothering him, though. "Beckett never said anything about explosives."

Thanks to their narrow confines, Ronon heard him. "You mean on the tracking device?" He laughed once, a sharp, bitter sound rather than his usual amused chuckle. "That's because there weren't any."

"Nekai lied about the explosives?" It made sense, though. What better way to keep the team together than to make them think they had to stay together?

"I wasn't sure," Ronon admitted, "not until Beckett examined me. But I'd suspected. I'd actually wondered about it back when I was still with them, that and a few other things." He shook his head. "Nekai needed to remain in control. So he kept us in the dark as much as possible, and lied to us when he thought it would help." He shrugged. "I tried removing the device myself, right after I got away, but I couldn't get the right angle. And I couldn't trust anyone to help me."

"Until you met us." Then Rodney flashed back to their first encounter with Ronon, and how the Satedan had taken Teyla hostage and had ordered Beckett to remove the tracking device at gunpoint. "Or maybe trust isn't the right word there, either."

Ronon grunted. "I trust you now," he admitted softly. Rodney was surprised how much he appreciated that simple statement. And he trusted the big guy, too.

Not that he was about to tell him that.

"So you think it's still Nekai himself?" he asked after a minute.

"I don't know," Ronon replied. "Maybe. Or maybe the others just kept up what he'd started." He shifted again. "I know one thing, though. They've taken it a step further."

"How's that?"

"When I left, Nekai was talking about killing anyone who crossed their path, Wraith or not," Ronon pointed out. "But this trap was way out in the middle of nowhere. No one was going to happen across it."

"So they're actively hunting humans now as well," Rodney agreed. "Swell."

He waited a second, but Ronon didn't say anything else, so after a minute Rodney leaned back and closed his eyes. But sleep wouldn't come.

"They don't know it's you, do they?" he asked finally.

"I doubt it," Ronon answered. "No tracking device, and I didn't see anyone watching us."

"Sheppard and Teyla might let your name slip."

That got one of Ronon's more typical chuckles. "They won't talk. At least, not the way the V'rdai are hoping. Sheppard won't give them anything."

"Well, what now?" Rodney asked. "We can't just stay in here forever."

"No, we can't," his companion agreed.

"So what do we do?"

Again he caught a quick glimmer of the Satedan's grin. "They're hunting us," he replied. "So we hunt them first."

CHAPTER TWENTY-TWO

RODNEY woke to a world of hurt.

"Oh, ow!" he complained, shifting slightly and producing a wave of sharp pain across his back, shoulders, and neck. Another twist and his legs and butt joined in, all protesting angrily.

"Shhh," Ronon warned beside him.

"What do you mean, 'shhh'?" Rodney snapped, but quietly. "We're trapped in a tiny cave somewhere on a godforsaken planet in the middle of nowhere! Who's going to hear me?"

"The people hunting us."

That shut Rodney up, but only for a second. "Oh right, because they're going around and putting their ear to every rock and cliff and hillside they can find, just on the off chance they'll hear us in this little cave nobody knows exists?" He tried stretching again, but only succeeded in banging his elbow, forearm, and wrist on the low ceiling. The new injuries joined the chorus of older ones in shrieking at his misuse of his own body.

"Sound carries," Ronon answered softly. "And we have no way of knowing if these walls have cracks in them. Our voices could be heard miles away."

"But if they were," Rodney argued, "wouldn't that make us impossible to locate by sound alone?" He grinned, and was pleased to discover his face was one of the only parts of him that didn't hurt. Thank God for small favors!

"Best not to chance it," was all his companion replied. Which meant Ronon knew he was right but couldn't admit it. The pleasure of winning yet another argument helped offset the pain of sleeping curled up in a hard rocky niche but didn't drive it away completely.

"What time is it?" Rodney asked, though he did whisper the question. "How long have we been in here?"

"It's almost dawn," Ronon told him. "We slept maybe four hours."

"Four hours? I'm useless without at least six."

"Guess you don't sleep much, then," his companion said, and Rodney could tell the big lug was grinning.

"Ha ha, very funny. So when are we getting out of this lovely little hole in the wall? Dawn?"

But Ronon shook his head — Rodney's eyes had apparently adapted enough to their environs that he could see the motion, even though the Satedan's features were still a blur. "Too early," came the answer.

"Too early? What are you talking about? We have to go find Sheppard and Teyla. We've got to get the Jumper up and running again. We've got to call Woolsey and let him know where we are!"

His companion turned and looked down at him. "They'll be waiting for us at first light," he explained. "It's the best time to hunt — the prey's still tired, not fully alert, and the early light can be misleading, even blinding at the right angles."

"Oh." Rodney thought about that. "So what do we do?"

"We wait until mid-morning. They'll be getting restless by then, which means they're more likely to make mistakes."

"Great. So what do we do until then?"

Beside him, Ronon leaned his head back against the cave's curving wall. "Sleep," he answered. And within seconds he was doing just that.

Swell. "I can't just go to sleep upon command!" Rodney whispered, but Ronon didn't react. The Satedan had demonstrated plenty of times that he possessed that military knack for falling asleep instantly, though Rodney knew if there was danger Ronon would be awake again at once and fully alert. But he didn't share that skill. He needed quiet, and calm, and a comfortable bed, and a soft pillow, and a warm blanket, and music playing, and —

Before he could even finish his list, Rodney was asleep.

"What is your name?" The masked figure loomed over Sheppard, leaning in close enough that he could make out angry blue eyes through the tinted goggles.

"Mickey Mouse," Sheppard replied. He resisted the urge to spit, but did deliberately stick out his bottom lip. That caused his answer — and the hot air that went with it — to angle directly into his questioner's face. The goggles fogged instantly, making the figure recoil and tear them off so he could see properly. Yep, blue eyes, and set in a narrow, pale-skinned face, Sheppard noticed. Human, unquestionably, but then he'd already figured their captors weren't Wraith. This just wasn't their style.

"Tell me the truth!" His interrogator struck him hard across the face, the blow knocking Sheppard's head back against the rock behind him.

"Sure," he answered, wincing slightly as he shifted away from the boulder. "What do you want to know?"

"Who are you, and why are you here?" The blue-eyed man demanded.

"We're here because you idiots tried to blow up our ship!" Sheppard snapped, and instantly regretted it as his captor struck him again. "Look," he continued more quietly, when the pain had died down enough for him to think clearly again. "What do you want from me? We're not a threat to you — hell, I don't even know who you are! And we only came this way because we picked up the distress signal you left on that shuttle. Let us go and we'll leave and you'll never have to see us again."

The man laughed, a short, bitter sound. "You think I'd fall for that?" he asked. "You were just in the area and heard the distress signal? You'll leave and never come back? Sure."

"I didn't say we were in the area," Sheppard pointed out.

"You've probably got scanners — you know we came through the Stargate. But yes, we'll leave you alone. We aren't interested in whatever you're doing. We only came because we thought you needed help."

"Or because you thought we were helpless," the man corrected angrily, "and wanted to take us when we couldn't fight back." He hit Sheppard again, but this blow was more of an afterthought, a casual backhanded slap not really meant to hurt but that showed how helpless Sheppard was at the moment.

And that was plenty helpless.

Their captors had half-led, half-dragged him and Teyla across several foothills and to a small ledge along one of the steeper hills. They'd both had their hands bound behind them already, and gags tied across their mouth, but once they reached the ledge their legs were tied as well. A small smokeless fire provided a little heat and light against the cold winds that had risen as the sun had vanished, just enough warmth to keep Sheppard and Teyla from freezing to death as they huddled together, shivering.

Two more strangers had arrived just after dark, carrying on a whispered conference with the original four, but that seemed to be the extent of the group. They'd kept their facemasks and goggles on, at least as long as Sheppard could see them, so he hadn't gotten a good look at anyone, but they were all armed, all wore the same armored jumpsuits, and all moved with the grace of experienced hunters. Which they clearly were, given how easily they'd captured him and Teyla.

The question was, what had they been hunting with that shuttle and now here on this miserable excuse for a planet?

And what did they do with their captures?

He'd apparently exhausted his captor's patience, because Sheppard found himself being hauled to his feet and dragged back to the fire at the center of the ledge. Teyla was still there, and Sheppard was glad to see she didn't look hurt in any way. Either these guys weren't willing to interrogate a woman or they'd simply decided to start with him and keep at him until he broke. Or died.

Sheppard hoped they were patient.

"Are you all right?" Teyla asked softly as the blue-eyed captor shoved Sheppard hard enough to make him stumble. She caught him on her shoulder before he could bash his head against the rocky ground, and with a few nudges and hip-checks helped him twist around so he could sit upright again.

"I'll live," he replied just as quietly, "or at least I will until they get tired of this game."

He'd wondered how sharp the blue-eyed man's hearing was. It proved to be sharp enough. "You think this is a game?" the man demanded, grabbing the front of Sheppard's shirt and hauling him up again, far enough that Sheppard's knees were off the ground. The captor was still hunched over at that point, and Sheppard realized he'd be as tall as Ronon if he stood up fully. Great.

"This is no game," the man continued, shaking him vigorously. "This is your life! You will tell us what we want to know if you wish to have any chance to survive to the morrow!"

One of the other captors approached, resting a hand on the first one's arm. This one was shorter, and something about the gait suggested female to Sheppard, though he couldn't be sure. If it was a woman, she was slender enough that any curves were hidden by her jumpsuit. "Enough," she said, and her voice, though deep, confirmed his guess as to her gender. "You won't get anything out of him that way."

The first one dropped Sheppard like a heavy trash bag. "Maybe not," he agreed, "but it makes me feel better."

The second captor studied Sheppard and Teyla for a second, and he wondered if he might have found a potential ally. Her next words crushed that hope. "I say just kill them and be done with it," she offered, her voice showing no more concern than if she'd been commenting on a distant rock formation. "Kill them, go after their friends, and move on."

"We need to know who they are, where they came from, and what they know," the blue-eyed man insisted. "They could be·bait!"

"They are bait," the woman replied. "Bait for their friends. Bait we're using in our trap. Not bait for a trap for us."

"How do you know that?" Those blue eyes were wide, darting here and there. Sheppard could almost smell the tall man's panic. "How can you be sure?"

"We're not part of a trap," Sheppard offered. "We were just trying to help." He was glad Rodney wasn't here to tell him "I told you so" about the danger of helping strangers, though he hoped the scientist would get here soon. Or rather, he hoped Ronon would get here soon, and would have Rodney safely in tow. He wasn't sure how much longer these people's patience would hold out.

His comment earned him a swift, hard kick from the woman. He managed to twist enough to take it in the side instead of the head, but the tip of her boot caught him right between two ribs, producing an explosion of pain all along that part of his torso. "Shut up!" she warned him in a hiss. "Bait doesn't get to talk!"

"Then why does he keep telling me to?" Sheppard muttered, winning a second kick for his sense of humor. I always knew being a smart-ass would be the death of me, he thought as he determined to lie there and shut up rather than give her another excuse. Not that it seemed she needed one.

"Leave them," one of the others called out — Sheppard thought it was the one who'd arrived last the night before — and the other two obediently turned and rejoined their three companions on the far side of the ledge. Sheppard waited until they were safely ensconced before crawling back over to Teyla and pulling himself up to a sitting position again.

"You really should stop antagonizing them," she advised once he was able to lean back against the rocks next to her and catch his breath.

'I know," he agreed. "But I can't help it." He grinned at her. "Besides, if I can get them angry they may get sloppy. And I'll take any advantage I can get."

"What will you do with it, though?" she asked. She gestured around them with tilt of her head and a shrug of her shoulders. "We are bound hand and foot on a ledge in a mountain range on an unfamiliar planet. They have our weapons and clearly know this planet well, plus they have set various snares across its surface. Even if we manage to escape this camp of theirs, where would we go?"

"I don't know," he admitted. He sighed. "But I'm sure the others are still out there." He deliberately didn't use their names, or give any indication how many there were, just in case their captors were listening somehow. "If anyone can find us, they can." "They" meaning Ronon. "We just have to stay alive until then."

Teyla arched an eyebrow. "So your plan on how to stay alive is by provoking our captors?"

"No, by not answering their questions," he told her. He lowered his voice to barely a whisper. "And as long as I'm irritating them, they'll respond by kicking and slapping me. They'll be too focused on that to consider killing me — punching is more immediate. It's when they calm down and decide we're useless that we're in trouble."

She nodded slightly, showing she understood both what he was suggesting and that they couldn't let their captors overhear. "Should we try feeding them information to make ourselves more valuable?"

"No. Once you start talking about real things it's hard to stop." Sheppard thought about the anti-interrogation courses he'd had, years before during his Air Force pilot's training. "Plus if we start trying to tell them some details while holding back or lying about others, we'll be inconsistent. Better to just not tell them anything. If they question you, give them nonsense answers. Ask questions in return. Start talking and veer completely off-topic. As long as they're listening, we're safe." Relatively so. A lot depended upon who these people were, what kind of training they'd had, and how hardened they were to cold-blooded murder. If they were hunters, they might be used to killing animals but not people, and especially not people they'd already captured and rendered helpless. If they were soldiers, they might be more callous. Sheppard hoped that wasn't the case — a good soldier knew when a hostage had outlived his usefulness, and was prepared to kill that hostage before he could become a liability.

Movement caught his eye, and he glanced up to see one of the other captors approaching them. This one was male, he guessed, and no taller than the woman had been but broader. His steps were heavier but just as smooth, with the grace of a hunter and the assurance of a leader. This had to be the group's commander.

"You said you came through a Stargate," the man said without preamble. He crouched down, putting himself at Sheppard's eye level, but stayed carefully just beyond lunging distance. The pistol at his side looked familiar, and at first glance Sheppard felt a chill. That was Ronon's pistol! But a second look corrected his mistake — the weapon did look very similar, but it was not identical. Still, that was odd enough to stand out. The only other time they'd seen weapons like Ronon's were with the Travelers, and Sheppard didn't think those nomadic people would suddenly stoop to kidnapping and torture, even if they did decide to abandon their ships long enough to descend to a planet. Could this man be a rogue Traveler, or have some sort of alliance with them? Sheppard hoped the latter wasn't the case. He and the Travelers' leader, Larrin, hadn't parted on the best of the terms, but he still hoped they might become allies — or more — some day.

"That's right," Sheppard answered. "But I'm sure you knew that already. Didn't you use one to get here yourself?"

The man ignored the question. "Why did you call it that?" he asked instead. "A 'stargate'?"

"Would you prefer 'ancestral ring'?" Sheppard asked him. "It's just a name," he answered quickly, as he saw the other man tense. "That's what we call it, because that's what it does — it opens a gate between the stars." He didn't bother to explain about the Stargate's history on Earth, or how Daniel Jackson had helped decipher that one and had translated the Goa'uld word "Chaapa'ai" as "stargate." He doubted his captor would care for the lecture, and he didn't want to risk mentioning anything about Earth or about Atlantis.

"Who is 'we'?" the man demanded, leaning forward slightly but still maintaining that safe distance. This guy was good, Sheppard realized. Careful and constantly alert but not on edge like the taller man. He'd be a hard one to provoke.

"My friends and I," Sheppard answered. "What do you call it?" He decided to take a risk. "Astria Porta? The Portal?"

The first term — the original Ancient name for a Stargate — got no reaction. At the second one, however, the man went rigid. He uncoiled a second later, though it took another moment before his fingers released their grip on his pistol. Interesting, Sheppard thought. "Portal" was what the Wraith called it.

"How did you access it?" the man continued after a short pause. From the way his words emerged half-hissing, Sheppard guessed he was gritting his teeth under that mask. Mentioning the Wraith term had definitely struck a nerve.

"You push these big flat buttons on this panel thing right in front of the ring itself," Sheppard answered, adopting a casual tone. "If you hit the right ones, the whole thing — " the man's hand lashed out and caught him on the cheek, not hard but a stinging blow nonetheless, and he stopped talking.

"How did you learn of the Stargates?" the man demanded. Sheppard noticed his use of the term and some of his feigned humor evaporated. This guy had been well trained, enough so that he knew to use Sheppard's own term rather than revealing his. That suggested a military background. And from their captive standpoint, that didn't bode well.

"We discovered one and managed to get it to work by accident," Sheppard told him, which was true enough as far as it went. The fact that this had been on Earth, galaxies away, and that there was now an entire agency dedicated to the Stargates and their use — that was all stuff the stranger didn't need to know. "How about you?"

"Where is your ship from?" the man asked next, again ignoring Sheppard's question completely. "We have not seen anything like it."

"I don't really know," Sheppard lied easily. "We just happened across it and liked it, so we took it." He shrugged. "No one else was using it at the time." The puddle jumpers had been docked in several hangars in Atlantis, of course, but it was interesting that the design was unfamiliar to the hunters. The Ancients had used them regularly, and several of the races here in the Pegasus galaxy recognized them from old descriptions and drawings. Either these people came from planets the Ancients hadn't visited, or none of them were in a position to have access to such archives.

The stranger studied him quietly for a moment. "You will tell us what we want to know," he said finally, his voice quiet and certain. "The only question is how much pain you and your companion will endure before you reach that point. For your own sake, I suggest you drop this pose and answer us fully and honestly when we return." Before the last word was out of his mouth he was rising to his feet again, and stalking quietly across the ledge to rejoin the others.

"Return?" Teyla asked once they were alone on their side again. "Where do you think they are going?"

Sheppard watched as their captors conversed quietly, then split into two groups. Four of them — including the leader, the tall man, and the woman — moved quickly and quietly to the end of the ledge, then turned and pulled themselves up onto a smaller outcropping perhaps eight feet over their heads. That piece of rock was evidently just one end of a jutting cliff, because once atop it the trio disappeared from view. The remaining two shifted to positions against the wall where they could watch Sheppard and Teyla easily, then sank down into crouches again, breaking open some sort of food bars and passing a canteen back and forth. They both kept their weapons ready, however.

He squinted up at the sky. The first tendrils of light were snaking across, filtering into the nighttime gloom and softening it as they touched. It was almost dawn.

"They're going to hunt," he answered Teyla, deliberately turning away from the guards so they would have a harder time making out what he was saying. "They're hunting our friends."

She nodded. "Dawn is a good time to hunt."

"Yeah, it is." He gave her a quick, reassuring grin. "But it doesn't work so well if your prey's waiting for you."

And if he knew anything about Ronon, the big Satedan would be doing exactly that.

Sheppard just hoped Ronon was ready for these three. Because they obviously knew what they were doing, and they were deadly serious about it.

Then again, so was Ronon.

CHAPTER TWENTY-THREE

"LET'S go."

Rodney came awake slowly, groaning as Ronon nudged him again with his boot tip. "Leave me alone," he whined under his breath. "Just let me sleep."

"No time. We've got to get moving."

"Can't you just kill them all and come get me when you're done?" Rodney asked, still refusing to open his eyes or uncurl from the position he found himself in. At least with his head resting on his arms he didn't have to use the cave wall as a pillow. He was sure once he tried to straighten up, however, his entire body would inform him of the folly of such a sleeping position.

"What if they find you while I'm gone?" Ronon asked him. "You going to be able to defend yourself against a pack of trained hunters?"

That was a valid point, and Rodney finally, reluctantly blinked and looked around. Yep, still in the cave. "Fine, I'm awake," he grumbled. "What time is it?"

"An hour or so before noon," came the answer. "Come on." Ronon turned and led the way back out of the cave, and Rodney slowly followed, after taking a minute or two to unbend himself and to rub some circulation back into his protesting limbs. Getting out of the cave and being able to stand up straight and stretch was a relief, though as he'd suspected it was followed by a fresh wave of aches and pains.

"Remind me never to go camping with you again," he told his companion, who seemed none the worse for the night's cramped accommodations. And the answering grin told him Ronon was enjoying his misery a bit too much.

"If you're all done," the Satedan said finally, "let's go."

"Where are we going, exactly?" Rodney asked as he followed the big man down out of the hills. He drew a food bar from one of the pouch-pockets along his leg and munched as they walked, then sipped a bit from the canteen hanging from his belt. It was a good thing Sheppard never let them go anywhere without emergency rations! The food, water, fresh air, and exercise were helping his brain unfog more quickly. "Are we going to go find Sheppard and Teyla?"

"Not yet," Ronon replied. He was walking half-crouched — which meant he was now only the height of a normal man, Rodney thought — and studying the ground before each step.

"What? Why not? We have to find them and rescue them before these old friends of yours kill them!" Rodney half-trotted to catch up, determined to face Ronon and convince him, when the big Satedan's arm shot out. Rodney ran right into the muscular obstacle and bounced off it, falling on the ground a few feet behind his previous position.

"What the hell are you doing?" he demanded, but Ronon now held up that hand, palm out, and Rodney quickly quieted. He watched as his companion crouched down and tapped the spot Rodney had been about to step upon. The touch produced a strange, muted echo. A second, harder tap, almost a punch, and the ground caved in, revealing a deep hole.

"How did you know?" Rodney asked, staring. He had almost stepped in that!

"They used a tarp," Ronon answered, standing again. "It was a little too even to match the terrain perfectly. And they dusted it with pebbles but they were too uniform about it." He shook his head. "Sloppy."

"Sloppy? It looked pretty convincing to me." Rodney stood as well and stepped forward to stare into the hole. It looked more than deep enough and more than wide enough to swallow a man whole. "Did they dig that, or just find it and cover it up?"

"It's a natural crevice," Ronon replied. "They're all over this area." He gave Rodney a hard look. "That's why you need to stay behind me."

"Okay, I got it," Rodney agreed quickly. He couldn't argue that Ronon was a better hunter and tracker, and he had no desire to fall into one of those concealed pits. "But tell me why we're not going straight to wherever these V'rdai are keeping Sheppard and Teyla?"

"Too many of them," Ronon told him bluntly. "Even if we find them and they don't see us, I'm guessing there're at least four of them, maybe more. There's no guarantee I can take them out before they shoot the hostages."

"What? Why would they shoot them?" Rodney shook his head. "Why not try to use them for cover, or to bargain their way out?"

Now it was Ronon's turn to shake his head, his dreadlocks flying. "They don't think that way," he explained. "They're hunters, and soldiers. They're used to dealing with Wraith. That means no bargains, no mercy, and no getting captured. Ever. If we attack they'll kill the hostages and make a run for it, hoping we stop to check the bodies."

Rodney gulped. "Okay, so we can't just hit them straight on. Got it. What do we do?" He tried to put himself in Ronon's shoes—and failed miserably. So he tried to think like Sheppard instead. That was a little easier, though horribly limiting. "We need a diversion."

His companion grinned. "Exactly. And I know just the one to get their attention."

"There!" Ronon peered quickly around the rock they were stooped behind, then drew back, his motion swift but smooth. Rodney craned his head to look as well, and though he had only the briefest glance before he was yanked back down, he had seen enough to identify what they were looking at.

"A ship!" He tried to organize the few details he'd seen. "Well, a shuttle, really. No hyperspace, probably no weapons, maybe not even any shields. But it could get us to the Stargate, and even if they don't still have that portable DHD you mentioned it must have some kind of communications array — I could contact Atlantis!" He was already halfway up again before a burly arm shoved him back onto his rear.

"No," Ronon told him. "No communications. Not yet. We can't let them find out about Atlantis."

Rodney started to object, then thought about it. Much as he hated to admit it, even to himself, his companion was right. There was no guarantee the V'rdai didn't have some sort of *commlinks* tied in to the ship's systems. After all, *they* did. And if that was the case, and he used the shuttle to call Atlantis, the V'rdai would all hear it. They'd know exactly where he and Ronon were, and they'd also know about Atlantis. They'd even have the city's subspace frequency. No, that wouldn't work at all.

"Okay," he agreed, "so we steal the shuttle, use it to find the others, head on back to the Stargate with it, and then Woolsey sends troops back to retrieve the Jumper."

That met with another headshake. "They'll have them up in the mountains, where a shuttle can't reach," Ronon explained. "And we don't want to leave the Jumper in their hands. They might be able to get it working again, and then they'd have access to the gates and to Atlantis itself." He looked pained for a second. "Adarr was a top-notch mechanic, and he could still be with them."

Rodney hadn't considered that, and he studied his companion for a second. They were going up against people who had been the Satedan's friends, his comrades in arms, for almost two years. If it came down to it, would Ronon be able to take them down? Then he shook himself. Why was he even asking the question? This was Ronon, for heaven's sake! He came close to knocking out his friends on a regular basis.

Still, Rodney was getting tired of having his ideas shot down. "Okay, I give up," he said testily. "You don't like any of my suggestions? Fine. Let's hear yours. What do you think we should do with that shuttle down there?"

So Ronon told him. And, after his initial disapproval, Rodney had to admit it was a good idea. Almost as good as if he'd come up with it himself.

"Fine," he said finally. "We'll try it your way."

"Fine." Ronon risked another look, then rose to a crouch and gestured for Rodney to follow him. "Let's go."

"What, now? Shouldn't we plan it out a bit more first?" Rodney was on his feet and following even as he complained.

"No time," came the reply. "They could show up at any second."

"Great. I just love pressure," Rodney muttered. He kept glancing around, expecting strangers to appear behind every rock and boulder — he didn't even know what these V'rdai would look like, so in his head they became monstrous figures with oversized, clawed hands and enormous jagged teeth and tusks and horns, a combination of men and a dozen different Earth predators. No one appeared as they made their way the rest of the distance out of the foothills, however, and the shuttle seemed quiet as they approached it.

"All right, let's see what we've got here," Rodney said to himself as he stepped up beside the airlock.

"Careful," Ronon warned — the big Satedan had his back to the hull and was scanning the area for danger, pistol in hand. "They might have rigged it."

"Thank you for that brilliant observation," Rodney snapped at him, pausing just long enough to glare at his companion, "but I think I figured that one out on my own. This is my area of expertise, remember? So you do the whole shooting-and-killing thing, and let me do my work. Okay?" He didn't even wait for the nod he suspected would never come. Instead he carefully cracked open the access panel and studied the mass of wires and chips inside.

The V'rdai had indeed rigged it. They'd done a decent job, too — anyone trying to type in the wrong access code would have gotten an exploding panel for their trouble, and it had enough of a charge to vaporize the would-be intruder's hand, arm, and maybe chest and face as well. Of course, they hadn't counted on a bona fide genius like Dr. Rodney McKay. It was child's play for him to disconnect the charge, reroute power around the password protection, and enter an override. He paused before he activated it, however. He'd just noticed the secondary wiring, and the small array it ran to at the rear of the panel.

"I've got it," he told Ronon, "and it was rigged. But there's more. They've got it wired so it sends out a signal every time it opens or closes. Do you want me to kill that as well?"

"No, leave that alone," Ronon instructed, which was what Rodney had thought he'd say. After all, if you were trying to lure people to you, you wanted them to know where you were. The very idea of deliberately attracting an enemy's attention made his skin crawl, but he shrugged it off and initiated the override. The airlock slid open with a low hiss.

"Okay, I got us in," Rodney told him, unable to resist a surge of pride at how easily he'd bypassed the shuttle's security. Was that the best they could do? Ha! "You do the rest."

It didn't take long for Ronon to get everything set up. "Now we wait," he said afterward, clapping Rodney on the back with his free hand. "Shouldn't be too long — they'd stay close enough to keep their ship somewhere they could reach it in a hurry."

Rodney nodded, eyes flickering to take in every inch of the desolate planet around them. Great, more waiting. He hated waiting. He especially hated waiting for crazed killers to show up and attack them.

But right now he didn't really have a whole hell of a lot of choice. So he stayed close to Ronon as they crouched behind the shuttle, and found himself in the ironic position of hoping their foes would hurry up.

It was at least ten minutes, though it felt like hours, before Ronon tapped Rodney on the arm. The Satedan gestured his head off to one side. Rodney stared in that direction until his eyes ached. Just as he was about to blink, he saw a shadow shift, then a second one. Finally!

The two of them waited, completely silent, and utterly motionless, as those same shadows shifted again. And then again. They were growing longer, but far too quickly for it to simply be from the sun sliding by overhead. No, this was something else.

After a few more minutes, one of the shadows detached itself from a large boulder and darted across the short space to the shuttle. Its companion joined it an instant later. As they reached the shuttle they gained solidity, mass, until they were two figures dressed in dark mottled clothing designed to blend in with their current surroundings. Both were armed and had weapons drawn. Facemasks and goggles completely concealed their features, but the second one's head swiveled about, taking in their surroundings. The first one's attention remained focused upon the shuttle itself.

Without a word, the first figure advanced to the airlock. It hesitated briefly, then peered inside. Rodney held his breath as the figure entered the shuttle. Almost . . .

The figure outside was checking all around them, covering the shuttle while its partner looked within. It spun about, however, when a gasp and a thud emerged through the open airlock, and then darted inside as well, a pistol in one hand and a knife in the other as it hurried to aid its partner.

The second its back was turned, Ronon ducked back around

the shuttle and fired. His shot hit the stranger square in the back, and the masked figure collapsed, weapons falling from its hands to hit the ground right beside it. Ronon was already moving, gliding back over to the airlock and through it to take out the V'rdai within as well. He'd rigged a simple snare just past the airlock, trusting the gloom and their foes' haste to prevent it from being noticed until too late. Clearly he'd been right.

Ronon reemerged a moment later, a bound figure slung over his shoulder. He stalked off toward the hills they'd descended from, and returned after a minute without his burden. Next he bound and gagged the one he'd dropped just outside the shuttle — revealing a square-jawed woman with dark skin and jet-black hair as he pulled off her mask — and carried her off to place her beside her partner.

While he was doing that, Rodney ducked into the shuttle. He hadn't entered it before, waiting behind it while Ronon deliberately left tracks through the airlock and then erased any others, so this was his first glimpse of the small spaceship's interior. It was very utilitarian, even more so than the Jumper, which wasn't exactly designed for opulence. But this shuttle had that particular look and feel that screamed military, with bare surfaces and sharp angles and gray metal. Even the seats looked uncomfortable, little more than hard benches. The good news was, military ships tended to have straightforward designs as well, and so it took him no time to find the panel he needed and make the appropriate adjustments. He did notice a DHD panel up front — probably the same one Ronon had told him about them taking from the Dart's debris, only now they'd apparently attached it to the ship instead of carrying it around separately — but left that alone. That wasn't his concern right now.

"All set?" Ronon asked as he returned from his second body drop.

"Just about," Rodney answered from within. A moment later he closed the panel again, wiped his hands on the bench and then on his pants legs, and rejoined his companion outside the shuttle. "Good to go."

"How much time did you give it?" Ronon asked.

"One hour, just like you said," Rodney assured him. "Trust me — this I'm good at."

The Satedan's simple nod was high praise indeed, coming from him. "I found their tracks," he said instead. "They were in too much of a rush to conceal them completely. It's this way."

Rodney followed behind, hoping wherever the V'rdai had been holed up wasn't more than an hour away. If it was, things could get a bit tricky.

Still, it felt good to be taking the fight to their attackers for a change. He was starting to see why Ronon and Sheppard enjoyed being so aggressive. There might even be something to this whole hunting thing.

Though he'd still prefer to relax with a good book.

CHAPTER TWENTY-FOUR

BOOM.

"What the hell was that?" Sheppard started, glancing around. The ground was shaking slightly beneath him, and he fell back against Teyla — she leaned into him as well, so that they were propping each other up.

"Seismic activity?" she asked quietly. She pressed her bound hands flat to the ground, trying to get a better feel for the vibrations that were already fading.

"I don't think so." Sheppard tilted his head a little so he could watch their captors. Two of the four who had left earlier had returned, and now they were all clustered in a group. Even without being able to hear them clearly he could tell they were upset about something — the tall thin guy and the woman and one of the others were gesturing wildly, and the leader was trying to calm them down.

"Something's wrong," he told Teyla softly.

"Wrong for them, or wrong for us?" she asked.

"Wrong for them." He continued to watch them. The tall guy was pointing off in one direction, and practically shouting. Sheppard strained to listen.

". . . our ship!" the man was saying. "What if I can't fix it? We could be stranded here on this rock!"

The leader replied, raising his hands to calm the others, but the tall man wasn't having any of that.

"And what if they were caught in the blast?" he demanded. "They could be dead already! And we've still got at least one of them unaccounted for!" An accusing finger waved in Sheppard and Teyla's direction had accompanied that last statement, and Sheppard tried hard to hide his smile as he turned back to Teyla.

"Sounds like they had a ship hidden somewhere nearby," he reported in a whisper, though right now it wasn't likely their captors would overhear them. Still, better to be safe. "That may have been the sound we heard."

"An explosion?" Teyla looked at him, and they both nodded. Ronon and Rodney.

"What's more," Sheppard continued, "two of their friends are missing. I'm guessing they went to check on the ship and haven't been heard from since." That smile was creeping up again. "Which means we're down from six to four. And they're off-balance."

"We are still tightly bound," she pointed out, raising her wrists to demonstrate. "Even with the odds improving, there is little we can do."

"We don't have to do anything," he answered. "Just wait. Our friends should take care of the rest."

The argument had concluded, he noticed, so he turned his head to watch their captors again, though he also folded his legs under him and leaned forward a bit. It was a more casual position, so he'd look less threatening, but he could actually kick up to a standing position in a hurry if he had to.

The tall man was still upset, but the leader had calmed him down somewhat. Now they exchanged a few final words, and then the group split in half. The leader and the angular woman moved to the back of the ledge and the outcropping there — within minutes they had vanished from sight. The tall man and his remaining companion grabbed their guns and stomped over to stand near the fire, and their captives.

"What do you know about all this?" the tall man demanded, glaring at Sheppard.

"About all what?" Sheppard replied, giving his best unconcerned shrug. "About you guys luring us in here, damaging our ship, capturing us, and torturing us for no reason?"

"You're the enemy!" was the angry response, and the tall

man half-started toward them before his companion pulled him back.

"The enemy?" Sheppard laughed at him. "How're we your enemy? We don't even know you! We didn't know you existed until you attacked us. So how does that work, exactly?"

"It doesn't matter," their other guard said. It was the first time Sheppard had heard him speak. Definitely male, with a deep voice that belied his short stature. Broad, though, and sturdy. Not someone Sheppard wanted to have to tangle with. Especially since this one was completely calm, his gun rock-steady in his hand. The tall man's was bouncing all over the place as he twitched and jumped at every sound and every shadow. "All that matters," the shorter guard continued, "is finishing this hunt and getting out of here."

"That won't be easy if that was our ship we heard," the tall man argued. "And I'm pretty sure it was." He glared at Sheppard again. "Your friends did this, didn't they? The ones we haven't caught yet. They found our ship and destroyed it!"

Sheppard held up his bound hands. "I have no idea," he admitted. "I've been here, remember? But if they did, let's face it — you earned it." He met his captor's glare with one of his own. "You attacked us. You hit our ship. Turnabout is fair play."

"What I don't understand," the shorter guard said, low enough that it was probably meant to be to himself, "is how they've evaded our traps. That takes skill."

The tall man snorted. "You're thinking about those stories again," he accused.

"So what if I am?" his companion asked. "Maybe they're true!"

"They're not," the tall man insisted. "Nekai said it was impossible, remember?"

"Well, maybe he's wrong!" Judging by the way the tall man recoiled, that was something people simply didn't suggest, and the shorter guard sounded defensive as he continued, "it could happen. He doesn't know everything!" Sheppard guessed that Nekai was their leader, the one who'd questioned him about the Stargates.

"He knows everything about Runners!" was the tall man's angry retort, and beside him Sheppard felt Teyla stiffen and glance at him. He fought the urge to look at her as well. He didn't want to give their captors any hints. But inside he was straining to take in everything they said, and doing his best to become invisible so as not to interrupt what was turning into a fascinating conversation.

"Maybe not everything," the shorter man said softly. "Look, it makes sense," he insisted. "Somebody got past our traps. Somebody managed to hide from us all yesterday and last night and this morning. That's not just a hunter, it's someone who's used to being chased. Someone who's good at disappearing. And that's a Runner."

"There are others with the same skills," the tall man claimed, but he didn't sound very convinced. "Fugitives, stowaways, refugees. It could be any of them."

"And would any of them be able to take out Misa and Castor?" the other guard asked. "I couldn't do that. Could you?" From his tone, he already knew the answer. "That's more than hiding, that's fighting. And who can hunt, hide, and fight? A Runner."

"There aren't any other Runners right now," the tall man said with as much certainty as he could muster, which to Sheppard's ear didn't sound like a whole hell of a lot. "There's us and there's the ones who died. That's it." Sheppard could feel Teyla's look boring into his back but he refused to turn around. Yes, he'd heard. These men were Runners. From the sound of it, all of them were . He'd never heard of a group of Runners, and he wondered if Ronon had. Did the big Satedan know he wasn't the only one? Did he know there were others who had banded together like this? If they got out of this, Sheppard had a lot of questions for his friend.

But right now he was too busy listening. "There's one," the shorter man was saying. His tone was strange — Sheppard would have described it as "faraway," like when someone talked about Santa Claus or the Easter Bunny or some other favorite childhood memory. Wistful, hopeful, but not completely convinced.

"He doesn't exist," his companion said bluntly.

"He might. Think about it. A Runner who's shut down his tracking device. A Runner who hunts freely, and can't be traced." The shorter guard was practically bouncing with excitement now. "If it's true, there's a way to do it. And that means we could do it, too."

"There isn't," the tall man insisted. "It can't be done. Nekai's seen what happens when someone tries." He seemed to feel that was the end of the discussion, and turned away slightly.

"Yeah, I know what he said," his companion continued, "but think about it. What if —"

He didn't get any further, because just then a shadow fell across him. The guard glanced up, just in time to see a tall, powerfully built figure dropping down on top of him. Sheppard almost shouted with relief! Ronon!

The Satedan landed hard on the guard, both boots coming down on the smaller man's chest and shoulders, slamming him into the ground. The guard grunted in pain and surprise, his pistol flying from his hand, and then collapsed. Ronon was already rolling off him, dodging away as the taller guard turned, bringing his weapon to bear.

Well, time to get involved, Sheppard decided. He sprang to his feet, lunging forward as he did so that his bound hands came up and struck the tall guard's forearm from underneath. The clumsy blow was enough to jolt the man's arm upward, throwing off his aim, and his first shot went wide. Teyla had gained her feet as well and moved around to the other side, flanking their remaining captor, and Sheppard saw another figure appear at the far end of the ledge, moving carefully. Rodney.

A shot flew toward them, its coloring a familiar crimson, but the tall man was partially shielded behind Sheppard himself, and Ronon's first shot sizzled past. It did make the guard turn, however, and Teyla took that opportunity to step forward and slam both fists into the tall man's side just below the ribs. The blow doubled him over and Sheppard hammered him across the back of the neck. He couldn't put enough force behind the blow, however, and the tall man shoved him away and backed up himself, putting himself against the rock wall.

"Get back!" he shouted. "I'll shoot you all!" His gun was waving wildly between them, though it didn't look like he'd seen Rodney yet.

"I doubt it," Ronon answered, straightening and stepping forward. "You were never a killer, Adarr."

The tall man stared, and his pistol dropped down to point at the ground between his feet. "Ronon? You're alive?" Sheppard couldn't see his face, but he was guessing the man's mouth was hanging open. "It's true?"

Ronon shrugged. "I don't know what's true," he replied, "but yes it's me, and yes, I'm still alive." He grinned.

The man he'd called Adarr was still in shock. "Nekai said —" His words trailed off. "I thought you were —"

"Dead? Captured?" Ronon moved closer, holstering his pistol as he did. "I did get captured again, actually. But that was a long time ago now. I escaped. And now I'm free. No tracking device, Adarr. The Wraith can't find me."

"What? But — how?" They were only a few feet apart, and the thin man seemed to suddenly realize that. "Stay back!" he insisted, starting to raise his pistol. "I mean it, Ronon! I will shoot you!"

Before he had the chance, however, Ronon had closed the

distance. The big Satedan covered the last few feet with a single quick step, one hand shooting down to trap Adarr's pistol and keep it pointed at the ground. The other fist rose and lashed out, catching the tall man hard on the jaw. Adarr crumpled without a sound, and Ronon caught him.

"You probably would have," Sheppard heard his friend admit quietly as he quickly tied Adarr's ankles and wrists. "I'm sorry."

"We have to hurry," Rodney said as he finally reached them. He drew a knife from his belt and began cutting Teyla's bonds. "The others could come back at any time."

Ronon nodded and drew his own knife. Within seconds Sheppard and Teyla were free.

"Took you long enough," Sheppard told his friends, rubbing his wrists. But he was smiling as he said it.

"Had to keep the rest of them occupied," Ronon answered, returning his grin. He turned serious again in a second. "Rodney's right," he admitted, though having to say that clearly galled him. "They could be back soon. We need to move."

Sheppard nodded and grabbed the guards' fallen pistols. Rodney had apparently paused earlier, where the guards had been camping, and he handed Sheppard and Teyla their P90s without a word. Then the four of them walked quickly back toward the end of the ledge — if there was another way off, Sheppard couldn't see it.

Ronon led, moving as quickly and quietly as ever, and Sheppard took the rear, making sure Rodney and Teyla were clear before he hauled himself up onto that outcropping overhead. Now wasn't the time to ask questions. But once they were safely away, Ronon had some explaining to do.

CHAPTER TWENTY-FIVE

"YOU'VE got some explaining to do, mister."

They had hiked for an hour or more, glancing around constantly in case the remaining strangers found their tracks. Ronon would lead them for a ways, then guide them to a clearing or a cluster of rocks or a small ledge and leave them there while he circled back and hid their tracks. Those had been particularly tense moments, with Sheppard, Teyla, and Rodney starting at every little sound or shadow. They'd have come close to shooting Ronon himself a few times if he hadn't simply appeared beside them and blocked their weapons before they could react — by the time they could wrestle free, their brains had registered who it was.

Eventually Ronon led them to a series of low cliffs. He knelt and brushed aside some scraggly bushes that were growing against the rock, and Rodney groaned.

"Again?" he whined. "Really?"

"Again," Ronon agreed. The displaced foliage revealed a dark hole in the stone — its smoothed edges and irregular outline suggested it was natural. Probably a fissure that had simply expanded over time. But now it was a cave.

Ronon gestured them in, and followed a few minutes later after sweeping away their remaining tracks and concealing the cave's entrance again. By the time he did, the others had shuffled deeper into the hidden passage, which widened and rose slightly as it went. Luckily this world didn't seem to have any native fauna, so they didn't have to battle a bear or a cougar for the prime location. There was a section where they could sit and stretch their legs out in front of them, and they did so, Sheppard on one side and Rodney next to him. Teyla was sitting facing them, and when Ronon returned he slid down beside her.

"We're safe for now," he told them quietly. "They won't find us here."

"Good, great, glad to hear it," Sheppard said. He did his best to glare at his friend in the near-darkness — some hairline cracks above filtered in just enough light for him to make out the others' outlines, but nothing more. "So let's talk. You first."

He could just barely see the Satedan's slow nod. "They're called the V'rdai," he said. "They're Runners who've banded together to hunt the Wraith instead of the other way around." He sighed. "I used to be one of them."

As Ronon explained about his past, and his association with these people, Sheppard marveled. Ronon was one of his best friends, someone he trusted with his life without a second thought. They'd fought together countless times, saved each other more times than he could count, and hung out together both at Atlantis and at some of the towns and cities they'd visited. Yet for all that, he'd never heard any of this before. He'd known about Ronon's upbringing on Sateda, and had heard a bunch of stories about Ronon's grandfather, who'd also been a military man. He knew about the Wraith's attack, and about Ronon's dead wife, Melena. And he knew far more than he'd ever wanted to about the Wraith and how they'd captured Ronon and turned him into a Runner.

But all this? A group of Runners? Ronon learning to hunt? This was all completely new to him.

Finally Ronon stopped talking and leaned back. He hadn't rushed, but Sheppard knew the big man was only telling them the crucial details. There were probably lots of stories there as well.

"Why didn't you ever mention any of this?" he asked finally. "You were with them for two years! You never thought it might be important to tell us there were other Runners out there? And that they liked hunting innocent bystanders just as much as Wraith?"

"I didn't know if I could trust you," Ronon answered sharply. "Not at first. And they were still my friends, and my comrades. I wasn't about to betray them." He shook his head. "By the time I knew you better, it didn't seem like the right time to say anything. They were hidden away, and I figured we'd never run into them." He sighed. "To be honest, I thought they'd all be dead by now."

"Why?" Teyla asked. "You are not."

"But I would be," Ronon told her. "If you hadn't found me first."

Sheppard thought about that one. His friend was probably right. Surviving on his own with the Wraith pursuing him for five long years was unbelievable. Eventually, Ronon's luck would have run out.

"Okay, so how do we keep them from killing us now?" he asked. "I mean, going up against six of you? I don't like those odds."

"Not exactly like me," Ronon replied. "None of them can take me in a fight—at least, none of the old V'rdai could. I don't know these new ones."

"Which ones are old and which ones are new?" Teyla asked. "We saw their leader, who the others referred to as Nekai. Then there was the tall man, Adarr."

"An angry woman, narrow build," Sheppard added to the list. "The short guy you landed on when you rescued us — thanks, by the way. And two more — I'm not sure if they were men or women."

"One was a woman," Rodney told him. "Dark skin, darker hair, strong jaw. Striking, if you like that type."

"The other was a man," Ronon finished. "Average height, reddish hair, green eyes, full beard. I don't know him, or the short one, or the dark-skinned woman. The angry woman, though — that's Lanara." Sheppard could hear the sneer in his voice. "She's probably Nekai's second in command now."

Sheppard noticed the last word. "She wasn't back then?"

"No, Banje was," Ronon said. "He was good, too. I'm glad we don't have to face him." He did sound relieved, but he also sounded sad, and Sheppard understood why. Other than Ronon himself, it was clear that being a V'rdai had only one possible end. If this Banje wasn't there, it must mean he was dead. "Lanara was Nekai's lover," Ronon continued. "She's dangerous, too. Angry, bitter, and a trained hunter. She's also got amazing aim with guns, knives, pretty much anything."

"You said Adarr was a mechanic," Rodney commented. "Before, when we were about to blow up their shuttle."

"He is — a really good one, too," Ronon agreed. "He was never much of a fighter, or a hunter. He used to be really friendly, actually, and talked all the time." He shook his head. "I guess he's changed."

"And Nekai?" Sheppard asked.

"He's an amazing hunter," Ronon admitted. "Decent in a fight but not great. Good tactician, but too controlling — he doesn't tell people what they're doing or why, just where to go."

Sheppard nodded. "Okay, so we've got three known quantities and three unknown," he summed up. "Did you kill the ones at the shuttle or just stun them?"

"Stunned them," Ronon answered. "Bound and gagged them, too." That made sense — Ronon had known some of these people, once been part of their unit, so killing them would be tough. Besides, killing the first two could have sent the others over the edge, making them crazed and completely unpredictable. Leaving them alive meant the others had to waste time untying them, but it also meant they were still angry but rational. And rational people could be outwitted.

"We need to know where they are," Sheppard said finally.

"And then we can figure out what to do about them."

"Not a problem," Rodney announced. "I should have thought of this earlier." He fumbled with his jacket, pulling something from one of its pockets, then leaned back against the rock wall again. He had both hands cupped in front of him, and after a second a faint glow appeared between them. As his eyes adjusted Sheppard saw the light was coming from a small, flat device Rodney was holding. A life signs detector !

But his excitement at realizing the scientist had brought such a tool quickly faded as Rodney frowned and shook his head. "That's weird," he said, tapping the screen several times in rapid succession — Sheppard guessed he was entering codes and commands. "I'm not getting any life signs except for us," Rodney reported finally, glancing up and around at the others. He scowled. "But that doesn't make any sense. We know they're out there."

"We are in a cave," Teyla pointed out. "Perhaps the rock all around us is interfering with the signal."

"It shouldn't," Rodney replied. "I adapted this thing myself, and it's got more than enough range. I'd explain how it worked but none of you would understand. Trust me, though — unless these cave walls are literally miles thick, they shouldn't pose a problem." He tapped in another command but continued to frown at the tiny screen.

"Maybe these rocks are special," Sheppard offered. "Maybe something about them makes them more resistant to whatever energy you're using for your scans."

Rodney started to shake his head, then stopped. "That could be it," he admitted. His fingers flitted across the monitor again, and then he raised it and turned slowly, scanning their surroundings. "Yes! The rocks here emit a low-level magnetic charge," he explained. "It's not enough to damage any electronics outright, but spread out over an area the charge creates a backdrop that swallows the scanning signal. Then the monitor filters all that out, leaving it with nothing." As was often the case, he sounded excited even though this put them in considerable danger. Sheppard fought not to roll his eyes. What was it about scientists that they could happily die if they got to discover a new weapon or principle in the process?

"That's why Nekai picked this place," Ronon said. "He knows all the tricks for hiding and ambushing, and he must know about these rocks' unusual properties. It's the perfect place to set a trap. He knows we can't find him here."

"Maybe, maybe not," Rodney told him. "I can't use the standard scanning frequencies, no. But that doesn't mean I'm out of options."

"You can scan for life signs with different energy?" Teyla asked.

"Not life signs, no," Rodney admitted. "But other things, yes." He glanced over at Ronon. "They're all Runners, right?" The big Satedan nodded. "But they all still have their tracking devices?" Another nod. "Then I can reconfigure the scans and set them to the same frequency as the device we pulled out of you." He retrieved a small tool from a breast pocket and used it to open the back of the monitor. Then he turned his back on the others and began fiddling with it, crouching and holding it close to the nearest wall so he could see by the reflected glow of the screen.

"You still remember that frequency?" Teyla asked. The surprise and even disbelief was clear in her voice.

Rodney didn't even bother to face her, but Sheppard knew the scientist would be wearing his usual smug expression. "Of course. I had to program it in when the Wraith recaptured Ronon and inserted a second tracking device in him, remember? When I used it then, it showed seven different dots. I had to guess which was Ronon." This time he did glance back over his shoulder before returning to his task. Yep, definitely smug. "Lucky for you I'm always right." Sheppard stifled a groan, but only because in this enclosed space it would have been deafening. "But now it'll only show them," Rodney concluded. He closed the device back up and turned back around, then started typing in new commands. "And it's a subspace frequency," he explained, "so the rocks won't interfere with the signals." He finished his adjustments. "There!"

He held out the monitor, and Sheppard glanced over at it. Sure enough, the tiny screen now showed six dots, all clumped together. But even as he watched, they wavered and became two dots, then one dot, then four, then back to two. "Why is it doing that?"

Ronon leaned over to peer at the screen as well. "It's the feedback," he explained. "That's why we all worked together in the first place — when we're that close, our signals overlap. The Wraith can't find us anymore."

"Ah, but the Wraith aren't me," Rodney said proudly. "This little baby has better filters than any of their hardware." He entered another command, then slid his finger along the edge of the screen, adjusting the scans' sensitivity. "All I have to do," he muttered, "is figure out the feedback level, and factor in that distortion. The scans will automatically compensate for it, adjusting their gain to bypass the effect, and — Voila!"

The shifting lights on the screen resolved into six clear dots — and stayed that way.

"Nice work, Rodney," Sheppard admitted. Much as the scientist annoyed him sometimes — well, okay, almost all the time — he really was handy to have around. "Okay, so now we know where they are, and we can track them." He studied the image, trying to mentally overlay a map of the area atop it. "That's not the ledge we were on, so they must have found a new hiding place."

"Standard procedure," Ronon agreed. "We knew that location, so it was compromised."

"Well, the good news is, they're nowhere near the Jumper,"

Rodney pointed out. "We can get back there and fix it and get the hell out of here. Good luck following us then!"

"We need to get the communications up and running first," Sheppard told the others. "Calling Atlantis and telling them what's going on has to be our first priority."

But Ronon was shaking his head. "No calls," he said. "That'll only make matters worse."

"Worse? How?" Rodney demanded. "You think having Woolsey send a squad to back us up and to stand guard while I repair the Jumper so we can get off this rock is a bad thing?"

"No, I think blowing up anyone coming through the gate — and maybe us with them — is a bad thing," the big Satedan snapped in reply.

That statement got Sheppard's full attention. "Wait, blow them up? What're you talking about?"

"Nekai will have rigged the gate," Ronon explained. "It was something he'd been thinking about before I left, and I'm sure he's long since figured out the details. Dial any place without disabling the charge — even if it's just to send a message through — and it'll activate. Probably has a motion-sensor trigger, so it won't go off until something moves within range. Then — *Boom!* Won't hurt the gate itself, but it'll probably vaporize anyone near it — and 'near it' could mean anywhere from a few meters away to half a light-year."

Sheppard frowned. It made sense, given everything the V'rdai had already done to them. But that only added another worry to the list. "They'll try to dial us," he reminded his friends. "When it's been thirty-six hours and we haven't checked in, especially since this was supposed to be a quick rescue mission. And when they can't reach us, they'll send a team through." That put a time limit on all this, and a tight one at that.

Ronon didn't seem too fazed, however. "Don't worry about that," he said. "They won't be able to dial the gate open from

Atlantis. Nekai has it locked down — until we dismantle his lock or he removes it, no one can access the gate from the other side."

Now Rodney was impressed. "So you think he perfected whatever he was using to do that? How?"

"I don't know," Ronon admitted. "Nekai never showed the rest of us that trick. He kept most of what he'd learned about the gates entirely to himself." In the faint light of the small monitor Sheppard saw the big man's mouth twist. "Just another way for him to keep us under his control."

Rodney looked disappointed, and Sheppard couldn't blame him. There was still so much they didn't know about the Stargates and how they worked! "Maybe it's something on his DHD," Rodney mused, already caught up in the problem. He noticed the surprise on Sheppard's face, though. "They scavenged one from a Wraith Dart — ask Ronon for the details. So maybe, when this mechanic of theirs jury-rigged it to his ship, he added a few features, and . . ."

"This world has no gate of its own ," Teyla pointed out, bringing all of them back to the problems at hand. "Which means we will have to get the Jumper repaired, return to the gate we came through and disarm whatever trap Nekai has set there before we can return to Atlantis."

Sheppard nodded. "So we get back to the Jumper and get it running again. Assuming we can."

"Oh, I can fix it, no problem," Rodney assured him. "I just need a little time. Preferably with no one shooting at me — for once. I'm sure I can figure out the lock on the gate, too, once I have a chance to study it." Sheppard believed him, too. For all his bragging and all his arrogance, Rodney really was a genius, and the leading expert after Samantha Carter on the functions and uses of the stargates.

"He'll have someone guarding the Jumper," Ronon warned. "A pair, of course. They always move in pairs."

"I noticed that," Sheppard agreed. "Why is that? That feedback loop you were talking about before?"

Ronon nodded. "Exactly. The signal gets even more distorted when you add more Runners, but as long as you have two of them within five meters of each other, the Wraith can't lock onto the signal." He grinned, white teeth visible even in the shadows. "But we can. We've got two other things going for us. I know how they think, what they'll do next. And I don't have a tracking device. They won't be able to find me with Nekai's monitor. That's even assuming Adarr tells him it was me."

"You think he won't?" Sheppard asked.

His friend shrugged. "I don't know. Years ago, I would've said Adarr would tell Nekai — or anyone else — anything. He's gotten hard, though. And he's worried. He might keep it to himself until he's sure what's going on and why."

"That will work to our advantage as well, if he does," Teyla commented. "They will have no idea who to expect, or what your skills are, or how much you know about them."

"Okay." Sheppard sighed and forced his fatigue away. There would be plenty of time for sleep later, assuming they made it out of here and back to Atlantis in one piece. "Ronon, it's your call. What do we do?"

The big Satedan grinned again. "I have a plan," he announced, though softly. Sheppard listened while his friend outlined his idea. Rodney and Teyla were paying close attention as well. When Ronon finished, they all considered it.

"It's risky," Sheppard said finally. "But it should work."

"It had better," Rodney grumbled. "Otherwise we'll never get out of here."

"It'll work," Ronon assured them. "I know what I'm doing." That much was certainly true. And the plan wasn't the worst Sheppard had heard, or even the worst he'd put into effect.

"Right, let's do it," he said finally. "First thing in the morning." He hunkered down, leaned his head back, rolled his shoulders to find a more comfortable position for them, and then shut his eyes. The fatigue was already rising up to wash over him in a soft blue fog. Within seconds he was asleep.

Rodney grumbled for a bit, complaining about damp caves and stone floors and hiding in caves and a whole host of other things. He shifted and wriggled the whole time, trying to find some imaginary soft spot on the hard rock, but his griping grew fainter and fainter, until at last he stopped talking altogether. That meant he must be asleep.

Teyla got up and switched sides so she was leaning next to Ronon. "Are you okay?" she asked him softly.

"Why wouldn't I be?" He had his eyes closed, and Teyla thought he'd probably been asleep until she'd spoken, but with Ronon it was sometimes hard to tell.

"These were your friends," she pointed out. "They saved your life, took you in, and trained you. They were your first family after you became a Runner. They gave you purpose." Ronon didn't reply. "And now they are hunting us," she continued after a minute. "They are trying to kill us. We may have to kill them in order to survive."

"They made that choice," Ronon replied. "Not me. They would have killed me long ago if I hadn't escaped." Now he did open his eyes to look at her. "We can't afford to show them any mercy," he warned, "because they have none."

Teyla tried to imagine the world from the V'rdai's point of view. "I can see where being a Runner would set you against everyone else," she mused. "It is a very solitary way of life, isn't it? You have to trust in yourself and no one else."

"There's trusting no one and there's attacking everyone," Ronon replied. "Two very different things."

"You attacked us when we first met," Teyla pointed out.

Ronon grunted. "You were armed and hunting someone yourself," he reminded her. "Besides, I let you live." Which was true. He'd been more than happy to kill the Wraith but he'd only stunned her and taken her hostage.

"But surely they have some valid basis for their caution," Teyla argued. "There are times when not doing anything is more dangerous than taking action. What about that village, the one that gave you back to the Wraith? You didn't attack them and they captured you and gave you to the Wraith anyway."

"One frightened little village," Ronon answered. "And they'd already paid the price for helping me once." He shook his head. "You kill when you have to," he declared. 'When it's you or them. Not when you think it could some day be you or them. Because if you think that way, anyone could turn on you. There's always a 'some day.' And you'll always be alone."

Teyla smiled at him and rested one hand on his shoulder. "You are not alone, Ronon."

Ronon nodded and smiled—a little. "I know," he admitted softly. Then the smile disappeared. "Unfortunately, neither is Nekai."

"I think you are wrong there," Teyla responded. "He has the V'rdai, yes, but from what you have said he does not trust them enough to share his secrets. They are loyal, but they know he is withholding something, and that makes them nervous." She shook her head. "No, I think he is alone, far more alone for all that he is surrounded by his followers."

"You may be right," Ronon admitted. "But tomorrow we'll make sure he's alone for real." With that he closed his eyes again, leaned his head back, and was asleep once more. Teyla sighed and closed her eyes as well. It looked to be a long day tomorrow, and she knew it would be better if she went into it rested and alert. At least, as much as one could be in damp, dark, drafty cave, packed in with three friends.

One of whom snored.

CHAPTER TWENTY-SIX

"THERE they are."

"Just like you said. Damn, sometimes I hate it when you're right!" Sheppard scowled and peeked again. They had woken shortly after dawn, and waited impatiently while Ronon had scouted the immediate area. When he'd returned and confirmed that it was all clear, they'd crawled back out of their cave shelter and stretched quickly. Sheppard had been happy about that part, at least. He still hated caves. They'd swigged some water from their canteens and chewed on some nutritious but boring ration bars — why couldn't anyone make those things taste good? Then Ronon had led them back here.

Now the four of them were crouched down behind some rocks, looking out at the small valley below and the Jumper nestled neatly within it. Not a bad landing for an emergency, Sheppard congratulated himself. And taking off wouldn't be a problem — none of the nearby peaks overhung the valley, so there was more than enough clearance for the little ship.

Provided Rodney could get it up and running again.

And, of course, assuming they could get past the two V'rdai who guarded it.

The Runners-turned-hunters weren't even bothering to hide, he noticed. Which made sense, since they knew he and his team knew they were here. Whew! Plus the Jumper was their obvious destination, so why pretend you don't realize that? Better to just plant yourself right in front of the door, guns at the ready, and take out anyone who approaches. It's what he would have done, and he was disappointed but not surprised to see that the V'rdai had thought along similar lines.

"You sure the rest of them won't be here somewhere, just waiting to jump out at us?" Rodney whispered anxiously.

"I'm sure," Ronon replied. "Nekai knows we'll have to come back here eventually, but he doesn't know if it'll be our first stop. So he's got two out scouting for us, and Adarr and one of the others working on their own ship." He held up the tracking monitor, which Rodney had grudgingly handed over after they'd exited the cave this morning. "See?" Sure enough, there were three pairs of dots on the screen, all widely separated.

"Okay, so what do we do now?" Rodney asked. He held up his hands when the other three glared at him. "Right, right, I know. I was just hoping you'd change your mind."

"Can't imagine why," Sheppard told him bluntly. "It's the perfect plan." He slapped Rodney on the back and rose to his feet, staying hunched so the rocks still shielded him from the guards' view. Teyla did the same. Ronon had already moved away, so quietly Sheppard hadn't even noticed. Damn, the big guy could move!

"Easy for you to say!" Rodney shot back in a hissing whisper, but he stayed put as the other three crept off to one side. Then they worked their way a little closer to the ship, splitting up so that Ronon was approaching it from one side and Sheppard and Teyla from the other. They settled into place and waited.

And waited.

And waited.

"Come on, Rodney!" Sheppard muttered under his breath. The sounds were still on his lips when Teyla nudged his elbow and gestured silently with her chin. Glancing in that direction, Sheppard saw something shift behind a boulder a little higher than they were, and directly in line with the Jumper's airlock. About time!

"Um, hello?" Rodney called out as he rose to his feet. "Anyone there?"

The two V'rdai were instantly alert, their bodies tensing

and their guns swinging up to point at him. But Rodney was just a little too far away for effective range.

Exactly as Ronon had planned.

"Don't move!" one of the guards shouted, and Rodney froze instantly except for his hands, which fluttered up as if to raise in surrender before stopping mid-motion. "Where are the others?" the guard demanded. It was a man, and Sheppard judged him to be about average in height, which meant the bearded man. The other guard, who had backed up against the Jumper's hull, was probably the dark-skinned woman Ronon had mentioned before. The same pair he and Rodney had jumped at the V'rdai ship. Which meant they would be extra- cautious about ambushes.

Great.

"I-I don't know," Rodney claimed, his hands twitching again until he finally lowered them. Slowly. "I — when we got away, they ran. We all ran, I mean. But they ran faster than I did. I lost sight of them. I don't know where they went. So I came back here. I was hoping they'd come back here too. But they're not here. You're here. And I'm here. Uh, hi?" Sheppard had to admit he was impressed. He'd never seen Rodney channel his own nonstop chatter and constant fear like that. He wasn't entirely convinced it was an act, but it didn't matter. What mattered was how the V'rdai reacted.

The two guards leaned toward each other slightly, muttering too softly for Sheppard to hear. Then the man moved forward, gun still up, slowly making his way toward Rodney. The woman kept her back to the Jumper itself and scanned the surrounding area. Smart. That way they were prepared if someone did jump out, and in a minute Rodney would be within range of the bearded man's gun.

Of course, Rodney knew that as well. "Hey, wait!" he whined, starting to back up a step but freezing again when the man waggled his head 'no'. "Look, let's talk about this! I'm sorry about what they did, okay? I had no part in that! I'm just the scientist, that's all! I just want to fix my ship and go home!" Sheppard tried not to bristle at Rodney's calling the Jumper "his" ship, and tensed, waiting for the right moment. "Look, you can come with me!" Rodney offered. "Your ship isn't working either, right? Well, let me fix this one and the three of us can get out here together! To hell with the rest of them!" Rodney was far too convincing when he said that, Sheppard decided.

But it was convincing the V'rdai as well. "You think we'd abandon our teammates?" the man asked, his voice a low growl as he continued to stalk toward Rodney. "We're not cowards! We're V'rdai! We don't run, we fight!" His attention was entirely upon Rodney now, and the woman's glances around the area had subsided as well. She was starting to believe that Rodney really was here alone.

Perfect.

"Okay, okay," Rodney tried again. "How about this, then? You let me fix my ship, and then gather up the rest of your crew and we all fly out of here together. I can drop you guys off anywhere you want — or you can drop me anyplace that has at least a small city, if you'd rather do it that way. How does that sound?"

"It sounds like you're desperate," the man answered, and Sheppard privately agreed. The guard was almost close enough to shoot Rodney now, and perhaps thirty feet from Sheppard and Teyla. It was time.

Sheppard nodded, and Teyla responded by rising to her feet. She had her gun out already, of course, and she aimed and fired as soon as she had a clear shot. It winged the V'rdai guard but didn't take him out, and he spun around to face her —

— and Sheppard's shot hit him full in the chest. The man collapsed instantly, falling in a limp heap on the hard rocky ground, his gun clattering as it dropped from his hand. Sheppard sighed. The man was dead, no question about it. He wished there had been another way.

"Castor!" The woman had dropped into a crouch as soon as she saw Teyla, and she squeezed off a shot but Teyla ducked back behind a boulder. Sheppard could tell she was trying to decide who to shoot at — Rodney was still frozen in front of her but too far away, Teyla was back out of sight, and he was standing there, bringing his own weapon around toward her. Easy choice. She turned to face him, raising her pistol as well —

— and Ronon shot her in the back. She crumpled without a sound, and not for the first time Sheppard envied his friend's unusual pistol. The P90s were lethal, but Ronon could set his weapon to stun or to kill. Sheppard could see the woman's back moving slightly with each breath. The big Satedan had only stunned her.

"Good plan," Sheppard commented as he and Teyla stepped out and hurried over to meet Ronon by the airlock. Rodney was already working his way down from his vantage point, and joined them a second later.

"Yeah, of course you liked it," he complained, carefully not looking at the dead male V'rdai. "You weren't the one playing bait!"

"I wouldn't have been half as good at it as you were, Rodney," Sheppard assured him, forcing himself to keep his tone light. That way he could avoid thinking about the man he'd just killed, at least for a little while. "You have that certain look of terror I don't think I could ever match."

"Ha ha," the scientist snapped. "If you've had your amusement, do you mind if I get to work?"

"By all means." Sheppard bent and grabbed the woman under the arms, then hauled her away from the airlock. Ronon was already moving the dead man off to the side, and Sheppard was glad he didn't have to shoulder that task. "Go right ahead."

"Thank you." Rodney turned and raised his hand to the door panel, but Ronon called out and stopped him.

"They'll have rigged it," the Satedan warned.

"I guessed as much already," Rodney snapped at him. "I have done this before, you know." He opened the panel and checked the wiring. "Just as I thought — the exact same configuration as last time," he said to himself. "Easy enough to disconnect." He snipped a few wires, rerouted something else, then closed the panel again and activated the door release. Nothing blew up as it lowered, so Sheppard figured he must have gotten it right.

While Rodney disappeared inside to make sure the V'rdai hadn't caused any additional damage or left any other presents, the rest of them turned to the two bodies. They stripped off the V'rdai's camouflaged jumpsuits, facemasks, and goggles, and Sheppard and Teyla quickly donned them and took up the guards' weapons while Ronon bound and gagged their captive and hauled her off behind some rocks where she wouldn't be found right away. He was still carrying the man's body away when Rodney reemerged.

"The interior's as we left it," he said. "They didn't break anything, so it's just the existing damage I've got to fix." He had his tools with him, and set to work at once, wrestling a battered panel open and removing a mass of burnt-out wiring and circuitry. "Excellent."

"Can you fix it or not?" Sheppard asked him. He had to raise his voice because the facemask muffled it. Plus the jumpsuit was armored in strategic locations, which made it stiff and heavy. How did the V'rdai stand it? At least Castor had been roughly his height, and these things were made to be a little loose, so it fit him well enough for appearance's sake. They were also dark enough to hide bloodstains, Sheppard noticed, and deliberately pushed aside the reminder that he was wearing the clothing of a man he had just killed. Teyla had had a little more trouble with hers, since she was shorter than the dark-skinned woman, but hopefully no one would notice her rolled-up cuffs.

"Of course I can fix it!" Rodney snapped. "I just have to replace a few things and reroute some of the systems. It won't be perfect, but it'll get everything up and running again, and it'll hold long enough to get us back home." Sheppard believed him. Rodney did have a very high estimation of his own abilities, but in all honesty there was a very good reason for that. And he wouldn't risk his own life on something he didn't think was fully functional.

"How long?" was Sheppard's next question.

"A few hours, at least," Rodney answered. He didn't bother to snap this time, because he was already focused on the task at hand. Which was fine. The sooner they could get out of here, the better. Sheppard hoped they might manage it before any more of the V'rdai came looking for them.

But he'd never been that lucky.

"Hey!"

Sheppard had been half-dozing where he stood, head bowed against the sun—it was close to noon, and the small orb was almost directly overhead, even its weak rays beating down on him like a sledgehammer. But the shout jerked him awake, and his hand reached instinctively for his P90 before he remembered that he was holding a pistol already and raised that instead.

The exclamation had come from a tall man gliding down from between the nearby boulders, and as Sheppard took in the other man's mottled gray coverall and headgear he snapped fully awake again. Right, the V'rdai. Apparently the second team had found them.

"What?" he called back, trying to make his voice sound like what little he'd heard from the man he was impersonating. Fortunately the facemask muffled him already, so that would help. He saw the short, broad-shouldered V'rdai right behind the tall one, glancing around as they approached. Teyla was

still next to him, Sheppard realized, and Rodney was somewhere, hopefully out of sight — he couldn't risk checking. But
where was Ronon?

"What do you mean, what?" the tall V'rdai — Adarr — replied.
He sounded downright pissed. "You were half-asleep!" He was
less than forty feet away now.

"So what if I was?" Sheppard said. "This is ridiculous!
They're not stupid enough to come back here!"

"They'll be here," Adarr assured him. Twenty feet. His
partner was just a little behind him, and Sheppard hoped
Teyla had a clear shot at the shorter man. He was planning
to drop Adarr any second now, but he didn't want to get shot
while doing it.

As it turned out, he didn't have to worry about that. Just
as the two V'rdai reached him, Sheppard heard a faint noise
from up among the rocks and a little to the left. It sounded
like someone brushing against a boulder, someone who didn't
know how to keep completely quiet — or someone who did and
was pretending he didn't.

Ronon.

The two V'rdai heard it as well, and both whirled around,
guns raised. Adarr was barely five feet away, but even so
Sheppard wasn't taking any chances. A quick step and his pistol
pressed against the back of the tall man's head, right above his
jumpsuit collar. He had just enough time to stiffen in surprise
before Sheppard pulled the trigger. Teyla had stayed against
the Jumper's hull but she'd taken careful aim, and she dropped
the shorter V'rdai an instant later.

Ronon had obviously been watching the whole time, because
as soon as both V'rdai were down he appeared from among
the rocks and quickly picked his way back down to them.
Sheppard helped him bind and gag the unconscious men,
and then Ronon took them one at a time to wherever he was
stashing the others.

"How're the repairs going?" Ronon asked after he returned.

"They're going fine," Rodney replied—fortunately he'd been inside the Jumper, recalibrating the controls to compensate for the engine modifications. "But they're not even close to done yet. I need at least another hour, maybe two."

"Two?" Sheppard shook his head. "I thought you said you were good at this, Rodney?"

"You think you can do it any faster?" the scientist told him sharply. "Be my guest." He had a diagnostic tool in his hand, and offered it to Sheppard. "No? Fine. Then trust me when I say I am doing this as fast as humanly possible—maybe faster—but if you actually want us to be able to make it all the way to the Stargate I need another hour at the absolute minimum!"

"Okay, keep your shirt on, Rodney," Sheppard said, raising his hands in surrender. "I give up."

"We all know you are working as quickly as possible," Teyla assured him. "We are simply anxious about the remaining V'rdai, that is all."

"There's only two left," Ronon pointed out. He pulled out the tracking monitor and held it where they could all study the tiny screen. Two dots showed, close together and a short distance from here.

"You think they heard what happened to their friends?" Sheppard wondered aloud. Most guns made a lot of noise when fired, and the V'rdai's pistols were no exception. The sound of each shot had reverberated across the tiny valley, and probably up into the hills beyond as well.

"I know they did," Ronon replied. He pointed at the monitor again, and Sheppard saw that the dots had now separated. One was stationary, but the other was moving farther from them. "That's Nekai," the big Satedan said, indicating the dot on the move.

"How do you know?" Teyla asked.

"I know how he thinks," Ronon answered. "They know we took down at least two of the others, and possibly all four. So he's worried. He wants to give us time to panic, to make mistakes. So he's giving us some space. He doesn't want to risk going after us unprepared."

"And the other one?" Teyla pointed at the first dot, which still hadn't moved. "That is the other woman, is it not?"

"Lanara," Ronon agreed. He half-sneered as he said her name, just as he had back in the cave. "She's too angry and too bitter to be cautious. She won't back down, no matter what."

"But they're making themselves vulnerable," Sheppard pointed out. "They're visible to the Wraith again because they split up."

"They must be more worried about us than about the Wraith," Teyla remarked. "We are the more immediate threat, after all."

"Lanara must be really worried if she disobeyed Nekai," Ronon agreed. "She's never gone against him before." He frowned and tapped the tracking monitor with one finger, lost in thought. Then a slow, nasty smile spread across his face.

"Of course, I don't blame her for being worried," he said, not bothering to be quiet about it. If anything, he raised his voice slightly, and it echoed faintly off the rocks all around. "She's got nothing without Nekai, and he's got nothing without the V'rdai. So if we kill all the others, that leaves him weak and her even weaker."

Sheppard saw what his friend was doing. "She didn't seem weak to me," he commented loudly. "Just angry."

"That's how she covers it up," Ronon explained. "She's always angry. It's just a cover, though. Inside, she's just scared. Scared of everything — and everyone. Scared to move, scared to fight, scared to run. That's why she clings to Nekai so tight. She's too scared to stand up on her own."

There was a scritching noise from somewhere off to one side, and Sheppard saw a flicker of light speeding toward them. He dove to one side, but it hadn't been aimed at him, and Ronon had been expecting it. The big Satedan spun to the side, and the throwing knife sailed past him, just missing his shoulder. If he hadn't moved, it would have imbedded itself in his throat.

"You missed, Lanara," Ronon called out. "You're getting sloppy. Is that why Nekai left you? Because you're losing your edge?"

Sheppard heard what sounded like a low growl from the direction the knife had appeared, and he turned, training his gun that way. But he didn't see anything except rocks and more rocks.

"You used to be a good shot," Ronon was saying. "Of course, that was years ago." He faced the same direction and spread his arms. "Want to try again?"

A second glitter, and another blade sped toward Ronon's throat. This one was easier to spot, however — perhaps because they knew where to look and what to watch for — and the Satedan actually caught it, grabbing the knife by the handle. The blade's tip was less than an inch from his throat.

"Definitely losing your touch," Ronon remarked, holding the dagger up and examining it. "I hope you have a lot more knives. We both know you're not going to face me directly — that wouldn't even be a contest."

Apparently that last dig was the final straw. Sheppard heard someone roar, definitely a person but someone driven to the limits, pushed so far she reverted to baser instincts and actions. Then there was a scrape and a clatter as Lanara burst from the rocks and charged them. She had a pistol in one hand and a third throwing knife in the other. And she was screaming as she ran, no words but just a long endless exclamation.

Ronon waited until she was ten feet away, then shot her in the throat. The impact actually brought her charge up short and knocked her off her feet. She groaned once, shuddered slightly, and then stopped moving altogether.

"Did you kill her?" Teyla asked, looking down at the woman but not making any move toward her.

"No," Ronon answered. He holstered his pistol and crouched down beside Lanara, removing her weapons before binding and gagging her. "She's just stunned." Without another word he hoisted her onto one shoulder and stood, carrying her off into the rocks and the shadows.

"I need to go after Nekai," Ronon announced when he returned. "Alone."

"Alone? Don't be ridiculous," Sheppard told him. "One of us" — he indicated Teyla and himself — "can come with you. The other can stay here and guard Rodney and the ship."

"I'm starting to enjoy this whole "Rodney is too important to risk' attitude," Rodney commented from under the Jumper's right wing. "You should definitely handle situations this way from now on."

"Shut up, Rodney," Sheppard said without turning around. "I'm serious, Ronon. You can't go after him alone."

"I don't have a choice," Ronon replied. "Rodney needs to fix the Jumper so we can leave. You need to make sure he's safe enough to do that. The V'rdai we captured could get loose. There could be other dangers here. And now the Wraith are on the way. You both need to stay here and protect Rodney. But someone has to go after Nekai. We can't leave him at our backs — we'd never wake up."

"I'll take care of him, then," Sheppard offered. "You and Teyla stay here with Rodney."

But the Satedan was already shaking his head. "You don't know Nekai like I do," he pointed out. "I know how he thinks. I know how he hunts. I can anticipate that. You can't."

Sheppard stared at him for a second. "You're just doing this to avoid having to put up with Rodney," he accused finally. Ronon laughed even as Sheppard sighed. He knew arguing about it was hopeless. And Ronon was right — he was the only one of them who stood a chance against the V'rdai leader.

"Good luck," he told his friend.

"Don't leave without me," Ronon replied. He was already turning back toward the rocks in the direction of the wrecked V'rdai shuttle — Sheppard had missed seeing that firsthand, but Rodney had told them all about it. Within seconds Ronon had slipped between two rocks and was only a shadow. A rapidly receding shadow.

Sheppard started to turn away when he noticed something. There was a small, dark shape where Ronon had been, a patch against the gray rocks. Too small to be a weapon, but too even to be a stray shadow or a natural indentation. Curious, he walked over to check it out. What he found was a small, dark metal square with a faintly glowing rectangle inset on one side. He recognized it immediately.

The tracking monitor.

"What — did Ronon drop it?" Teyla asked when he rejoined her and showed her the device.

"Not likely," Sheppard answered, studying the object. "He's not that careless, and this is too important." He tossed it from hand to hand. "I'm betting he left it behind deliberately. This way we can tell exactly where Nekai is."

"But he cannot!" Teyla pointed out.

"No, he can't," Sheppard agreed. "He'll have to do it the hard way."

"Do you think he will be all right?" Teyla asked, scanning their surroundings again.

"I think he'll be fine," Sheppard replied. "I hope we can say the same for us. Rodney, hurry it up!"

"Don't rush me," Rodney snapped, still working. "Unless you want to crash before we even make it off of this planet's ridiculous surface!"

Sheppard shook his head. Ronon had completely disappeared already. Barring any sudden problems, Sheppard knew he wouldn't see his friend again until they were almost ready to leave this place. Or until Ronon had settled his dispute with Nekai for good.

CHAPTER TWENTY-SEVEN

RONON paused once the Jumper was out of sight. He had to shift his focus now. It was all too easy to fall into camaraderie and carelessness when he was with his friends. He knew he could count on them to watch his back, even Rodney. But out here, it was just him against Nekai. One on one. He had to be completely alert, as sharp as he'd ever been, and fully self-sufficient. There wasn't anyone to cover for him if he made a mistake, and any errors could be fatal.

Taking a deep breath, Ronon closed his eyes and forced himself to relax. Being tense when hunting wasn't a good thing. People assumed it was because if you were tense you were alert, cautious. But tension actually made you paranoid and jumpy—you started at everything, overreacted, overcompensated. And when you were up against someone clever, someone who could plan and prepare and set snares, that meant you could get distracted by obvious dangers and overlook the more subtle signs that pointed to a trap. Better to be calm, cool, and careful. Nekai had taught him that.

Nekai had taught him a lot.

But not everything, Ronon reminded himself. Yes, Nekai had taught him how to hunt. But he'd had six years since then, five of them completely on his own. He'd learned new tricks, things the V'rdai leader probably didn't know because he didn't have to. There were a lot of situations a lone Runner came up against that a group never would, and because of that Ronon had been forced to adapt and to find new solutions.

And he had. He'd grown. He'd improved. He'd become a better hunter than he'd ever been with the V'rdai, and a better Runner than any of them. He thought about what he'd heard Adarr and that other V'rdai saying—the legend of a lone Runner who'd evaded the Wraith for years, and who no longer had a tracking device so he could strike at will. All true. And to them it had sounded like an impossible fantasy, a fairy tale. But it was his life.

He was more than a match for any of them now.

Even Nekai.

Which didn't mean this was going to be easy. He had to watch out for overconfidence. Nekai knew it was him by now, of course — Adarr would have told him after he'd helped Sheppard and Teyla escape. So the V'rdai leader would be setting traps and leaving clues with Ronon in mind. He knew how Ronon thought, how he hunted, how he fought, and he'd take full advantage of that knowledge.

Except that Ronon had changed. And he was willing to bet Nekai hadn't.

That didn't make the man any less dangerous. But at least it was a familiar danger, and one Ronon thought he could work around.

He was about to find out if he was right.

A few hours later, Ronon stopped and crouched to study the ground. He'd backtracked to the ledge the V'rdai had used as their staging area and base camp when they'd captured Sheppard and Teyla. The spot was long since deserted now, of course, and scrubbed clean of any trace of the V'rdai, but Ronon had felt it was as good a place as any to start. He knew Nekai had been here, after all, so he figured he could start here and then expand his search outward, circling until he found the Retemite hunter's tracks.

Most of the ledge was bare rock, which meant no tracks except for bits of stray dirt the V'rdai had apparently tracked in from elsewhere. That wasn't much help — there was too little dirt and it was too scattered to yield even one partial bootprint, much less a clear set of tracks. But the outcropping the hunters had used as their entryway led to a small clearing between several small boulders, and enough dirt had collected there to give the rocky surface a solid coating. The space had been brushed clean, of course, but staring at it intently Ronon saw what looked like a hint of prints nonetheless, visible as faint depressions just beneath the top layer. He smiled. They'd been left by a man, average height judging by the stride, a little heavy from the weight of the indent but still light on his feet from the evenness front to back.

Nekai.

Ronon's smile changed to a frown. His old mentor was getting careless — or was he? Nekai had shown nothing but cunning in the trap he'd laid to damage their Jumper and bring them here — never mind that the initial idea had been Ronon's, all those years ago — and in the snares Sheppard and Teyla had described when explaining how they'd been captured. And Nekai knew he was liable to be followed and even hunted now. Why would he be so sloppy, then? To come back here, where Ronon was sure to look for him, and then not brush the tracks clear completely? Something didn't add up.

Ronon studied the small clearing again. Then his gaze drifted to the rocks just beyond them, the cluster those almost-vanished tracks directed him toward. He crept over to the nearest boulder there, and then stretched as high as he could, his fingers scrabbling for purchase. After a second he managed to get a passable handhold with his right hand, and hauled himself up far enough to wrap his left arm around the top.

Not the most graceful climb, but it did the job, and a few seconds later he was straddling the boulder. From here he had a clear view of the areas in front and in back, and he studied the stretch behind the boulder as closely as he could from this vantage.

There! Not three paces past the boulder was a spot that seemed a little too even, with the barest suggestion of a circu-

lar border around it. A snare! Ronon almost laughed aloud.
Nekai had lost none of his guile! The faint track had been a
trap, designed to lure him between those boulders and straight
into that snare — he was willing to bet another mark lay just
beyond the trap, to draw his attention there instead of to the
ground beneath his feet. It was a good trap, and he'd almost
fallen for it.

Almost.

Ronon considered the scene again. If he'd been Nekai setting up this ruse, he'd have walked along, brushing away his
tracks behind him and deliberately leaving a few just visible
for bait. Then he'd have circled back, set the snare, perhaps
added a second snare just beyond that next boulder in case the
prey had gotten past the first unscathed, and then kept going
in the other direction. He'd have scaled those boulders on the
far side to avoid leaving additional tracks, so he wouldn't have
touched down on dirt again until — there!

Keeping the spot he'd selected in sight, Ronon clambered
from boulder to boulder, keeping low so anyone watching would
have a hard time picking him out from a distance — his clothes
didn't blend in as well as the V'rdai's mottled jumpsuits, but
his coat was close enough that it wouldn't clash. At one point
as he crawled across a portion of rock something crumbled
beneath one hand, and lifting his palm Ronon saw that it was
now dusted with dark brown. Dirt! But dirt wouldn't collect
here on its own — it would have been deposited lower down by
rain and swirled away by the frequent winds. This had been
brought here more recently, and only a little bit.

Just enough to have been trapped in the soles of a man's
boot, and dislodged as he climbed from one side of the clearing to the other.

Ronon smiled again. This was the real trail — he knew it.
Nekai had thought to fool him, and most likely had circled
around to some nearby vantage where he could spy upon the

false trail he'd laid and see if anyone set off one of the traps. But by following his real path, Ronon could overtake the V'rdai leader and get the drop on him.

Not that Nekai wouldn't anticipate the possibility. There'd be traps along this trail as well, Ronon was sure of it. But he knew they might be there, so he'd be watching for them.

Nekai was about to find out what it felt like to be on the wrong end of a Runner's hunt.

As he stalked after the older man who had once been his friend and mentor, Ronon thought about the irony of it all. Here he was, a Runner chasing a Runner, a hunter pursuing a hunter, a man using skills against the very man who had taught them to him. It was, in some ways, the ultimate test of Nekai's long-ago training, and a true contest between them. That was at least part of the reason why Ronon had left the tracking monitor behind for Sheppard. Of course he had wanted Sheppard to have it in case something went wrong here and they needed to know where Nekai and the other V'rdai were, but that wasn't the main reason. He hadn't wanted to use the device to follow Nekai. It would have felt like cheating, and it would have tarnished his victory — if in fact he won this contest. But Nekai deserved his best effort, his full attention and utmost skill, and that meant a lot more than staring at a little screen and closing in on the dot it revealed.

Ronon was still musing on this when he came across another clearing, this one a bit larger than the tiny area by that rocky outcropping. He had been following Nekai's tracks for over an hour and had already eluded one concealed pit and a nasty coiled branch. This was by far the largest empty area he'd passed through, and all his senses went on high alert as soon as he set foot within it. Nekai's bootprints had led him down out of the foothills and there was brush here instead of boulders, and dirt deep enough to support them and some bristly grass and a few scraggly trees as well. Ronon considered. This was the perfect place for an ambush, with the ground soft enough to conceal snares and the trees scattered around the edges, thin but sturdy and with long, springy branches. It was exactly where he'd set his trap, if he were the one hunting.

Pausing for a minute, Ronon dropped to his haunches and ran his fingers lightly along the ground. He could feel the smooth arc a branch had made as it had been brushed across the dirt, obscuring all traces of Nekai's passage but leaving those faint marks of its own. This was definitely the place.

Reaching into his jacket and his belt, Ronon extracted what he thought he'd need. A minute's preparation, then a few more, and he was ready. Or at least as ready as he could be. A lot would depend upon how much Nekai had changed over the years, if he had at all. Rising to his feet again, Ronon studied the trees around him. They bent together over this clearing, their leaves eager for sunlight and forming a loose canopy up above so that the entire space was dappled with shadow. Some of those branches looked sturdy, and Ronon studied two in particular.

Finally he sighed and shook his head. Nekai was close, he was sure of it, and he'd done everything he could to be ready. There was nothing left now but to finish this.

Ronon drew his pistol and started across the clearing, studying the ground carefully before setting down each foot. Despite his care and caution he was still startled when he felt the dirt beneath his right foot shift slightly, and then a tight loop close around his ankle. There was a sharp tug and a whoosh up above as the hidden rope released the bound tree branch and it snapped upright, and Ronon felt his world tilt upside down as he flipped over and hurtled into the air, feet-first. His head spun as he struggled to regain his equilibrium and his breath while the world tilted around him. Damn, he'd never get used to being snared!

Nekai had chosen well, and by the time Ronon's eyes were clear again and his breathing steady he was a good six feet off the ground, which was more than high enough to render him helpless. Only one ankle had been trapped but he couldn't reach high enough to grab the snare, and it was tight enough that he couldn't loosen it at all. His gun had fallen when he'd sprung the trap, and lay several feet below his grasping fingers. His knife, meanwhile, was still snugly in its sheath in his boot — the same boot caught in the rope! He tried grabbing for it, but just bending and trying to grasp his own ankles was enough to make him flop down again, gasping for breath. No good. He was well and truly stuck.

Well, I wanted to finish this, Ronon thought, letting himself dangle by his foot and feeling the blood rush to his head and hands. It looks like I'm about to get my wish. He just hoped Nekai showed up soon, before the lightheadedness made him pass out. He'd hate to be unconscious for their big showdown. But Ronon had a feeling it wouldn't be long at all — Nekai was too good a hunter to leave his snares unattended for extended periods.

The only question was whether the V'rdai leader would be surprised or pleased when he discovered his most recent catch.

CHAPTER TWENTY-EIGHT

IT WAS difficult to judge time with the blood pounding in his head and throbbing at his temples, but Ronon doubted it was more than ten minutes before he heard rustling among the brush on the far side of the clearing. Then one of the trees swayed slightly, its slender trunk and long thin branches moving more than could be accounted for by mere wind. Ronon glanced in that direction, then swung himself around to face away from it, squinting up into the sun, and waited.

A minute later, the foliage directly ahead of him parted without a sound and a figure emerged, pistol in hand and leveled at his head. It was classic Nekai, creating just enough noise to attract attention from anyone watching and then circling around to catch any potential ambushers flatfooted.

Of course, this time the only person here was Ronon himself, and he wasn't exactly in a position to hide. But Nekai had obviously wanted to be sure.

The V'rdai leader was wearing the same goggles and facemask as the rest of his team, so Ronon couldn't see his expression, but he noticed the way the shorter man paused just within the clearing, studying him intently. If he'd had to guess, he'd have said his old mentor was surprised but not stunned, as if he'd seen something he'd been warned to expect but had refused to believe.

"Ronon," he said finally.

"Nekai," Ronon replied. "I'd say it's nice to see you, but I can't."

"That's sort of the point," his former mentor agreed, but he reached up and pulled off the facemask and goggles. He looked much as he had the last time they'd faced off, though the hair was a bit grayer and the face a little more lined, especially around the mouth and over the brow. "Better?"

"Much." Ronon swung lightly back and forth. "Why so surprised to see me? Didn't Adarr tell you I was here?"

"He did," Nekai admitted. "But I didn't believe it. I couldn't. I thought you were dead."

"Almost was," Ronon said. "More'n a few times, in fact. Just not quite yet."

Nekai circled around, and Ronon knew the Retemite was checking to make sure he didn't have any concealed weapons on him. He saw the other man's gaze flick up to his boot sheath, then visibly dismiss the knife there as clearly out of reach.

"You don't show up on the tracking monitor," Nekai said finally, stopping in front of Ronon again. He was still a good twenty paces away, much too far for Ronon to reach even if he'd had his knife in hand. His tone was level, almost mild, as if they were discussing the weather, but Ronon saw the way the other man's eyes narrowed and his mouth tightened. Annoyed? Incredulous? Worried? Or some combination of the three?

"No tracking device," Ronon explained, trying to keep his own tone just as casual. His words came out rough, though, because his tongue felt heavy in his mouth from all the pressure pounding down on his head.

"Oh?" Was the only response Nekai made to that statement. If it had been any of the other V'rdai, the comment would have met with shock, amazement, jubilation, or terror. Or all of the above.

"I had it removed," Ronon continued after a few seconds. "Funny, no explosion." He tried to glare but that wasn't easy when his eyes felt like they were going to pop out of their sockets.

Nekai started to respond, but his shrug made it clear whatever he said would be another breezy explanation and Ronon cut him off before he got the first word out. "Don't bother lying to me," he said sharply. "We both know there was never an explosive there."

For a second it looked like the Retemite would still argue, then he did shrug. "It was a necessary falsehood," he admitted. "As long as all of you thought you couldn't remove the tracking device, it forced you to stay together. It kept the unit bound by common need."

"It kept us under your control, you mean," Ronon shot back. "Just like the way you never let us near the Stargate, never told us the way you locked it from use or scrambled the last location you'd dialed. The same way you never told us your plans in advance, and didn't bring new members to the base until you had them entirely under your thumb."

"I did what I thought was best for the team!" Nekai snapped. "We needed each other to survive!"

"You needed us to follow you!" Ronon shouted, all those half-buried resentments finally emerging. "You needed blind obedience from each and every one of us! And when I dared to question you, you tried to kill me!"

"I obviously didn't try hard enough!" Nekai shouted back. Then he stopped, shut his mouth, closed his eyes, and took a deep breath. When he glanced at Ronon again, the V'rdai leader was in control of himself once more. "I'm glad to see you survived," he said softly, and his eyes were surprisingly kind. "I'm glad you found a way to remove the tracking device — I wasn't lying about seeing another Runner die from trying, just about the explosives. He carved open his own back and sliced through his own spine attempting to pry the damn thing out. Bled to death while I stood there, helpless, my hands soaked in his blood." He glanced down at his hands, one still clutching the pistol, as if he expected to still find them crimson-stained. "The fact that you got yours out and survived — it's a miracle."

"I had help," Ronon told him truthfully. "We could remove yours too, if you stop all this. Yours and the others. You could all be free of those devices forever."

He'd thought the offer would tempt his old mentor, but Nekai's jaw tightened instead. "Who's 'we'?" he demanded, his voice harsh with suspicion. "The Wraith? Did you fall in with them? Are you one of their loyal lackeys now?"

This time the blood Ronon felt surging through him had nothing to do with his upside-down state. "Come a little closer and say that," he warned, his voice no more than a growl. Now he was the one forcing himself to calm down. "No, not the Wraith—you know I'd never go near them except to kill them." He took a deep breath, considering what he was about to say and how Sheppard—and Woolsey—would react once they found out. If he lived long enough to tell them. "I found other friends. Good friends." He decided he had to risk it. "I found Atlantis."

"Atlantis?" Now the Retemite was staring openly, his mouth gone slack. "Are you joking?"

"It's no joke," Ronon said. "The lost city of the Ancestors. Only the Ancestors have long since gone. There are people there now. Good people. They're using Atlantis as a base and trying to reach out to the galaxy. They're fighting the Wraith."

Nekai was still digesting this information. "Atlantis," he said again to himself. "No wonder they knew how to use the rings! The technology they'd have access to! The weapons!" He was clearly imagining exactly what he could do with such resources. Then he glanced up at Ronon, greed plain in his eyes. "And you're working with them?"

"I'm one of them," Ronon replied simply. It was true. He'd started out as just a local who helped them, but he'd long since become one of the team. Atlantis was his home now, more than any other place, even more than Sateda. Maybe more than the V'rdai base had been.

"You could get us access," Nekai started, and Ronon knew he'd have to nip those thoughts in the bud right away. He didn't want his old mentor planning to invade his home.

"You don't need access," he assured the shorter man. "You could join us. All of you could. We could use your skills. You could go on fighting the Wraith, but with friends and allies and full use of the Stargates. And they can remove your tracking devices. You won't have to run anymore."

He could see Nekai was considering the possibilities, and held his breath. Would it be this simple? Could his old leader truly be swayed into signing on with Atlantis? If he could bring the entire V'rdai back to the city, he was sure Sheppard would vouch for their skills as hunters. Woolsey wouldn't trust them at first, which was fair enough, but he was too canny to discard such valuable men and women without giving them a chance. He'd test them out, see how they worked with the rest of the Atlantis, and see if they could be trusted. Much as they'd done with Ronon himself, when he'd first met them. But if they upheld their end, the V'rdai would eventually be welcomed fully. They could stop running and have a real home again.

His own musings were cut short as he saw Nekai's expression change. The hopefulness faded, and his puzzled look deepened into a frown and then a scowl. Uh-oh. Clearly the Retemite's paranoia had only grown worse over the years.

"So you're saying if I cut you loose and we all accompany you back, your new friends will take us all in?" Nekai asked slowly.

"Yes."

"There has to be a catch," Nekai stated. "What is it?" He glared at Ronon, and finally Ronon sighed.

"No more attacking noncombatants," he said. "You can go after the Wraith, and you can defend yourself, but you can't hit people unless they attack you first."

Nekai was already shaking his head. "Absurd," he declared. "There are no noncombatants. Not anymore."

"There are thousands of them!" Ronon insisted. "There are whole worlds who want nothing to do with the Wraith. Who want nothing to do with any of us! They only want to be left alone. How can you even think of them as combatants?"

"They may say they're not involved now," Nekai answered, "but it never lasts. The Wraith show up and tell them 'hand over the Runners or die,' and they turn on us in a heartbeat. They truss us up and offer us as gifts before the Wraith say a word, in the hopes it'll appease their masters." His mouth twisted into an ugly grimace. "They've long since chosen sides, and they picked the Wraith. That makes them as bad as Wraith themselves."

"Can you really blame them for trying to save their own lives and their own families?" Ronon asked. "Wouldn't you, if you were in their shoes? That's not the same as fighting you. They're innocents who're being used."

"No one's innocent," Nekai insisted. "And everyone turns on you, sooner or later." His eyes were stone-hard as they skewered Ronon with a sharp gaze. "You did."

"You attacked us first." Ronon pointed out. "We wouldn't even be here otherwise. You lured us in with that shuttle decoy, and then damaged our ship so we had no choice but to land here. If you hadn't we'd never have known you were out here."

Nekai shook his head. "I'm not talking about here and how," he said, dismissing his own recent actions with a wave of his hand—the same hand holding the pistol, Ronon noted as its barrel waved disconcertingly close to his face. "I'm talking about when you left. You turned on me!"

"You were wrong!" Ronon shouted down at him. "You slaughtered people who wanted nothing but to help. They were defenseless, and kind, and you butchered them!"

"It was my call!" Nekai shouted back. "I was in command. And you disobeyed."

"They weren't a threat." Ronon insisted.

"I don't care if you thought they were or not," Nekai argued. "I gave you an order, and you didn't carry it out. We were at war and you rebelled."

"It wasn't war!" Ronon bellowed. "They weren't our enemy! They were just people, people you murdered. That doesn't make you a soldier or a hunter — it makes you a killer!"

"And you were too good for that, I suppose!" Nekai screamed at him. His face was completely red now, and Ronon could see the veins bulging out on his forehead and along his neck.

"Yes, I was!" Ronon replied, his voice hoarse. "And I thought you were too. Too bad you proved me wrong."

"I did what I had to do!" Nekai answered. "It was us or them, and I chose us."

"So did I," Ronon said, his anger starting to drain away. "I just wasn't willing to turn into them in order to do it." He saw his old mentor stiffen as the implication hit home. There could be no doubt which "them" Ronon had been referring to.

"You might as well have," Nekai responded after a moment. "You walked away from us, from your team, from your friends. From me. You left us behind."

"Only because you gave me no choice," Ronon reminded him. "It was leave or die, as I recall. And I was in no mood to die." He stared at the man in front of him, the man who had taught him so much, the man who had given him a reason to live. "But I never truly left."

"Yes, you did." Nekai's answer was filled with bitterness. "And when you did, you went from being one of us to being one of them."

"If that was true," Ronon told him, "why didn't I hunt you like the Wraith did? Why didn't I try to find you and kill you? I could have — I knew how you thought, how you fought, how you hid. Even if you abandoned the base once I left" — he could tell by the way the other man looked away that they had — "I could have figured out where you'd gone or at least narrowed it down enough to locate you if I searched hard enough." He'd begun swaying from the force of his exclamations, and now he stilled himself so those swings slowed and gentled and finally stopped, leaving him to lock gazes with his old friend. "But I never did," he said. "In all those years, I never once came after you. I didn't agree with what you were doing but I left you alone."

"I left you alone, too," Nekai replied quietly. "Do you think I didn't know how dangerous you were? I probably should have gone after you and killed you, just in case you turned on us. But I didn't. And I could have found you easily enough — I still had my tracking monitor, and you still had a device in your back." He shook his head. "But I didn't. I left you alone. I didn't think you'd ever turn on me, on us. I kept tabs on you from time to time, but you never came after us so I never went after you either." He looked down at the pistol in his hand, studying it as if it were new to him somehow. "When your device disappeared, I thought you were dead."

"Or that I'd figured out you were lying about the devices and the explosives," Ronon accused, "and I'd somehow managed to remove mine." He tried to flex his hands, though his fingers were tingling and going numb. "You must have heard the rumors that I was still alive, or that some Runner was, anyway. I know you did. The others had."

"I heard them," Nekai admitted. "And a part of me wanted to believe them. I liked the idea that you might have escaped your fate, stopped Running, found a new life." The scowl returned and his voice grew harsh once more. "But I had to think you were dead. And the others had to think that, too. If they thought there was a chance they could survive on their own — if they knew someone else had done it, that you'd done it — they'd have started considering leaving themselves. They'd stop thinking as a team and they'd become separate people again. I couldn't risk that." He glared up at Ronon. "And neither could they.

None of them would have survived on their own."

"Why not?" Ronon asked. "I did. For five years. Until I found friends."

"Or masters," Nekai sneered.

"Friends," Ronon repeated sharply. "No one forced me to do anything. I chose to go with them." He smiled, thinking back on all the adventures he'd had with Sheppard and Teyla and the rest — yes, even with Rodney. "They've helped me, Nekai. The way you did once, but without the paranoia and the secrecy. They forge alliances with others instead of seeing everyone as an enemy."

"So now you do what they want, and consider yourself lucky," Nekai retorted.

"No, I do what I want and our interests coincide," Ronon corrected. "They understand that I have my own goals, and sometimes we clash but they're always willing to help me in the end." He studied the Retemite glowering up at him. "I killed the one who tagged me, Nekai. He caught me again, tagged me with another tracking device, and then dropped me on my own homeworld so he could hunt me. And I killed him. And a whole lot of others. But I didn't do it alone. My friends came to find me, and they helped me." He thought back to that final showdown with the Wraith commander, and how he would have died if Beckett hadn't killed the Wraith with the Jumper's guns. "I couldn't have done it without them."

"You could have done it with us," Nekai suggested.

"Maybe so."

"We were a good team, once."

Ronon smiled, remembering. "We were a great team."

"We could be again." Nekai had been holding his pistol the entire time, but now he holstered it. "Come back with me," he urged. "Come back to the V'rdai. It's where you belong — tracking device or not, you're still a Runner. You're still a hunter. Come back and we can hunt together again!"

It was tempting. Ronon admired and trusted Sheppard, and liked Teyla—he even admired Rodney for his mind if nothing else. But they weren't like him. They never had been. They couldn't understand what he'd been through and they didn't have the same sort of skills he did. Sheppard was pretty good in a fight, and Teyla could hold her own as well, but neither of them were hunters. To be with the V'rdai again meant living and working with the only people who really knew what it was like to be a Runner. And it meant being with other hunters, and being able to set traps and ambush prey together without a single word.

Yes, it was tempting. And if he could go back to the V'rdai the way it had been when Nekai had first brought him in, with Setien and Turen and Adarr and Frayne and Banje, Ronon knew he might have accepted.

But that was a long time ago. Most of them were dead now. Adarr had changed. Nekai had changed. And the V'rdai had changed with them.

"I'll come back," Ronon said finally. "If you give up attacking innocents."

Nekai ground his teeth together. "There are no innocents." he insisted again. "There's only us and them. That's it! No other choices, nothing in between!"

Ronon sighed, though it was the answer he'd expected. "You're wrong," he told his former friend. "And I can't be a party to that."

The shorter man sighed as well. "I'm sorry it's come to this," he said, and he did sound disappointed and regretful. "But if you're not one of us you're one of them, and I can't let someone with your skills and your knowledge of us go free." He drew his pistol again.

"So that's it?" Ronon asked him, his entire body tensing. "You're going to shoot me?"

"You don't leave me any choice." Nekai raised his gun and

pointed it at Ronon's head, still keeping more than ten feet between them.

"Put the gun down," Ronon urged. "You owe me a better death than that, at least."

"It'll be quick," his old mentor assured him. "One shot and it's over. You won't feel a thing."

"I'm a hunter, and a Runner," Ronon reminded him. "Don't take me out with a pistol. If you're going to kill me, use a blade, at least. Give me a warrior's death."

Nekai considered for a second, then nodded and holstered his pistol a second time. "Fair enough." He drew a long knife from his belt instead. "I'll still make it quick, and as painless as I can." He raised the blade and approached Ronon slowly. "I really am sorry."

"So am I," Ronon answered. "So am I."

Nekai was less than five feet away now. Ronon hung as still as possible, watching as the other man took one slow step after another — and then stopped. The Retemite crouched down, and brushed at the leaves and dirt scattered in front of him. Then he grinned and lifted a loose rope coil from where it had been hidden just in front of his right boot tip.

"Did you think I'd forgotten?" he asked as he straightened again. "Your final hunting test, when you set a snare for me and then let yourself get caught by mine so I'd get careless? I'm not stupid, Ronon, and I don't fall for the same trick twice."

"It was worth a shot," Ronon muttered as his former mentor tossed the snare aside, sidled over to right a bit, slid forward another step—

—and yelped in surprise, the knife flying from his hand, as something snapped tight around his foot and ankle. Ronon had a quick glimpse of the other man's shocked expression as he shot upward, his feet yanked out from under him by the snare closing and the tree branch it hung from snapping aloft again.

At the same time, Ronon felt the tension of the rope holding him lessen. This is going to hurt, he thought just before the rope came plummeting downward, and he followed it headfirst, his weight no longer supported by anything. He curled in, twisting in mid-air so he hit the ground with his rear first and then his back and sides and legs.

Pain exploded through him, both from the sudden impact and from the reawakening of nerve endings as blood flowed again to legs and upper arms and receded from hands and head and chest, but Ronon couldn't let that distract him. He forced his body to uncoil, leaping to his feet, and drew his boot knife as he moved. One quick slash and it was over.

"There," he said, sheathing his knife again and then stretching, letting his body work out some of the kinks it had gotten from its recent suspension. "Now we can talk more freely."

Nekai glared down at him, their positions now reversed, but his eyes were still wide from shock as well. "How did you do that?" he demanded. "I found your snare!"

"The first one," Ronon agreed. "Which made you cocky, so you missed the second one." He grinned up at his former teacher. "I figured you'd remember what I'd done, but who'd look for two snares right next to each other?"

"How did you know which way I'd move?" Nekai asked, then shook his head as he answered his own question. "I'm right-handed, and you remembered that," he realized. "You knew I'd approach you head-on if we were talking, and then I'd shift to the right once I'd spotted the first snare. Smart." There was clear admiration in his tone. "You're still as good as ever, Ronon. Maybe better."

"I am better," Ronon agreed. "I had to be. I had to survive on my own all those years." He gestured up at the trees. "The first time, I didn't think to link your snare and mine. This time I did — when your branch rose, it released the counterweight on mine." He rubbed his backside and winced. "Of course, I could have done with a shorter drop, but it couldn't be helped." He bent and scooped up Nekai's belt and pistol, which lay where they'd tumbled when he'd cut them loose. He was far enough out of reach that, even if Nekai could get to one of his many knives, he wouldn't be able to attack with it. He'd never been that good at throwing them, and doing so while upside down would be almost impossible.

"What now?" Nekai asked. "You kill me instead?" Even hanging there, he kept his cool.

"I could," Ronon pointed out. "And you were ready to do the same to me." Ronon made a point of drawing his knife again, tossing it end-over-end so the handle smacked back into his palm — and then sheathing it once more. "But I won't."

Instead he gazed up at the man he had once called mentor, leader, and friend. "I didn't kill the others, either. Except for Castor — I'm sorry." He saw Nekai's surprise in his eyes and the twitch of his mouth. "The rest are alive, just bound and gagged not far from our ship. Of course, they know now that the stories about me are true. And they know you've been lying to them. You won't be able to control them like that anymore. You'll have to start telling them the truth. They're your team — you need to trust them."

"I would have trusted you," Nekai grumbled.

"But you didn't," Ronon replied. "You never let me in on your plans, any more than you did the others." He shook his head. "It doesn't matter. No matter what you may think, I didn't betray your trust. I'd think not killing you or the others would prove that." He studied his captive. "I'm not your enemy, Nekai. And neither are most people. You need to learn that."

Ronon turned to go, then stopped. "But if you ever come after me or my friends again," he warned, his voice dropping, "I will hunt you down. And I will kill you. It's your choice."

"So you're just going to leave me here?" Nekai called out as Ronon began to walk from the clearing.

"That's right," Ronon replied over his shoulder. "I know you'll figure a way out of that eventually, if the others don't wake up and get loose and find you first." He met Nekai's gaze. "I'd hurry though, if I were you. You've been by yourself for a while now — the Wraith will be homing in on your signal." He could tell that had hit home. "Good luck."

Then he was beyond the trees, and out of sight. He paused long enough to set Nekai's belt and pistol down on a nearby rock, somewhere he was sure the other man would find them. No one deserved to be defenseless before the Wraith. With that done, Ronon straightened and began jogging back toward the Jumper, and the others. Back toward his friends. He hoped Rodney had the Jumper fixed by now. This hunt was over, but if they didn't hurry they might get caught up in another one, and Ronon preferred to face the Wraith on his own terms, not theirs. He frowned and picked up the pace. It was time to go home.

CHAPTER TWENTY-NINE

"THAT'S ridiculous!"

"That's exactly what I said!"

"No, not that way. *Your* way. What you're saying is ridiculous!"

"I know it is! Yet we did it anyway and look where it got us."

"That's not what I meant. I am definitely not agreeing with you!" Sheppard scrubbed at his face with one hand, as if that could rub away Rodney's statements.

"Yes, you are!" Rodney insisted. "I said it was ridiculous right from the start, and you just agreed with me!"

"I didn't agree that helping was ridiculous! I said you're calling it ridiculous was ridiculous! You're just — aaahhhhh!!!" Sheppard threw his hands up in disgust. He could never win! Arguments with Rodney never worked because there were two kinds of logic — real logic and Rodney logic. And never the twain would meet. But in Rodney-logic, Rodney was always right. Period.

It was a relief to spot something moving beyond the boulders, and Sheppard quickly turned all his attention upon the half-seen disturbance. He raised his pistol and took aim as best he could, sighting on the faint play of shadows across the rocks —

— and relaxed as Ronon stepped into view.

"Everything okay?" Sheppard called out as the Satedan approached them. His pistol was safely in its holster, which Sheppard took to be a good sign, though he knew all too well how fast his friend could draw and fire.

"Everything's fine," Ronon replied as he rapidly closed the distance. He wasn't running and didn't look back, but he was moving quickly nonetheless. "It's time to go."

"Good thing I fixed the Jumper then, isn't it?" Rodney muttered as he opened the airlock and preceded the rest of them inside. "But don't thank me or anything. I'm just saving all our butts yet again. It's what I do."

"Yeah, and it's a good thing the rest of us took care of those hunters trying to kill us," Sheppard couldn't help retorting, "and that Ronon dealt with their leader all by himself, otherwise they'd have cut you down long before you could finish. But that's okay—that's just what we do."

"Yes. Well." Rodney gulped. "It's a team effort, of course."

Sheppard bit back his smile as he took the controls and powered up the Jumper. The engines hiccupped a little and the liftoff was a little jerkier than he'd have liked, but the ship seemed to be spaceworthy again. "So long, mudball," he said under his breath as the small world fell away behind and beneath them. "Don't bother to write."

"Did you get the cloak working again?" Ronon was asking Rodney as Sheppard zeroed in on the local Stargate and gave the Jumper as much speed as he thought she could handle.

"Of course," came the immediate reply.

"Good. We're going to need it."

"Expecting trouble, Ronon?" Teyla asked him from her customary place beside Sheppard.

"Always," the Satedan answered. "But especially now."

"You figure the Wraith are on their way," Sheppard guessed. "Nekai and his partner split up after we took down the others, so he was exposed long enough for them to get a lock on his location." He didn't need to see his friend's nod to know he was right. Part of him was a little surprised Ronon didn't want to stay and kill whatever Wraith actually showed up, but he figured that was less about Ronon losing his hatred for them and more about him realizing they might not make it back to Atlantis if they didn't leave now. Fighting long odds was one thing, but throwing your life away against impossible odds was another. And Ronon was too canny and too determined to go for the latter.

"Gate's coming up," he announced a few minutes later. "At current speed, we'll hit it in two minutes max. Rodney, how close do you think we need to be for you to unlock it without setting off whatever booby trap Nekai left for us?"

"There's no way to say for certain," Rodney answered, all snark set aside as he focused on the situation at hand. "If it was tied to his DHD, we disabled that already, so there may not be a problem at all. If he hacked the gate itself, he might have programmed a feedback loop or some sort of recursive error like an impossible dialing combination — if that's the case I should be able to break it as soon as the Jumper's within its usual dialing range. If he figured out a way to hardwire the lock, however, I'll need to remove it from the gate itself."

They looked at Ronon, but he shook his head. "When I was with them, we rarely took ships through a Stargate," he explained, "and the DHD wasn't attached to anything. They've done that since. There's no telling what else they've added." He frowned. "But Nekai isn't good enough with computers to hack into anything. And he prefers to keep his solutions simple and direct. He'll have the explosives on the gate itself, and the lock, too, I'm guessing."

"Right, gate it is, then. I'll put us a little ways off, just in case that motion-sensor's already been activated." Sheppard adjusted their trajectory slightly, and a minute later started firing the braking thrusters. The Jumper slowed and then came to a stop. The Stargate hovered in space a short ways ahead of them and off to one side, starlight and stray wisps of sunlight casting the glyphs on each face into deep shadow.

"I'm on it," Rodney announced, snapping his helmet into place — he'd pulled on the spacesuit as soon as they'd lifted off from the planet and Sheppard had decided not to argue about it. The others had donned their MOPP suits, just as a precaution. "Hopefully this won't take long."

"I can help," Ronon offered, but Rodney shook his head.

"You'd only get in my way," the scientist explained, but not meanly. And it might even be true with something like this — Sheppard could see how two men, both trying to deactivate a bomb, could trip each other up. Especially if they had different ideas about what needed to be done.

Ronon shrugged and settled back into his seat as Rodney opened the bulkhead door and stepped through to the cargo hold. A minute went by and then they felt the Jumper rock slightly as he opened the ceiling hatch and slipped through it.

"I've reached the gate," Rodney reported through the suit comms a few minutes later. "And I found the explosives, Your friend didn't do things by half-measures, did he? There's enough here to blow up anyone coming through, plus our ship, and possibly that planet we just left as well."

"He liked to be thorough," Ronon agreed. "Watch out for a secondary charge tied to the first — cut the first without deactivating the second and it'll go off and ignite the larger charge along with it."

"I see it," Rodney acknowledged. "Nasty. I can take care of that, though — short loop here to bypass that, a shunt over here to reroute this, a . . ." his words trailed off as he worked, though Sheppard could still make out an indistinct mumbling from time to time. This part he wasn't worried about, though. It would take a lot to out-paranoid Rodney McKay.

Finally Rodney spoke again. "All set," he said. "I'm coming back in."

"Nasty piece of work," he explained once he was safely back in the Jumper again.

"What about the lock?" Teyla asked. "Did you have any luck discerning how he managed that?"

"Oh, that's taken care of," Rodney assured her. He grinned, clearly pleased with himself. "Turns out he went low-tech on the lock — magnetically clamped an iron net across the outer ring, then ran a small electrical charge through it. The charge actually courses through the ring as well, tripping whatever sensors it's got, and the gate thinks it's butted up against something big and solid and utterly immovable. The gate won't open as long as that charge remains — it thinks it's buried, specifically against a slab of iron or some other highly magnetic mineral, and its own safety protocols keep it locked up tight." He held up what had looked like an empty mesh bag he'd been trailing when he returned, and which the others now realized was the net in question. "Clever, too — I wouldn't have thought of locking a gate that way, but it definitely works. I'll have to keep it in mind next time I go somewhere and don't want Woolsey sending babysitters after me."

"Except that we're usually through the gate in front of you," Sheppard told him dryly, provoking a snort from Ronon and a smile from Teyla even as Rodney grimaced. As he made the crack Sheppard repositioned the Jumper, aiming it at the gate, and was just inputting Atlantis's dialing code when an alarm flashed on one of the consoles.

"Someone is approaching in hyperspace," Teyla warned, scanning the readings. "They're targeted on the Stargate, and about to drop back into normal space. The energy signature is Wraith."

"Cloaks up!" Sheppard announced, activating the Jumper's stealth technology. Then he skipped the little ship sideways so it was on the gate's far side, and spun it on its axis until it was pointing a little ahead of the Stargate. This way the Jumper's guns would be facing whatever came through — assuming they popped out of hyperspace facing the other way. He tried not to think about what would happen if they were facing this direction instead.

He watched intently, hands poised above the controls, as the patch of space just off to the side of the Stargate flickered and shimmered. It blurred and seemed to bend and swirl, and then a long, blunt nose pierced that disruption. A vaguely triangular body followed, jagged and dangerous and too unevenly textured to be strictly manufactured. And it just kept coming, growing larger and larger as more slid through the subspace window and dominated the space around them.

"Hive ship!" Teyla whispered unnecessarily. They had all seen the Wraith command ships far too many times already. As they watched, the Hive ship took up a position a short ways in front of the Stargate — though with its back to the gate, Sheppard was happy to see — and then smaller, sleeker vessels burst from its sides and streaked toward the planet Sheppard and his crew had so recently left behind.

"They're after Nekai and the other V'rdai," Sheppard said, a little amazed despite himself. He'd guessed the Wraith would be closing in on the Runner-hunters, but he'd figured a few Darts, not an entire Hive ship! Ronon's former friends must have pissed the Wraith off one too many times. He glanced at Ronon, and thought he saw a flicker of concern and maybe guilt for a second, but then his friend's face went back to its usual scowl. What was he thinking? Was he regretting leaving them there like that? They could have brought the V'rdai with them, trussed up in the Jumper's cargo hold, but what would they have done with the Runners then?

"Can you get us out of here?" Rodney asked from behind him, interrupting Sheppard's musings. "Or are we stuck?"

"We're not stuck," Sheppard assured him. "I just have to figure out our next move." He thought about it, and gauged the distances involved. "Okay, I think this'll work. Teyla, I need you to dial another gate for me — not Atlantis but one we know, and one we can visit without anyone shooting at us."

"What about the Tower?"

"Do it," Sheppard agreed. They had visited that planet, and its ruined remains of a Lantean city-ship, some time ago, but still maintained good relations with the people there. "Don't activate it yet, though — wait until I give the word."

"Understood." Teyla's fingers danced across the dialing console, and then she paused and waited. While she was doing that, Sheppard slid the Jumper quickly but quietly behind the Hive ship, putting them between the Wraith and the gate. Even at this close range the Wraith wouldn't be able to penetrate their cloak without a targeted scan, and why would they scan behind them when they were already focused on the prizes they expected to find on the planet nearby?

"Get ready," Sheppard warned once they were in position. "Okay, now!" He gunned the Jumper's engines as Teyla activated the gate. He watched the familiar flicker of light and lightning, followed by the burst of color and light and what looked like, but wasn't, water as the Stargate activated, the flume erupting from its center like a volcano. The energy-surface was still settling when they pierced it and entered the distortion that carried them across the stars. A minute later Sheppard was able to shake his head and clear it enough to regain control of the Jumper and to notice the planet down below. The single spire rising above the trees was unmistakable.

"Okay, find us a different gate now, one out in space somewhere," he instructed, and took them back through the second Teyla had entered their new destination. He jumped them twice more before he felt it was safe to head for Atlantis itself — it wasn't that the city didn't have defenses, or that the Wraith didn't know where it was, but he still didn't like the idea of anyone tagging along behind him.

But finally he shut down the Jumper, safe within Atlantis's docking bay, and pulled off his helmet. "We're home," was all he said, but it was enough.

For now. He sighed as he stood and made his way toward

the airlock, knowing Woolsey would be waiting to hear all the details of their mission, and what had happened to delay them afterward. Sheppard glanced over at Ronon, who stared back at him, his face as blank as usual, and wondered exactly how much he should say about the men and women who had attacked them, or their connection to the big Satedan he considered one of his closest friends.

CHAPTER THIRTY

"WELL, it's about time!" Mister Woolsey was sitting in his office as usual, and set aside whatever report he'd been studying as Sheppard led his team in. "We've been trying to contact you for almost thirty-six hours. It was supposed to be a simple rescue mission."

"Things didn't exactly go as planned," Sheppard told him, stopping in front of the Atlantis commander's desk and standing more or less at rest, military style, with his hands behind his back, legs slightly apart. One of the things he did like about Woolsey was that the man didn't stand on ceremony, but he also knew the former NID agent appreciated an observance of basic protocol. It also gave him the opportunity to gesture to his three teammates, warning them to keep quiet and let him handle this.

"Elaborate, please," was all Woolsey replied, leaning forward and steepling his hands. Clearly Sheppard wasn't going to get off the hook so easily.

With a sigh, Sheppard began his report. "The distress signal was a trap," he explained. "The shuttle was empty but had been rigged to show fake life signs. It also had a bomb set to detonate when we reactivated our engines. Ronon realized something was wrong and Rodney confirmed the falsified readings, but we didn't manage to get away in time. The explosion damaged our Jumper and we had to set down on the nearest habitable planet." He took a breath. "Which was exactly what the people who'd set the trap had planned."

"They called themselves the V'rdai," he continued. "They're freedom fighters, waging war against the Wraith — and anyone they think might be working with them." He shrugged. "We just happened to be in the wrong place at the wrong time."

"So what happened to these V'rdai?" Woolsey asked. "Did they attack you on the planet's surface? Are they still at large? Why didn't you contact us to let us know your situation?"

"The Jumper's communications systems were down and we were too far from the gate to access it," Sheppard continued. "Rodney had to repair them, and the engines, and the life support. Teyla, Ronon, and I fended off the V'rdai while he got us spaceworthy again."

"I take it you were successful, since you're here and not there," Woolsey remarked dryly. When he'd first come to Atlantis he'd seemed devoid of all humor, but since then he'd displayed a wry sense of humor, and often slipped barbs into conversation — especially if he was irritated or didn't like someone. The fact that he was making quips now meant Sheppard still wasn't out of the woods yet.

"We got out of there," Sheppard agreed carefully. "Ronon and Rodney also found the V'rdai's ship and destroyed it, stranding them on that planet. And when we left, a Hive ship had just arrived."

"A Hive ship?" Woolsey considered that. "They must have angered the Wraith a good deal to warrant such attention. A shame we couldn't enlist them as allies, then."

"Not a chance," Sheppard told him. "They were too paranoid to work with anyone."

"We tried to contact you, when ten hours had passed and you hadn't checked in," Woolsey told them. "We couldn't get through. Then we tried sending a ship to search for you, and couldn't activate the gate. Why not?"

"The V'rdai had set up some sort of interference," Sheppard answered. "They used a charged metal net to fool the gate into thinking it was obstructed, and that shut it down temporarily. Rodney figured out the problem and removed the net once we were able to reach the gate, but up until then nothing was going in or out."

Woolsey was studying him closely. "Very well," he said after a moment, and Sheppard tried not to sigh in relief. "I'm glad you all made it back safely. There is nothing pressing for you at the moment, so I suggest all four of you take the opportunity to clean up, eat, and get some rest." He turned back to the report on his desk, clearly dismissing them.

"That's just what I had in mind," Sheppard agreed. He turned and gestured for the other three to precede him out. Together they left the command area and walked down a hallway leading toward their respective quarters. Sheppard was already looking forward to a nice, long shower. But first he had a few questions of his own.

"What happened with Nekai?" he asked Ronon once the four of them were well away from anyone else. Teyla and Rodney stopped and turned to hear the answer as well.

"I let him go," Ronon replied. He stopped as well, but only because otherwise he'd have to shove past Teyla and Rodney.

"That's it?" Rodney asked. "You let him go? You're not going to explain that one?"

Ronon turned to stare at him. "No." After a few seconds Rodney looked away.

"Never mind that," Sheppard said, though he'd dearly love to know what Ronon and his former leader had talked about. But he trusted Ronon to tell him if he needed to know, and respected him enough not to pry. As long as he got an answer to a different, more pressing question. "Will he be a problem again?"

"I hope not," Ronon admitted after a second. "I don't think so." He frowned. "But if he does, I'll be ready." He pulled a small device from one of the many pockets in his jacket, held it up just long enough for Sheppard to realize it was a small black rectangle that gave off a faint glow from the other side, and then pocketed it again.

Sheppard started when he realized that Ronon had just shown him a tracking monitor, and outright stared when he felt his own pockets and discovered he no longer had the device. He'd last checked it as they'd left the planet, but obviously at some point since then Ronon had found a way to steal the device back. He was just letting Sheppard know he had it and would use it if necessary. Sheppard had only gotten a glance of the device itself. He had no idea whether it had shown any dots on its screen. But he knew that Ronon would keep an eye out, and would let him know if anything suggested the V'rdai were coming after them or after Atlantis. And that was good enough for him.

He turned to continue the slow trek back to his quarters, when Ronon laid a hand on his shoulder. "Thank you," the big Satedan said softly.

"For what?"

"For leaving out the V'rdai's history — or my former place with them," Ronon answered.

"Oh, that." Sheppard shrugged and tried to look like he didn't care. "I didn't want to confuse Mr. Woolsey with unnecessary details." He grinned at his friend, and Ronon mirrored the expression.

"Yes, there is no reason to mention it, since the V'rdai are no longer a threat," Teyla added.

Rodney just shook his head. "You're all ridiculous."

This time, Sheppard decided to let it go.

Some things just weren't worth fighting for.

And some things were.

ABOUT THE AUTHOR

Aaron Rosenberg likes to mix things up.

Perhaps it's because of his history—born in New Jersey, raised in New Orleans, schooled in Kansas (under the tutelage of science fiction legend James Gunn), now living and working in New York. Or it might be his work experience—creative director for an animation studio, script editor for a film company, submissions reader for a publishing house, English comp and lit teacher at two colleges, graphic designer for an insurance company, and desktop publisher for a publishing house.

Whatever the reason, Aaron just can't stick to one media or one genre. He's written novels, short stories, children's books, roleplaying games, webcomics, essays, reviews, and educational books, and has ranged from mystery to horror to science fiction and fantasy to contemporary fiction.

"I just like to tell stories," Aaron explains, "whatever the genre or the format." He's won awards for his roleplaying work (an Origins Award and a gold ENnie) and his fiction (a Psi Phi Award and two Scribe Award nominations), and is constantly finding new stories to tell and new ways to tell them.

Recent fiction projects include the Stargate Atlantis novel *Hunt and Run*, the Chaotic junior novel *The Khilaian Sphere*, the middle-grade book *Pizza Puzzles #1: The Case of the Secret Sauce*, and the first-ever Eureka novel, *Substitution Method* (written under the house name Cris Ramsay). Recent game projects include the *Supernatural Hunter's Guide, Eclipse Phase: Sunward, Warhammer Fantasy Roleplay*, and the *Call of Cthulhu* supplement *This Sceptre'd Isle*.

You can keep up with his exploits at gryphonrose.com or follow him on Twitter at gryphonrose.

STARGATE SG·1.

STARGATE ATLANTIS™

Original novels based on the hit TV shows STARGATE SG-1, STARGATE ATLANTIS and STARGATE UNIVERSE

AVAILABLE NOW

For more information, visit www.stargatenovels.com

Series number: SGU-01

STARGATE UNIVERSE: AIR

by James Swallow
Price: £6.99 UK | $7.95 US
ISBN-13: 978-1-905586-46-2
Publication date: November 2009

Without food, supplies, or a way home, Colonel Everett Young finds himself in charge of a mission that has gone wrong before it has even begun. Stranded and alone on the far side of the universe, the mismatched team of scientists, technicians, and military personnel have only one objective: staying alive.

As personalities clash and desperation takes hold, salvation lies in the hands of Dr. Nicholas Rush, the man responsible for their plight, a man with an agenda of his own...

Stargate Universe is the gritty new spin-off of the hit TV shows Stargate SG-1 and Stargate Atlantis. Working from the original screenplay, award-winning author James Swallow has combined the three pilot episodes into this thrilling full-length novel which includes deleted scenes and dialog, making it a must-read for all Stargate fans.

Order your copy directly from the publisher today by going to www.stargatenovels.com or send a check or money order made payable to "Fandemonium" to:

<u>USA orders:</u> $10.95 ($7.95 + $3.00 P&P).

<u>Rest of world:</u> $13.95 ($7.95 + $6.00 P&P)

Send payment to: Fandemonium Books, PO Box 2178, Decatur, GA 30031-2178 USA.

Or check your local bookshop – available on special order if they are out of stock (quote the ISBN number listed above).

STARGATE ATLANTIS: DEATH GAME

by Jo Graham
Price: £6.99 UK | $7.95 US
ISBN-10: 1-905586-47-7
ISBN-13: 978-1-905586-47-9
Publication date: July 2010

Colonel John Sheppard wakes up on an alien world, in the wreckage of a Puddle Jumper– and can't remember how he got there.

As he puts the pieces together, he discovers that his team is scattered across a tropical archipelago, unable to communicate with each other or return to the Stargate.

Prisoners of the local population, Sheppard and Teyla are taken as tribute to the planet's Wraith overlord, while McKay, Ronon, and Zelenka team up to mount a daring rescue...

Series number: SG1-15

STARGATE SG-1: THE POWER BEHIND THE THRONE

by Steven Savile
Price: $7.95 US | £6.99 UK
ISBN-10: 1-905586-45-0
ISBN-13: 978-1-905586-45-1
Publication date: August 2010

SG-1 are asked by the Tok'ra to rescue a creature known as Mujina.

The last of its species, Mujina is devoid of face or form and draws its substance from the needs of those around it.

The creature is an archetype – a hero for all, a villain for all, depending upon whose influence it falls under.

And the Goa'uld Apophis, understanding the potential for havoc Mujina offers, has set his heart on possessing the creature...

STARGATE SG-1: FOUR DRAGONS

Jack takes matters into his own hands to save Daniel

STARGATE SG·1.

FOUR DRAGONS

Diana Botsford

Based on the hit television series developed by Brad Wright and Jonathan Glassner

Series number: SG1-16

by Diana Botsford
Price: $7.95 US | £6.99 UK
ISBN-10: 1-905586-48-5
ISBN-13: 978-1-905586-48-6
Publication date: August 2010

Shortly after Daniel Jackson returns from his time among the ascended Ancients, he volunteers to join an archaeological survey of Chinese ruins on P3Y-702.

But after accidentally activating a Goa'uld transport ring, Daniel finds himself the prisoner of the Goa'uld Lord Yu.

Blaming himself for Daniel's capture, Jack O'Neill vows to go to any lengths to get him back – even if it means taking matters into his own hands.